THE EARL EXCHANGED GREETINGS WITH NEWMARCH, WHO WAS JUST TAKING HIS LEAVE OF CLARE.

"I trust I am not intruding, Miss Winchester?" he asked with what had almost become typical formality.

"Not at all, sir, why should you think so?"

"Newmarch," he stated testily. "You seem to be spending an uncommonly great deal of time with him. I saw you together on Friday last, at the opera." When she did not reply, he said more pointedly, "But, perhaps, you were too . . . occupied to have noticed me."

"On the contrary, I did see you—with Mrs. Marlowe."

There was a long pause, during which he stood scowling and twisting his heavy signet ring, as Clare fussed over a bowl of flowers. The arrangement entirely ruined, she sighed and looked at him shyly. Hoping she sounded offhand, she asked, "If you saw us, why then did you not speak?"

"Well, ma'am, why did not you?"

Suddenly aware of the foolishness of their behavior, they lapsed into embarrassed laughter.

"Oh, my, I am afraid we must sound like a pair of silly children."

"Not you, certainly, Miss Winchester," his lordship assured her gallantly, "the fault was entirely mine. But you are correct in another respect, I should have spoken to you first." He looked warmly into her eyes. "Perhaps you would care for a walk in the Green Park? It is but a short carriage ride from here and such a beautiful day is too fine to waste indoors."

"That would be very enjoyable, but I think we shall be unable to convince Evelyn to join us."

"I had no intention of inviting her, Miss Winchester."

WATCH FOR THESE REGENCY ROMANCES

The Changeable Rose

Jessie Watson

Zebra Books
Kensington Publishing Corp.

http://www.zebrabooks.com

To my mother and father

One

"Of course, I do realize that my convenience means little, Clare dear, but I must say you were uncommonly long at your toilette. Why, we might have been late for our little visit with Lucy." Plump hands clutched a reticule, absurd in its comparative smallness, to an ample bosom. "Not that I blame you, of course. No doubt it was entirely the fault of your flighty abigail. I cannot think why you keep her."

The young woman thus addressed might have been thought unmoved by, perhaps even deaf to, these remarks. Actually, she had been enduring this carping for what sometimes seemed to be forever, and, in truth, she had long ago schooled herself to disregard the older woman's expressions of discontent. Still, even one as good-natured as Clare Winchester could not be expected to possess an unlimited supply of tolerance, not even for the beloved aunt who embodied the last of what she could call family. Since departing their house in Edwardes Square earlier that day, Clare had listened to an endless catalogue of grievances. Most of them were variations on the same theme, their reduced circumstances, and she was nearing the end of her patience.

Their progress toward Bond Street was temporarily halted by the peremptory passage of a carriage and pair followed closely by several lumbering carts. The London streets were filled to bursting with people on foot or horseback, in hackneys, sedan chairs, and fancy carriages. Most folk were intent on their destinations, for there was too much bite in the February air to take to the outdoors for the less practical, albeit more fashionable, reason of "being seen." Clare's nose, bright pink with cold, crinkled at the acrid smell of fried fish as a vendor handed a greasy, newspaper-wrapped package to a customer and raised his voice to join the peculiar medley of church bells and other street sellers hawking their wares at near earsplitting levels.

"Buy My Hot Spice Cakes!"

"Coffee!"

"Penny-Pies, 'ere! Penny-Pies!"

Somehow, her aunt's voice managed to rise above this impediment. "I do not see why we could not have taken a carriage to Madame Claudine's, Clare. All this noise and the dirt and these wretched people. Oh!" She gave a little scream as an urchin, chased by a sinister-looking man, dodged past them into the filth-ridden gutter and across the road to lose himself in the crowd. Watching his progress, Clare silently urged the child on. She suspected he was one of the many children forced into a chimney sweep's life of terror and pain, a life that often ended too soon as the result of his master's cruelty.

"As I was saying, Clare, if you would only pay attention," the nagging voice continued, "a carriage would have been more the thing, especially in this cold."

Their way at last clear, the two women stepped into the street. "Aunt Maude, please. We took a carriage this morning from our house to Lucy Elwyn's in Half-Moon Street and it is just a short walk from there to Madame Claudine's."

"Well, of course, my dear, we had to take a carriage after your Molly took so long in dressing you."

"No, Maude, we took a hackney to your friend's house because it is too far to walk. I am sorry if I was delayed, but I cannot have kept you waiting above five minutes. And do, please, stop this talk of Molly. You know she is as dependable and devoted as anyone could wish. She very kindly works for us, as do Mrs. Musgrave and Estelle, for less than they could get elsewhere." She chose to ignore Maude's observation that a henwitted girl like their maid, Estelle, would be hard put to find honest work anywhere else unless she were willing to pay her employer.

"Fortunately, Aunt, we are not as badly off as we once thought we would be. Still, hiring a hackney in this circumstance seemed to me a luxury that we could easily do without. Do you not think so? Come, we cannot bicker here in public. You've been looking forward ever so long to your appointment with Claudine, let's not spoil it."

Her aunt's only response was a dissatisfied "humph," but the remainder of the trip was completed in their more customary, easy chatter.

Madame Claudine's was not an establishment of unusual size, but its rich appointments assured all who dared enter of its undisputed position in the forefront of Regency fashion and its patronage by members of the ton.

My Lady's entrance was not heralded by anything so crass as the tinkling of a bell. Rather, Claudine employed a proper young woman whose sole function it was to greet the modiste's clients. Awaiting Madame's ministrations, customers browsed through pattern books and the latest edition of *The Ladies' Cabinet* or wandered about enjoying the solicitous attention of a number of assistants. The deeply piled primrose carpet preserved the quiet of the shop, and the walls were hung with a figured silk of a pale shade of blue. A few dainty mannequins were placed here and there to display Madame's finer creations.

The shop was filled with all manner of goods to delight the eye and whet the vanity of every female who entered. Light filtered through the mullioned windows, igniting sparks in shimmering silks shot with silver or flecked with gold. Shelves held crepes, delicate organdies and tulles nestled beside brightly striped tarlatans, sarsenets, dimities, and lighter-than-air lawns. An entire wall was given over to a

vast array of soft muslins in pastels and the all-important
white, some sheer as gossamer, mulled, sprigged, or dotted.

A tall bureau, its wood soft and shiny as satin, stood in
one corner, its contents plundered by the artful hands of the
staff. Its drawers were agape and a profusion of lace tumbled
out lavishly, its fairness shown to advantage against the high
luster of the old, dark wood. In the wake of My Lady's skirts,
the trimmings wafted and danced lightly like the streamers
on the dustcap of some mad countess.

No dressmaker worth her price, and no lady who could
afford to pay it, would complete an ensemble without ribbons, and ribbons there were to tempt the fancy of the most
settled of matrons and the drabbest of dowds. Long dowels
held dozens of spools tightly wrapped in satin, velvet, gros-
grain, and moiré in fresh, crisp greens, lavish purples, and
blushing pinks. The very bottom tier held a succession of
mourning colors, from black and shades of grey to lavender,
in various widths and fabrics.

Clare and her aunt were led to a brocade-covered settee
from which they watched the bustling staff cater to the demands, whims, and uncertainties of several women. Some
twenty minutes after the hour appointed for her fitting,
Maude was greeted by the tall, gaunt modiste. The Frenchwoman's cool demeanor, while correct, made clear her opinion that Maude and Clare's visits were not of sufficient
frequency nor their purchases of the magnitude to deserve
the charm that she reserved for her wealthier clientele.

"If you will be so kind as to come into the fitting room,
we shall see if the final alterations meet with your approval.
However," she added, surveying Maude's plumpness with a
keen eye, "I fear that Mademoiselle may have added a pound
or two about the waist since the last measurements were
taken."

Clare overlooked the brusqueness of the woman to whom
her family had once given more than a fair amount of custom.
Maude eagerly accompanied her toward the rear of the shop,

all the while protesting that her waistline had not changed a hairbreadth.

Clare turned her attention to two women arguing the merits of several shades of yellow moiré. Her thoughts wandered back to her own trips to Bond Street, when the most important decision of the day was choosing between a sprigged and a dotted muslin for her latest walking dress. More often than not, she bought both, blaming the extravagance on the demands of her busy calendar.

She sighed at the recollection that such demands were made no longer. Her father's loss of much of his fortune had effectively set both her and her aunt outside the drawing rooms of the beau monde. Though Clare was inured to her quiet life, she still sometimes longed for late night revelry and the steady round of calls made and received. While the remains of her father's estate permitted them to live comfortably, Caulfield Hall, their country residence in Surrey, was long since gone to settle his debts, as was the large town house in Curzon Street, and the days of luxury had gone with them.

She listened as a pretty girl described a daring gown she wished made up for the coming Season. The girl's mother registered shock at her daughter's outrageous idea, while Clare flushed a rosy pink and shook her head. If only . . .

Her musing was interrupted by a commotion emanating from the far side of the shop. All heads turned to see an assistant staring down her nose at a well-dressed but disheveled and obviously distraught girl of some seventeen years. Her hands clasped to her bosom, she gave every appearance of pleading for her life.

The shop girl's strict training forgotten, her well-modulated tones were rapidly rising to a resonance never before heard in Madame's millinery. "Young woman, be so kind as to depart these premises immediately. I have already told you that Madame has no need of additional help and, if she did, I am sure that you would be the last sort of person she would be likely to accept into her employ."

The girl burst into tears. "Oh, please, miss, if you could only just inquire. I should be ever so careful and would w-work very hard." Brightening a bit, she added, "And I know a good deal about clothes, all those things which are au courant." Her voice trembled dangerously. "I am certain that I could be of help to Madame Claudine."

"Ha! You? Yes, I am sure you know a good deal about a lady's wardrobe, for you . . ." Further comment was precluded by the appearance of Madame herself. Her presence, like that of everyone else in the room, having been drawn by the clamor, she advanced toward the unfortunate girl with murder in her eyes.

"What is the meaning of this outrage, Bickell?" she demanded of the assistant. That woman, now quaking with fear herself, explained that the girl had come seeking employment that she, Bickell, Senior Shop Assistant, had denied her.

"And now, if you please, Madame, she has the effrontery to claim a knowledge of a lady's wardrobe, but I should say she is nothing better than a common parlormaid. Why, just see the dust and grime on her dress."

"Thank you, Bickell, I have eyes." Glaring, she turned on the frightened girl and spit, "I should say that your knowledge of fashion is limited to your frock. For though it has been badly used," she observed with distaste, "one can see it was made with care and style. Perhaps you stole it from your mistress."

"No, Madame," protested the girl, her voice a curious mixture of astonishment and desperation. "This dress is my own and . . ."

"Enough! Get out of my establishment at once, or I shall have you removed for stealing and disturbing the peace of these gentle ladies." This last was uttered with a frightened, ingratiating smile in the direction of the assembled company that, doubtless, had not enjoyed anything so much in months. The threat proved too much for the girl. Trembling and crying, she fell into a swoon and landed softly on the primrose carpet.

"Shocking!"

"How dare she, a mere housemaid?"

"I have never seen the like!"

The comments flew among the women, but only Clare and Bickell, the latter perhaps recalling her own days of seeking employment, paid the least heed to the unconscious intruder. Clare pushed her way through the crowd to kneel at the girl's side and began chafing her wrists.

"Oh, Lord, miss, what are we to do now?"

"First, we must rouse her," Clare answered. Never subject to vapors herself, Clare did not carry salts. Looking over her shoulder, she spied Maude amid the onlookers, a large, beribboned bandbox tucked under one arm. "Aunt, quickly, give me your vinaigrette," she called. After some fumbling, Maude withdrew the desired bottle and handed it down to her niece.

Madame, fearing a loss of custom, was moaning and wringing her hands. Those ladies not too busy expressing their disgust at the baggage on the floor, assured her of their continued loyalties. After all, where else could one go for gowns in the highest kick of fashion and a delicious bit of scandal besides?

Passing the vinaigrette beneath the girl's nose, Clare opined that she must have fainted as much from hunger as from fright, and asked the assistant to fetch a hackney. Ever alert to the prospect of a ride, Maude again came forward and knelt beside her niece.

"Why, Clare, whatever do you mean to do?"

"I mean to take her home to Edwardes Square, Aunt. What else can I do?" she whispered. "The poor thing has no employment, and, if this swoon is any evidence of her present circumstances, she probably has nowhere to go."

This plan elicited a gasp of horror from Maude. Clare glanced over her shoulder at the chattering women. They all were too high in the instep for her taste, but, though she itched to tell them so, she knew it would accomplish nothing.

The girl's long eyelashes fluttered open, revealing large blue eyes, and she moaned softly as she tried to rise.

"There now, you are in good hands. I shan't let anyone take you away." Clare spoke soothingly as she helped the girl to her feet and kept a steadying arm about her waist. The crowd parted and they walked toward the door, Maude trailing reluctantly behind. A lovely, grey-eyed woman who had entered the shop a few minutes before, stood quietly to one side and watched, a pleased expression on her face.

Bickell returned to apprise Clare of her success in hailing a carriage, and the three women, Maude blathering about appearances, passed into Bond Street.

Rain was drumming against the windows of Clare's bedroom as Estelle laid a fire in the grate. Her task finished, she opened the curtains to the colorless, wet morning, toppling a chair in her wake.

"Sorry, miss," she whispered.

"It's alright, Estelle, I was already awake." Waiting for the room to warm, she snuggled deeper into the bedclothes and recalled the events of the previous day.

Their small staff had greeted them with inquisitive glances, as Clare had bustled the stranger upstairs to the guest bedroom. She had been able to coax her into swallowing some broth but, in response to Clare's questions, the girl had claimed to remember nothing and pleaded exhaustion. Molly had helped her to bed, and the girl still had not stirred when Clare peeked in at her before repairing to her own room for the night.

Clare stretched away the last of her drowsiness. The chit must be awake by now, she decided, and rang for Molly to help her to dress.

She sat back and sighed as Molly brushed her glossy brown curls.

"Well, miss, I hope you had a good rest. You certainly deserve it after that dust-up with your aunt last night."

"That's enough, Molly." The warning denied her abigail further comment, but she went on with a familiar hint of amusement in her voice. "You know that we must make certain—allowances for Aunt Maude. She simply cannot adjust to our more quiet mode of living. Truly, she means no harm."

The pretty maid could not contain a disbelieving sniff, as she met her sweet-tempered mistress's hazel eyes in the glass. "Humph," she said, "and after all this time?"

"Molly, please. Help me decide what to wear." Molly extracted a dress from the not-very-extensive collection in the clothespress and held it up for approval. "No, not that one. I cannot think whatever made me purchase it, for it makes me look even shorter than I am. Yes, the blue muslin will do very well."

As it was not Maude's habit to rise for the morning meal, Clare was assured of a peaceful half hour in the breakfast room. She sat leisurely, sipping her coffee. Molly had been quite right—she and her aunt had argued the previous evening.

Maude's complaints in Bond Street had paled in comparison to the strident protests she had registered upon their return home. Not content to confine the argument to the subject at hand, she had echoed the griping that Clare had heard so many times over the past few years.

"If your father had not squandered nearly all of his money and lost our home . . ."

"Aunt, thinking always of the past will not bring it back. My dear father was, perhaps, not as judicious as we would have liked, yet we do live most comfortably, if not as we were used to. We must be thankful for what we have."

"Thankful, you mean, that Marcus died before dissipating his entire fortune."

"Maude! Let us not have this quarrel again," her niece

had countered firmly. "My father's death came all too soon, even had his living meant penury for us."

"Of course, my dear, I meant no ill will, though now he's dead, it hardly matters, I suppose. But even you must admit that my sister, Alicia, your dear, departed mother, married a spendthrift. He frittered away a handsome inheritance, a lovely estate, on the Lord only knows what mad schemes, leaving us without a feather to fly."

"My parents adored one another. Their marriage was a true love match."

"Yes, and my poor sister dead so young, leaving Marcus to rear you. Why, if he had but heeded my counsel . . . But, alas, he always indulged you. I cannot help but think that had it not been for your wild behavior, you might have made a suitable connection, for I was convinced that Mr. Portman meant to offer for you. Instead, here you are close on thirty years of age and on the shelf."

Clare fought to hold her temper. "Maude, this is the outside of enough." She spoke sternly and with a tone of finality. "I do not care a fig that I am unwed, and, unless I can have the kind of union that my parents enjoyed, I hope that I shall never go to the altar. And you must confess that our surroundings here are quite pleasant and certainly suit our needs. We do manage . . ."

"Well, yes, my dear, of course we *manage* . . ." interrupted her aunt in a conciliatory whine.

"Yes, we do. Our staff, though greatly reduced, is most adequate. And, if we cannot afford to keep our own carriage, with careful budgeting, we can allow some little luxuries, such as your appointment with Madame Claudine. With what I have and your small income, we cannot go there as frequently as we once did, but, since we no longer go into society, what does it matter?"

"Well, I am sure that I never meant to appear ungrateful for any charity you may care to extend to me."

"Oh, Aunt." Clare's exasperation showed in her voice. "You know that all I have is yours."

"Well, the Lord only knows how charitable you are. Who else would take in a total stranger such as that girl and then lodge her abovestairs, *and* in the only guest room?"

Clare's mouth took on a hard line as she remembered her reprimand. "Who else, indeed? Do you think any of those toplofty females in Claudine's would have so much as cast a crust of bread her way? Aunt, how can you be so heartless? Surely we cannot turn the poor creature out into the street, and what better place for me to see to her needs but in the room next to mine?" Incapable of dealing with this simple logic, Maude had flounced off to her room, vowing not to infringe on the "houseguest's" privacy, and had not been seen since.

Clare emptied her cup and gave silent thanks for small blessings. Informing Estelle that she would take more coffee in the guest room, she mounted the stairs. The girl was sitting up in bed devouring the last crumbs of her breakfast when Clare entered. She looked a trifle pale but, overall, much improved and seemed oddly at ease in a lady's bedchamber. Responding respectfully to Clare's cheerful greeting, she lowered her gaze and appeared a bit nervous.

"Well, I am pleased to find you coming along so nicely. You are quite well? Have you had enough to eat?"

"Yes, thank you."

"I trust you have no objection to my taking coffee with you? Perhaps you would prefer cocoa?"

"Oh no, Miss Winchester, I am quite old enough to drink coffee . . ." She stopped, apparently in fear of divulging too much about herself.

Clare pretended not to notice her hesitation and for the next few minutes chatted about the unhappy change in the weather and pondered her guest. The girl, a pretty, slender brunette, obviously was reluctant to leave this comparative luxury and resume her search for employment. Clare smiled knowingly and patted the girl's hand. While Clare was neither hungry nor homeless, she knew well the feeling of being an outsider.

But, reality could not be postponed forever. She sipped her coffee, then said gently, "Now, I think you must tell me your name and circumstances."

The girl blanched and began to tremble. "Oh, please, Miss Winchester, I have told you, I can remember nothing."

"Now, now, that was yesterday, and you were quite overwrought, but surely now you are recovered sufficiently to recall the events which led to your presence at Madame Claudine's?" Clare insisted kindly.

At mention of the awful scene, the girl shuddered and turned her face away. "I remember nothing," said a voice muffled by pillows.

Perceiving that determination was called for, Clare pressed on. "You may think me birdwitted, child, but I assure you, I am not in my dotage yet. Now, cease this foolishness and tell me the truth, for I wish only to help you. Tell me for what sort of work you are trained, and I shall endeavor to find you employment. No one need know of the incident at Madame's. Are you a housemaid?"

At this, the girl burst into tears. "No! If I tell you, then he—he will come after me and I am so afraid of him . . ." She now bordered on hysteria, and Clare, hard put to calm her, began to wonder just who her little "housemaid" really was.

Two women sat before a crackling fire in a cozy room. One, elderly with a kindly moon-shaped face, was busily tatting, the other, the one with the distracted air, was tall and razor-thin. Her spine formed a perfect parallel to the rigid line of the straight-backed chair on which she perched, but restless hands betrayed her anxiety.

Miss Merrow rose and, for perhaps the fifth time in as

many minutes, crossed to the casement window. She peered through the rain-spattered glass to the gently curving carriage drive two stories below, and beyond that to the park that formed the perimeter of the manor. Nothing appeared on the landscape save the elms and poplars that had stood for centuries and now waved their branches gracefully before the cold, wet wind.

She sighed and turned back to the warmth of the fire and the older woman who had been observing this ritual for the better part of two hours. "Nanny Somerset, where can he be? He was expected midmorning, and it has just gone three o'clock."

"Miss Merrow, first you are terror-stricken at the thought of his arrival, and now you are champing at the bit at his delay," Nanny remarked. "Really, I do not understand you."

Miss Merrow came to rest again, like an exhausted bird, on the edge of her chair. "Well, of course, I do not *wish* to see him, Nanny, it is only this waiting which is so very trying. Oh, dear, whatever am I going to do?" she croaked.

"Now, Amanda. We are all upset—such a childish, selfish thing to do—but, really, you must calm yourself."

"Calm myself! When he learns what has happened, there will be no escaping his rage!" The nervous woman shuddered visibly, her fingers absently pleating the skirt of her dull green merino gown.

"Tut, you paid too much heed to that henwitted sister-in-law of his, may she rest in peace. I tell you, he will put all to rights," Nanny nodded sagely.

Elsewhere in the spacious house, servants bustled. Footmen polished already gleaming silver as housemaids laid fires, aired sheets, and arranged hothouse flowers in crystal bowls and tall, china vases. Belowstairs, Cook was lovingly putting the finishing touches to a truffle pie.

"There," she said with some satisfaction, "that should please him, for this was always one of his particular favorites.

Still, I cannot see as how he'll have the stomach for it. Not after the news that's waiting for him."

The sound of carriage wheels could be heard on the drive. Hurriedly, footmen snapped to attention, and housemaids adjusted frilled caps and apron bibs as each stepped into the neat receiving line assembling in the great paneled hall. Gresham, the aged butler, smoothed his white gloves and solemnly opened the door. His usual unshakably dignified countenance broke into a broad smile.

"Welcome home, my lord. May I say, on behalf of the entire staff, how pleased we are to see your lordship at home once again."

Swinging the heavy door wide as he spoke, Gresham stepped aside. Footmen inclined their heads, and housemaids dropped curtsies. The center of all this attention crossed the threshold and paused as several of the younger maids gazed worshipfully from under lowered lashes. The man's broad shoulders were impressively defined in a well-cut coat of midnight superfine and his hard-muscled legs were shown to advantage by close-fitting biscuit-colored trousers tapering smoothly into gleaming Hessians.

His Grace, the seventh earl of Northrup, surveyed the assembly. His slow smile was first revealed in a pair of bright blue eyes that crinkled with pleasure above even, white teeth. He inclined his head, capped in short, but very natural waves of the deepest black.

"Thank you, Gresham. It is good to be home again."

Two

Clare had been able to calm her guest only through repeated and fervent assurances that she would not ply her with more questions, and, thence, she made rapid progress. Two days later, she could be found wrapped in a hastily altered dimity dressing gown and reposing on a chintz-covered chaise before the fire. Clare, seeing the ease with which the girl accepted her seeming status as "guest," was convinced that she was much more than a mere housemaid and determined to reopen the subject of her identity.

"Well, my girl, you are looking remarkably fit. I trust you feel much improved?"

"Yes, Miss Winchester, much better, thank you."

"Good," she said firmly. "Now, let us return to our discussion of two days ago." The girl paled. Clare decided to continue her previous line of reasoning to see where it would lead. "Only tell me of your experience, and I shall do everything I can to find you a comfortable situation. I would be happy to keep you on here, but our needs are small and, at the moment, are most adequately met." Maude would have an attack of the vapors if she heard that. She pondered a moment. "Failing my efforts, there is always the Registry, I suppose," she said thoughtfully.

"But I am not a domestic," the girl uttered with simple dignity.

"Then I say it is high time you told me exactly who you are."

There was a great pause, during which the girl took a deep breath. "Very well, I shall tell you. But you must swear not to tell him that I am here."

"I cannot and shall not make such an unfair promise. Someone, after all, must be very worried about you."

"Oh, I hardly think he will be worried at all, he . . ." Observing Clare's stern expression, she stopped mid-sentence and took another breath.

"My name is Evelyn Hallisey and I am the niece of the earl of Northrup. My mother died several years ago and Papa was killed in a carriage accident last year." Clare's expression changed to one of compassion and then to shock. Niece to an earl! However did the chit get herself into such a hubble-bubble?

"Since Papa died, I have lived on at Northrup Court with my governess, who insists on staying even though I am far too old to require her services. She is kind," the girl allowed, "but, oh so strict. When I would ride, she counsels that I could be hurt and she will not allow me to ride with my dearest friend, Peter, though we have played together since we were in leading strings."

A smile tugged at the corners of Clare's mouth. "And do you heed your governess, Evelyn?"

"Of course I do!" Then, a bit sheepishly, "Well, not always, Miss Winchester. But it is only because she will be so stiff-necked. When she finds I have been out riding alone or with Peter, she flies up into the boughs and begins sermonizing—as if I were not an expert horsewoman and Peter not perfectly capable of protecting me," she assured her listener.

"Perhaps you are a bit hard on your governess, dear, she wants only what is best for you."

"Yes, that is what she says. She tells me I am too willful by half and, when I protest, she warns of what *he* will do."

At this, Clare interrupted. "Just who is the terrible monster who frightens you so?"

"Did I not tell you?" Evelyn queried innocently. "It is my

uncle, Evan, the earl." This simple explanation given, she sat back, satisfied, and awaited its awful impact on the ever-so-dim Miss Winchester.

"And is he so very cruel, your uncle?"

"Why, I am certain he must be, ma'am, for you should hear Miss Merrow, that is my governess, go on about his awful temper."

"Whatever do you mean? Where is this mysterious man?"

"Oh, I have not seen him in years and years. In truth, ma'am, I hardly even remember him. You see," she continued with infinite patience, "he was often in London when I was a child. Then, later, he thought it his duty to join in the fight against France. My papa, who was the younger son, was not very strong. Since he could not fight, he offered to take over the duties of the estate until the war was over, you know. When my father died, Uncle Evan was fighting in the Peninsular and thus prevented from returning immediately. Then, a few weeks ago, he was wounded, and so he is finally on his way home." She gave a small shudder.

"Oh my," Clare said sympathetically.

"Oh, it is but a leg wound, ma'am. I am sure it does not signify, for Nanny is always saying how strong and healthy he is," Evelyn assured her with a lack of concern attributable to robust youth and a sheltered upbringing.

"I am glad to know that his prospects for a speedy recovery are so good," Clare drawled. "But, despite what Miss Merrow has told you, surely you are eager to renew acquaintance with your uncle, are you not?"

At this, Evelyn's eyes widened. "Eager? I have never dreaded anything so. Merrow has been in a rare pet this past month—ever since she discovered me riding alone again. But for that birdwitted housemaid, she never would have found out, and she vowed to tell all to my uncle upon his arrival. She said he would punish me severely because he is very stern, and he probably would not allow me my Season in London this year."

"Good heavens!" Clare interjected drily, during the pause provided for just this purpose.

Evelyn nodded at the seeming sympathy of her listener. "You may well understand my trepidation, ma'am. I simply cannot live under the thumb of such an odious man. That is why I ran away."

"But to what purpose, my dear? What will you do? Surely you cannot think to enjoy a Season as a shop girl?"

The girl lost some of her bravado. "W-well, no, of course not. I would rather give up the social whirl and any thought of an eligible connection, however, to escape the horrid fate that awaits me at home. I had planned to find employment as a shop assistant in an establishment such as Madame Claudine's. I thought that I could save enough of my wages to open a millinery of my own and be free of my uncle once and for all. But, alas, that seems impossible." Her chin began to tremble.

"We were on our way back from Aston Clinton and I escaped from Miss Merrow at a posting inn. I bought a seat on the next coach for London. We rode all through the night and did not arrive until very early in the morning. My father's solicitor keeps me on very short strings, and I spent most of my money on tea and cakes, because I thought to find a position without delay.

"I walked all day, I had no funds to hire a hack, and several dandies had the audacity to ogle me," she confided in shocked tones. "I inquired at every shop in Oxford and Bond Streets, but no one would hire me." The girl was fast approaching tears. "And that is when you found me at Madame Claudine's."

Clare, who listened to all this with astonishment, now contained a smile. "Evelyn, dear, there are many women seeking just such a position, and I would venture to say that most of them probably start off doing much more menial tasks—in the workroom, perhaps. And, truly, dear, I hardly think you would be suited to the position. Do you know that some shop assistants often are required to work eighty hours a week?"

The girl was astounded. "You cannot mean it. Why, that is inhuman!"

"Quite, but true. And as for your own establishment, I daresay you would earn barely enough to feed yourself."

Evelyn dissolved into tears. "Oh, Miss Winchester, what am I to do?"

The earl of Northrup looked as if he would shake the poor governess until her teeth rattled and, in fact, he was dangerously close to doing just that. "Miss Merrow, are you telling me that you have lost my niece?"

"N-not exactly *lost,* my lord," the governess stammered, dabbing her eyes with a very damp cambric square.

"Be so kind, Miss Merrow, as to cease these waterworks and tell me 'exactly' what *has* happened to Evelyn," he commanded in a low voice.

"W-well, my lord," she began slowly, "we were returning from a visit to Lady Longleigh at Aston Clinton, when our lead horse threw a shoe. Fortunately, we were just a few yards from The Bell, and so we stopped there. Evelyn and I went into the inn to escape the cold and refresh ourselves. Oh, my lord, I never meant—that is, I was so careful, I left her for just a moment, and—and . . ." At this, the tired woman began to weep once again.

During this narrative, the earl had stood looking out of the window, a muscle flickering ominously in his jaw. At the sound of her sobs, his hands, which were clasped behind his back, clenched into two powerful fists. He turned slowly to face the woman and bellowed, his normally deep, resonant voice a thundering baritone. "I command you to desist this ninny-hammered bawling, madam, for I will not tolerate it. Be thankful that you still have a position, for I vow I am sorely tempted to turn you off without a testimonial! Now, get on with it!"

The unfortunate governess only cried the harder, and the image of the earl dissolved into a blur. Throwing up his hands in a gesture of complete frustration, he turned to Nanny, who was watching the episode from her seat by the fire.

She put down her tatting and looked at him reproachfully. "Come, come now," she prompted, "pull yourself together and tell his lordship what happened." Merrow was too far gone to respond to this advice, however, and her sobs, if possible, became louder.

Herself miffed with the silly female, Nanny took the liberty of motioning her to a seat. Wishing to get as far away from her tormentor as she could, but not daring to leave until he dismissed her, Merrow took refuge in a chair on the other side of the room. Nanny sighed and turned back to the earl.

"There, you see? You have frightened her out of her wits."

"An amazingly easy accomplishment, you will agree. Still, you know I have ever had an aversion to exertion." His words were laced with sarcasm, as he took a seat across from the old woman.

"My lord, she is indeed terrified of you. You have that effect on a good many people, those who don't know you as I do, that is. Why must you be so intimidating? If you had but desisted in your bellowing and been a little kinder and more patient, I daresay she would have enlightened you."

"That creature is an idiot. And I would point out to you that I still do not know what has become of Evelyn. Now, perhaps I might impose on your benevolent nature to leave off the cataloging of my sins"—his voice rose a bit—"and tell me what the devil has happened!"

"Of course, dear, only do be still while I explain."

The earl allowed a small smile of exasperation. No one dared to speak to him in such a way. No one, that is, except Nanny. He winced as a sharp pain coursed through his leg and, extending it toward the soothing warmth of the fire, he waved his hand for her to go on.

"Well, they reached The Bell, and poor Miss Merrow went to bespeak a private parlor for them and that naughty chit sneaked away," she related simply. "Merrow looked high and low, naturally, and eventually learned that a young miss fitting your niece's description had boarded the coach bound for London more than an hour earlier.

"We have, of course, contacted various persons in that city, including your lordship's solicitor, Mr. Barnes, in an effort to find her, but so far we have learned nothing."

"My God, the child has been gone these four days. Anything can have befallen her. Do you realize how many people there are in London? She could be anywhere—assuming she is still alive!"

"Never say such a thing, my lord. Of course she is alive, and you will find her. I know it."

"Have you any idea why she ran off?"

Merrow's tears had at last begun to subside and she sat, sniffling and out of earshot in her seat across the room. Nanny nodded. "It is my opinion that Evelyn ran away because of the nonsense Merrow here had been feeding her."

"What do you mean? What has this peabrain told her?"

"This peabrain—er, that is, this misguided woman has been using you as threat to try to keep the chit in tow. She has often heard your old valet and Gresham speak of your, er—exacting and, er, dominating nature. Oh, of course only in the most respectful of terms," she assured him.

In truth, Northrup's demands were those of one used to having his way, but they were never unreasonable and always heartily approved by the servants in question, both of whom would have balked at working for someone with less discriminating taste. She glanced at him and noted that, though his face registered some surprise at her disclosure, it showed no malice. Ah, she thought, but he was ever good-natured and fair, even as a child. Most people, she realized, could not see beyond his frequently sardonic veneer.

"And, then, Evelyn's mother, if I may say so, your lordship, did her best to feed the woman's wild imaginings."

He rolled his eyes at the mention of his late sister-in-law. They had ever been at odds. The delicate, mindless woman had always been cowed by his arrogant, commanding presence and, obviously, she had filled Merrow's empty head with all manner of nonsense. Strange, he thought, not for the first time, that his brother, Kit, so practical and intelligent himself, should have wed such a creature. As for himself, if he were to consider marriage, something he was loath to do, but for the need of getting an heir, the woman would have some measure of independence and a sharp wit—in short, spirit. Nanny went on.

"Well, your dear brother, may he rest in peace, had the right of it. Evelyn is a willful child and is ever giving poor Merrow the slip. Apparently, she, having no personal knowledge of men, conceived that you are a monster, and she often tried to intimidate the girl with threats of your terrible temper. Naturally, I did my best to convince her otherwise, but I seem to have had little success." She did not add that in the last few minutes he had put paid to any inroads she might have made against Merrow's prejudices.

"Good God," he interjected.

"Indeed. Evelyn loves to ride out alone, though Merrow forbids it . . ."

"I should hope so," the earl snapped. "One would like to think she serves some useful purpose."

"As you say. Well, after she, that is, Evelyn, was caught riding without a groom this last time, the silly woman promised you would thrash her and, doubtless, refuse to take her to London. And that," Nanny finished at last, "is why I think she ran off."

"Evidently the child is stupid as well as spoiled and selfish."

"I must remind you, sir, that Evelyn is no longer a child. She is seventeen and has been anticipating her first Season in London with much relish."

"Not with *too* much relish, I sincerely hope, Nanny. I must own that I had not looked forward to taking over the care of my niece. Kit wrote of her headstrong ways, but this is quite the limit. Perhaps I shall give her cause to believe Merrow after all, for it will require the greatest effort to keep myself from beating her, I promise you. A London Season, indeed!"

"As to her comeout, you must do as you think right. I know you will not beat her, though the good Lord knows she deserves it." She paused. "It is good to have you back, my boy. I have missed you sorely." Smiling warmly, she wiped away a tear. "If I may say so, you should never have left. You might have been killed, heaven forbid, and now with your dear brother gone . . ." She shook her head sadly.

"Aye, Nanny. I, too, miss him deeply," he said softly. This was the closest Northrup had come to expressing to anyone the loss he felt at his brother's death. The grief, the devastation, brought on by the news, which had at last found him, fittingly, on that awful battlefield, had been suffered privately.

"Why you left is still beyond my ken. That silly Letitia was not worth such a sacrifice," she said, her lips pursed with distaste.

He gave her a sharp look. "Madam, your tongue sometimes makes me wish I had pensioned you off!" She sat, her hands once again busy with her tatting. In a moment, he smiled indulgently. "That was a long time ago, Nanny. I thought it best, and I also believed it my duty, to aid in our country's struggle. But, all that is ended now, for me anyway, and I am home to stay. I want only to find my niece and then spend my days here in the quiet of the country.

"Please have a word with this—woman. Perhaps you can lay to rest her hallucinations about me. I shall notify you of what I find in London." With that, he turned and, limping slightly, left the room.

Three

It had taken some time and not a little effort on Clare's part to quiet her guest after her latest bout of hysterics. The obvious and proper solution to the problem was to return Evelyn to her uncle, but Clare hadn't the heart to broach the matter, given the girl's emotional state. Surely, the man could not be the monster portrayed by Miss Merrow. And yet, she reasoned, some bit of truth must have sparked charges such as these. Clare determined to write Northrup forthwith to apprise him of Evelyn's whereabouts; for, even an ogre, she told herself drily, must be anxious about his niece's disappearance.

Her letter on its way to Northrup Court, Clare was just worrying how to give the news to Evelyn, when Estelle tapped at the bedroom door.

"Excuse me, miss, you have a visitor in the Blue Saloon."

Clare smiled. One of Maude's pretensions. They had but one room suitable for entertaining callers and, while it was decorated in that particular color, to refer to it as Maude insisted Estelle do, caused Clare to envision an endless number of luxuriously appointed drawing rooms, each tricked out in a different color!

"Who is there, Estelle?" her mistress prompted.

"The Viscountess Castlereagh, miss," she replied, pleased with herself.

"Lady Castlereagh?" Clare gasped, jumping from her chair. "Good heavens, why did you not say so?"

"But I did, miss, just now," she replied innocently.

Clare stood before her mirror patting stray curls into place. Really, she thought with exasperation, the girl would never learn her duties properly. Still, one could not fault the maid's lack of propriety, for not since before her employ had they received so exalted a visitor.

"Yes, very well, no damage done, I suppose, Estelle." She smoothed an imaginary wrinkle from her willow green morning dress. "Do I look alright?"

"Yes, very nice, as always."

"Thank you, Estelle. Do you serve tea and cakes when I ring," she called over her shoulder, as she hurried from the room.

Lady Emily, an old family friend, had always been kind, but it had been some time since the two had met. Whatever could the woman want? She entered the drawing room to find a handsome grey-eyed woman, around middle age, seated on a settee.

"Clare, dear," she said, extending a beringed hand.

Clare smiled broadly and dropped a curtsy. "Good day, Lady Emily, how wonderful to see you again. I am honored, ma'am."

"It has been much too long, Clare." Her guest smiled and patted a spot beside her on the settee. "My dear, you are looking quite lovely."

"You are most kind, Lady Emily."

"I daresay you are wondering what has brought me here after all this time." She raised a hand to Clare's polite objection. "Tut, tut, of course you are and have every right to. The fact is, child . . . Forgive me, I still see you as a gay, young miss capturing the hearts of every young buck in town." Clare flushed. "Just so. That, my dear, is precisely why I am here."

"Now, Lady Emily, please," Clare began.

"Hush. We have had this discussion before, you and I.

You were the victor then, but that will not be the case this time, I assure you."

Clare sat meekly, her hands folded in her lap, for she knew better than to gainsay Lady Castlereagh.

"I think it is time you came back into society. Yes, yes, I know what you are going to say. The ton was not kind to you, and I must agree, but you, child, should not have given in so readily and hidden yourself away."

"I beg pardon, ma'am, but truly I had little choice. It is true that my father's losses necessitated some substantial changes in our lives, though we were never at point non plus. But many people chose not to associate with one of less affluent circumstances, and some made it quite plain that my company was no longer desired."

"Yes, people can be cruel," Lady Emily allowed, "but I see no reason why you should remain shut away here in Edwardes Square. I collect, then, you could join in town life on a modest scale. Am I correct?"

"Well, yes, ma'am, that is so, but . . ."

"No 'buts.' It is high time you began to live again."

Clare's hazel eyes took on a wistful air, and Lady Emily, sensing her advantage, pressed on.

"You know, dear, pretty as you are, you are not growing younger. We must set about finding you a husband," she explained with candor.

"Dear ma'am, I fear you would go too far. The ton may see fit to accept my presence now that I have done my penance, provided that I do not take on any airs or try to rise above my present station, but marriage—I think not." Clare said this with an effort at determination.

"Fustian! I could not, in good conscience, countenance your previous behavior, Clare," she stated bluntly, "as I told you at the time." Clare blushed. "But allowance must be made for your tender years and the lack of a mother to guide you. Alas, Marcus, your dear father, was a kind man. Too kind, in fact, for he indulged your headstrong ways, when he should have curbed them."

"Yes, ma'am."

"Well, the ton loves to talk, no matter how small the transgression, but it was a long time ago and best forgotten." Lady Emily chuckled. "When I consider your attendance at the Cyprians Ball, of all places, and those daring gowns you sometimes wore . . . How did you ever convince your poor papa they were all the crack and worn by every young miss that year?"

Clare gave a faint smile. "You will recall that my father never went into society. He knew not what the ladies were wearing that Season and generally was caught up in his reading. Gaining his consent really was not all that difficult." She sighed. Speaking of her father ever made her glum, and to remember the ways in which she had tricked him gave her a pang of guilt.

In fact, Clare had been as gullible as had her father. She had believed her friends when they told her that it would be a harmless lark for a respectable girl to dress in a daring gown and sneak into the notorious annual Cyprians Ball. Once inside, she quickly saw that they were wrong, for the place was filled with demi-reps, dandies, and apparently respectable gentleman, but certainly no ladies. She had stayed but a few minutes and fled the Argyle Rooms in shame. Fortunately, her appearance there was so brief and the customary company so much more tempting than that of a green girl, that later no one could say with absolute certainty if she had attended. Nevertheless, the rumor and the gossips persisted and had damaged her reputation.

The older woman laughed. "Your father was rather naive, or he would not have lost his fortune," she remarked frankly. "Still, he was ever one to enjoy a good joke." She patted Clare's hand in understanding, then asked brightly, "What was it they called you, Clare? Ah, yes, The Changeable Rose, that was it," she recalled, pleased with her memory.

Clare wished to sink into the floor but, instead, rose and tugged at the bellpull. "Tea, Lady Emily?"

"Thank you, that would be nice. Yes, The Changeable Rose. Some of the mamas swore you used tincture of rose to heighten your color and, by heaven, they were right," she chuckled, oblivious to her hostess's discomfiture. "What I do not understand, dear, is *why* you painted, since your complexion is not so very pale."

Clare was spared the necessity of responding, as Estelle entered the room. The girl set down the tea tray and left, shutting the door softly behind her.

"I was a foolish, self-centered girl, ma'am, and I have learned my lesson, believe me," Clare said slowly, as she poured.

"I am sure of it, dear. But your crime was not so very terrible. Why, many of us, probably most of us, paint, and some of the gels today . . . No. Your actions were rather improper, but hardly real cause for ostracism. Why, that popinjay, Tobias Portman, was about to offer for you, I was convinced of it. He was quite willing to overlook your everlasting blush and your daring necklines, provided you brought a handsome dowry to the union. No, it was the loss of your fortune that was your real sin and the true cause of your expulsion, not your so-called reputation."

Clare sat quietly, her tea untouched. Lady Emily sampled a seedcake, nodded her approval, and continued.

"Then, one good thing did come of all that. You were saved from being wedded to Portman, whom I am sure you realize now is but a clown. Well, as I have said, that is all by the way."

"Oh, no, Lady Emily," Clare objected, "people do not forget easily, and, truly, I am accustomed to my quiet life, as I said before."

"Gammon! I ain't a nodcock, child. 'Tis plain you are just afraid of what folks will say. Well, I have never cared about how they talk of me, and you must try to do the same.

At any rate, the ton will not dare to snub you—not with me to sponsor you," she noted with satisfaction. Lady Castlereagh was married to the British Foreign Secretary, and was herself a patroness of Almack's. If her eccentric behavior was considered outré by some members of the ton, her position made it nigh impossible for them to shun her.

"You are good-hearted, Clare, always were. You may wonder what finally brought me here. Well, I was present at Madame Claudine's on Tuesday and witnessed that spectacle—insipid Frenchwoman, I've a good mind to let slip the truth about her origins; that would teach her. Anyway, I saw your kindness to that child, and I determined that you should at last be shown some kindness yourself. So, here I am," she ended, reaching for another cake.

"Who is the child, by the by? She looked simply awful. Perhaps I can assist you in finding her a situation."

At this, Clare giggled. "I hardly think so, ma'am. Only just wait until I tell you who she really is." Clare launched into a detailed recitation of the events of the past few days.

The viscountess gasped. "Northrup's niece, good gracious."

"I cannot recall him, ma'am."

"No, indeed, you would not, my dear, for Northrup must be about seven and thirty by now."

"You are acquainted?"

"My, yes. I have known him since he was a young man. He was the coveted prize of a number of Seasons, so very good-looking and quite rich, a prime catch. He broke many a heart," she recollected with an appreciative grin. "But then that witch, Letitia Wentworth, caught him. They were nearly betrothed some time ago. She was a beauty—still is—and wellborn, but a selfish hussy, if ever there was one. But there, Northrup loved her. He was besotted, they said."

"What happened? Evelyn made no mention of the countess of Northrup."

"Of course she did not, for they never married. Letitia

threw him over for Thomas Marlowe. Northrup was so cut up by the affair that he convinced the old earl to buy him a commission, and he has been out of the country these several years."

"Oh my, how sad."

"Most unfortunate, yes, but for Letitia, not Northrup. He was too good for the likes of that jilt, as I told him many a time. Of course, he would hear nothing against her. She, on the other hand, led him a merry chase. Believe me, she would have been better off with a man like him. He could have kept her in tow and stopped those selfish tantrums. Well, despite her attachment to Northrup, she took a fancy to Tom Marlowe and dangled after him, for he indulged her. Not that she needed his money, you know, for she was quite well off, but spoiled and greedy. She broke off with Northrup and married Tom, and that was a nine days' wonder, believe me. The poor man died a little over a year ago of a lung ailment."

"That's awful," Clare exclaimed.

"So, Northrup has come home to take his rightful place at last," the older woman mused. "I am glad of it. He will make a fitting earl. Shall I see him for you and break the news about Evelyn?"

"Thank you, Lady Emily, I have already written to him. He should receive my missive quite soon."

"Very well. I shall be on my way, Clare dear, but not before I have your promise to come to tea tomorrow. You may bring your aunt, if you must." She twinkled.

"I should be delighted, ma'am." Clare smiled. "And Maude will be most pleased to join me, I am sure."

Seated in Lady Castlereagh's richly appointed drawing room the next day, Clare was filled with a sense of well-being that she had not experienced in some time. She smiled at Maude, who clearly was thrilled at Lady Emily's attention.

After all, she, too, had suffered her isolation these last years, and her ebullience now was understandable.

The time passed quickly, as Clare listened to the latest on-dits with an eagerness never before felt, but borne of her endless days spent in nothing more exciting than walks in the park and working her petit point. For a girl once forced to her bed for several days after a dizzying round of parties, routs, and gentlemen callers, the latest gossip was not only fascinating, but a miraculous panacea.

"Dear ma'am, I fear you must be bamming me." Clare giggled breathlessly at her hostess's description of a particularly outrageous dandy.

"Indeed?" queried that lady, her brows raised in mock displeasure. "I assure you, Clare, I speak the truth." She nodded solemnly.

"But no, violet pantaloons!"

The viscountess burst into shrill laughter herself. "The final joke came with his sneezing fit. The man obviously was not accustomed to snuff, for his neckcloth, which doubtless took his valet hours to fashion into that intricate Trone d'Amour, came undone and fell down about his yellow coat!"

She was regaling her two guests with the details of Caro Lamb's latest escapade, when a footman entered, coughed discreetly, and announced the earl of Northrup.

The earl entered on the heels of the servant. Unlike the Regency buck whose raiment had so amused the ladies, his morning dress was tasteful, a coat of claret-colored superfine over a deep grey waistcoat edged in black silk, and trousers.

He crossed the room in careful strides and Clare realized that his silver-headed stick was not an affectation, but a necessity, as evidenced by the manner in which he favored his right leg. She grimly recalled Evelyn's cavalier attitude toward his injury and mentally castigated the girl.

Northrup took Lady Castlereagh's two hands in his.

"Emily," he smiled winningly. "I am glad to see you and to find you just as lovely as ever."

She looked up into his face and Clare would have sworn the woman nearly blushed. "Northrup, Evan. It is good to see you again." She squeezed his hands. "You are recently arrived in town?"

"Yes, Emily. I am just come down from Northrup Court, and I have a problem of some importance to discuss with you."

Clare watched this exchange with interest. Truly, the man was a devilishly handsome specimen. No jangling fobs for him, she noted. His neckcloth was fashioned in a simple Irish Knot, and his sole concession to jewelry was a heavy and seemingly very old signet ring that adorned his right hand.

She inspected his distinctive profile from the corner of her eye, noting a finely drawn nose and strong chin. His smile was boyish and sensuous at the same time . . . Clare blushed furiously. Good heavens, the man had turned and was looking straight at her, amusement playing in bright blue eyes.

Lady Emily looked from one to the other and apologized. "Clare, Evan, do please forgive my rag manners. Evan, I should like to introduce Miss Clare Winchester and her aunt, Miss Maude Beauchamp. Clare, Miss Beauchamp, may I present the earl of Northrup?"

The earl turned respectfully to Maude and bowed. "Your servant, ma'am."

"How do you do, my lord," she breathed.

During this interchange, Clare was able to regain her composure, and she looked up at him from under a heavy fringe of lashes and smiled.

Lady Emily motioned her guests to their seats and rang for a fresh tea tray. It was apparent to Clare that the earl had not been at home to receive her letter, and she felt rather awkward at having to make her report in person. As she pondered the best way to broach the subject, Maude, buoyed by such exalted company, chattered for some minutes.

Clare looked up to find the earl's eyes on her and, while Maude drew her next breath, interjected, "My lord, I believe that I can solve the problem to which you referred."

"Indeed, Miss Winchester," he queried stiffly, as he accepted a cup of Earl Grey from his hostess.

"Yes, my lord. You are, I think, searching for your niece, Miss Evelyn Hallisey, are you not?"

The earl sat forward and placed his cup on a lacquered side table. "What do you know of my niece, Miss Winchester?" he asked sharply.

"She has been a guest in my house in Edwardes Square these last few days," Clare replied. The earl looked baffled and, once again, she related the events that had introduced her to the runaway.

He listened, captivated by the tale, but with his lips set in a grim line. Until now, Clare had kept this information from Maude, for as long as her aunt believed the girl a housemaid, her privacy was secure. Upon hearing the story, the older woman's eyes widened. Before Clare could tell the earl that an explanatory letter awaited him at Northrup Court, Maude interrupted.

"Why, Clare, this is all too awful. That poor child," she shook her head in newfound sympathy. "Good heavens, the earl must have been driven to distraction with worry. What were you about? Why did you not advise him of this earlier?"

"Yes, Miss Winchester, I would like to hear the answer to that question myself," Northrup stated evenly. His voice was low, and his eyes had turned a deep midnight. "Perhaps, like most members of your sex, you consider your social engagements of more significance than returning a runaway child to her family."

Clare was taken aback. Naturally, she had expected that he would be upset upon hearing the story, but this was the outside of enough! She bristled at the injustice, but before she could retort, Lady Emily intervened.

"Northrup, please! You should beg Miss Winchester's pardon. She took pity on your niece when most people would have drowned her like a stray kitten. Furthermore, Clare has posted a letter to the Court to apprise you of the situation."

He looked toward Clare, who nodded her confirmation of this testimony. "It seems I do owe you an apology, Miss Winchester. I most humbly beg your pardon."

Clearly, apologizing was something that the earl was not often called upon to do, and Clare glanced back at him, her eyes flashing. No small wonder that Miss Merrow was afraid of him. Heartened by the knowledge that she would never have to see him again once he removed Evelyn to his care, she was able to feel more tolerant of his behavior. She nodded primly. "Please do not distress yourself, my lord."

The earl understood that he had not yet restored himself to her good graces. "You are too kind, ma'am. Now, when may I unburden you of my wayward niece?" he inquired stiffly.

"Truly, sir, the child has been no real trouble. If you have no objection, I think perhaps not before tomorrow morning, you see . . ." At this point, Clare hesitated. She had determined to discuss the girl's fears with him, indeed, she could not send her off to Northrup Court without doing so, but she was uncertain how to approach the subject with others present.

"Your kindness and generosity are deeply appreciated, ma'am, but I assure you, no longer necessary. I shall follow you to your house now and remove my niece."

"Well, my lord, to be candid, I do think it best that . . ."

"Miss Winchester, you will kindly allow me the right to know what is best for her. Now, if you have no further objection, may we go?"

She had expected and wanted no more than a simple thank-you for her efforts, but his high-handed, gruff manner was infuriating. "Sir, I should never presume to tell you how to care for Evelyn or to keep you from her. I have only her best interests in mind. I had thought her apprehensions about you were entirely the result of her governess's creative mind, but I confess I begin to see why the poor girl is so frightened of you!"

"Please, Miss Winchester, do not spare my feelings, I beg you," he drawled sarcastically.

Clare flushed. "Oh, dear, I hadn't meant to . . ."

"Not at all. Before I departed the country, I was advised of my niece's, er, opinions of me. I shall endeavor to convince her otherwise, naturally, and shall deal with that ninny-hammered governess upon my return."

Despite herself, she felt a twinge of compassion for him. To have lost a brother and been wounded in the war must have been bad enough, but then to come home and learn that his niece's fear of him had driven her to run off alone to London! She smiled warmly and shook her head. "My lord, I am convinced that all her fears will be allayed once you meet again and she realizes that you are not going to devour her. If you will allow me to impart the news of your arrival tonight, I am certain that she will be prepared to make you a proper greeting in the morning."

Northrup smiled, some of the light returning to his eyes. "It would appear, Miss Winchester, that, for the present at least, you are far more capable than I of handling the brat. Add to that the debt of gratitude I owe you for being so kind as to take her in, and I can hardly deny you your wish. I shall come round to Edwardes Square at ten tomorrow morning."

"Very good, my lord, we shall expect you. And now, Maude, I think we must be going, for Lady Emily and the earl must have much to say to one another." Clare rose from her seat.

"Oh. Why, yes, of course, my dear," Maude's voice was distinctly reluctant.

Both Lady Emily and the earl protested, but it was plain

that Clare's surmise was correct, and the two women took their leave.

When they returned home, Maude was still berating her niece. "Really, Clare, I think you might have told me. Why, to have the niece of an earl under our own roof."

"That," Clare responded drily, "is why I did not tell you. The child had quite enough excitement, Aunt. I wished to keep her as quiet as possible."

"What I do not comprehend," her aunt continued, as if Clare had not spoken, "is why she is so afraid of her uncle. True, he did display a lack of propriety when he took you to task so unjustly, but I think that can be put down to his distress over Evelyn. And you know, dear"—she shook her finger at Clare—"you should have told him sooner. Why, to number the earl of Northrup among our acquaintances, just as we are about to make our return into society. Only think of it!"

Clare let out an exasperated sigh as she untied the ribbons of her bonnet. "Aunt, I remind you that, after tomorrow, we shall probably never see them again. And as for our return to society, I have already explained that it must be in a small way and not altogether what we were accustomed to."

The older woman, still heedless of these explanations, removed her gloves and tossed them onto the sideboard with a flourish. "Yes, dear, in a small way, of course." Her aunt giggled as she traipsed upstairs with a youthful vigor that Clare had not seen in many a day. She found it impossible to be at odds with her aunt, for she sometimes believed that Maude missed the beau monde a good deal more than she herself did.

She was at sixes and sevens over how to break the news of Northrup's arrival, and decided that an unusually tasty supper would serve to fortify her own nerve, if not Evelyn's. Their cook, Mrs. Musgrave, was just concluding a purchase from the fishmonger's boy, when Clare entered.

"Afternoon, Miss Clare," the old woman grinned. "I've just got some nice fresh turbot from Sam."

"That is wonderful, Mrs. Musgrave, for I would like tonight's supper to be particularly tempting. Not," she added diplomatically, "that you do not always excel the finest cooks in London."

The cook beamed at the compliment. "Very kind of you to say so, miss. May I suggest, then, to go with the baked turbot, a pigeon pie and a nice celerata cream?"

"Perfect. And perhaps some of your special biscuits?"

"Of course, miss."

Mrs. Musgrave had been with the Winchester family for many years, and the move to Edwardes Square had reduced her standing among her peers. Still, she well knew that it was the rage for most of the ton to have a man in this position, and felt fortunate to have both the job and a considerate mistress.

Wasn't it just a year ago that Clare had paid her cook's passage to Winchelsea so that she could visit her ailing sister? Smiling to herself, she recalled how Clare and Estelle, between them, had prepared all the meals while she had been away. She sniffed, and her mistress a lady born and bred. It always pained her to think of Clare sitting on the shelf. But this special dinner—her hopes rose.

"Ahem, will there be company to dinner then, miss?"

"No, Mrs. Musgrave, just the three of us. But our guest will be coming down to the dining room tonight, so you needn't prepare a tray."

The cook's face fell. "As you say, Miss Clare."

Clare put an arm about her old retainer's shoulder and squeezed her gently. "Thank you, Mrs. Musgrave. You are indeed a treasure."

The supper was as flavorsome as Clare knew it would be. She watched with amusement as Evelyn spread butter on her third hot biscuit, pronouncing them "prodigious good." Clare had hoped that her aunt would make herself scarce, but when the meal finally ended, Maude suggested that the three remove to the Blue Saloon. Seated in a comfortable satinwood armchair, Clare picked up her needlepoint. Evelyn glanced about the room and bemoaned the absence of a piano.

"I regret to say we do not have one, Evelyn," was Clare's reply. "A pity, for I enjoy playing."

"Not have a piano, but why, ma'am?" the girl asked innocently. "At home, we have the most beautifully tuned instrument. Without a husband and children, Miss Winchester, whatever do you do to occupy your time?"

"I do manage, Evelyn," she drawled. "There are other things in life besides a husband and little ones, you know." Honestly, the girl's candor would have to be curbed, but she had no doubt that her uncle could accomplish that.

"Good Lord, what other things?"

Clare smiled. "Well, there is walking in the park or stitching new covers for the chairs in the dining room," she explained, holding her half-finished canvas aloft. Maude sniffed, and even Clare was at a loss to feel much enthusiasm at her words.

"How deadly dull!" the girl exclaimed.

"Indeed," Maude remarked. "Perhaps you would like a hand of piquet, dear?"

Before Evelyn could give her consent, Clare put down her needlework and interposed. "Not just now, Maude, for I would like to talk with Evelyn," she said pointedly.

The woman smiled and folded her hands in her lap. "Alright, dear, I'll just wait until you are finished."

Clare closed her eyes in exasperation for a moment. She expected that Evelyn might cause a scene and felt it would be better if Maude were not involved. "I should like to speak with Evelyn *alone,* Aunt."

"Oh! Well, I am sure I know when I am not wanted, Clare." She sniffed. "You had only to say so." So saying, she walked briskly from the room.

Clare turned to Evelyn, who was eyeing her with some

apprehension. Clare had been dreading this moment, but it was impossible to delay any longer. She drew a deep breath and began. "Evelyn, dear, I wish to speak with you of your uncle."

"Oh, please, Miss Winchester, I do not wish to talk of him. I do not wish even to think of him."

"Yes, I am well aware of your feelings, Evelyn, but talk of him we must, for he is here in London," Clare explained gently.

"No!" the girl gasped, "He cannot be!"

"He is."

"But, then, he must not be told where I am, you must hide me. You will hide me, will you not?" she begged, her voice rising in desperation.

"I have told you before that I cannot do such a thing, Evelyn. The earl knows of your whereabouts, for I met him quite by chance this afternoon at Lady Castlereagh's. I told him then and he . . ."

Her next words were drowned by hysterical weeping as Evelyn shot from her chair and began pacing the room. "But you cannot—you—you would not do such a thing," she fairly screamed. "I th-thought that you were my friend. I-I thought you would protect me!"

Clare was completely out of patience. "Cease these histrionics this instant, my girl," she commanded. "You shall not act out a Cheltenham tragedy in my drawing room for all of Edwardes Square to hear." The girl only sobbed the louder. Clare rose, grasped her shoulders, and shook her soundly. Evelyn's bawling stopped abruptly, and she stared at Clare in astonishment.

"That is much better. Now that you have remembered your manners, be so kind as to sit down and listen to what I have to tell you."

She related the details of the afternoon. Not wishing to upset her guest further, she deliberately avoided mention of the earl's harsh rebuke. Rather, she emphasized those qualities that she felt would place Northrup in the best light—his smiling blue eyes and the genuine concern that she had seen on his face and heard in his voice.

"And so you see, Evelyn, I think there is no reason for you to fly up into the boughs. To be honest, you should expect a thorough scolding, but there," she said, as she patted her hand, "even you must concede that is no more than you deserve." The girl's eyes grew wide. "Now, no more of your tears. Truly, your uncle seems a kindly, fair man, not at all the demon your Miss Merrow conjured up."

Evelyn had at last begun to show signs of weakening. "You know, the earl has not had an easy time of it, either. When you lost your father, remember that he lost a brother. In addition, that injury which you shrugged off so lightly appears to be causing him no little amount of discomfort." Evelyn had the grace to look contrite.

"You must realize, however, that the responsibility of guardian to a young woman is heavy and one which is quite new to a man who has been a bachelor all of his life." Clare played her final card. "I daresay he is as nervous as you are, Evelyn. You may find it necessary to make allowances for him now and then, but, in truth, I believe the two of you will deal well together, once you become acquainted. I think he will be quite surprised to see how grown-up you are."

"Very well, ma'am," Evelyn agreed, "if you think it best, I shall meet with him."

Clare hid a smile. "Thank you, dear, that is most kind of you. I am sure your uncle will be grateful. And now, why don't you go up to bed, for you're quite knocked up and you will want to be bright and fresh when you meet him in the morning."

Evelyn went off to her room without further complaint, and Clare, fatigued by all that had transpired, followed soon after.

Clare awoke refreshed and, for some inexplicable reason, more than usually eager to greet the day. Generally, she left the choice of her garb to Molly, who delighted in sorting through the small, attractive assortment of gowns, but this morning she was curiously particular. When Molly presented a brightly printed challis, Clare rejected it with a wave of her hand. "I think not, Molly. Perhaps the jonquil cashmere with the embroidery at the hem."

"Why, of course, miss, that would be the very thing."

The yellow gown did indeed become its wearer, the soft wool falling gracefully from under her bosom. As Molly dressed her hair, Clare sat lost in thought before her mirror. She saw neither her abigail's questioning gaze, nor the dreamy look in her own reflection, but rather a pair of laughing blue eyes that seemed to intrude upon her from nowhere.

". . . or the satin, miss?"

Clare suddenly realized that Molly was awaiting a reply, but for the life of her, she could not have said what the question was. "I'm sorry, Molly, I was woolgathering," she smiled, the blue eyes now flown from her thoughts.

"I was asking, miss, if you prefer the velvet or the satin ribbon for your hair."

"The satin, I think."

"Yes, miss." The maid obediently wound the ribbon around Clare's hair. "Are you feeling quite the thing?"

"Molly, I am quite up to snuff, I assure you. In truth, I have not felt so good in some time."

"Ah, of course, you must be relieved to get rid of that weepy miss, at last. She has been a trial to you, miss."

"Not at all, Molly. Perhaps you would like that challis you chose. I noticed last week that some of your own gowns are becoming frightfully shabby."

"Thank you," she said brightly, once again removing the dress from the clothespress. She held it close to her, one hand about the bodice, the other flaring the skirt as she danced about the room. "Oh, isn't it lovely? Only wait until Edward, that is, Mr. Reynolds, sees me in this!" she crowed.

Clare sat in the window seat and watched her abigail with

pleasure. The two had been together since Clare was twelve and Molly just fifteen. Smiling, she recalled the circumstances that had brought them together all those years ago, for, of course, at that tender age Clare had no need of a lady's maid.

Molly's parents had been too poor to keep her at home, and, after a series of unsuccessful positions, the girl had finally arrived at Caulfield Hall, where she was set to work in the scullery. Within days, Mrs. Musgrave had reluctantly expelled her from the kitchen. "Else we shall have to replace every bit of china and crystal in the place," she had explained to Clare's father.

Despite the differences in their positions, the two girls had liked one another from the first. Clare knew that banishment from the scullery meant dismissal from the Hall, as there was no simpler task to which the skinny girl with the wide, grey eyes could be put. She had gone to her father and pleaded her case for a personal maid in her most grown-up and ladylike manner. Marcus Winchester had, initially, rejected the request out of hand, but Clare persisted and, in the end, he indulged her, just as he always did.

Clare and Molly had been together ever since. If truth be told, they were nearer to being friends than employer and maid, their close relationship based on mutual respect and affection and the hardships each had helped the other to weather. Clare remembered with gratitude Molly's support when Winchester had died, and her refusal to seek other employment, which surely would have paid her more than Clare could now afford. She recalled, too, Molly's sobs, when her own mother had passed on and had insisted that she sleep on a truckle bed set up in her own room for the next month.

Smiling at her maid now, she teased her. "And just who is this Edward Reynolds you speak of, Molly? Have I met him?"

Molly came to rest companionably on the edge of Clare's bed and rolled her eyes. "Oh, la, miss, he is ever so strong and handsome. He is footman to Lord Ashby," she explained, wrinkling her nose at his lordship's name, "so I do not think you have seen him. He says that Lord Ashby is a very hard man."

"Do I take it aright that Mr. Reynolds has replaced the wonderful Paul in your affections, then? Has he offered for you?"

"Oh, Paul!" Molly dismissed her former beau with a toss of her curls. "He cannot hold a candle to Mr. Reynolds. But no"—she sighed—"he says he will not speak for me until he finds a better position, so that he can provide properly for a wife. Oh, but that could take ever so long, miss."

"Now, do not fret, Molly, good things are worth waiting for, after all. And I am gratified to learn that your Mr. Reynolds has such foresight." Glancing at the old ormolu clock on the mantel, she rose. "Goodness, the earl should be here any minute. I must check on Miss Hallisey, for it is likely she has been dawdling." Casting a last critical look in her mirror, she left the room.

A short time later, Estelle, with uncharacteristic grace, announced the earl into the drawing room. He was only just above average height, but his figure never failed to impress those about him, male as well as female. Despite his slight limp, he crossed the threshold with an easy assurance that made him equally at home on the ballroom floor and in the fencing ring. He paused by the fire to observe the scene before him and awaited an invitation to advance.

Evelyn sat as if glued to her chair. Her cheeks white and her eyes dark, she stared at him as if fully expecting he would sprout horns and a tail. Clare welcomed their visitor, giving him an apologetic smile, and turned back to the girl. "Evelyn, you are forgetting your manners! Get up and make your curtsy to your uncle, or he will think you sadly lacking in the graces expected of a young woman of breeding."

Evelyn rose hastily, greeted the earl with a barely audible whisper, and stood, her eyes cast downward, awaiting further direction. Northrup acknowledged Clare with a neat bow and crossed the room to his niece. She stood stock-still, not daring to raise her eyes, nervous fingers shredding a flimsy handkerchief.

"Look at me, child," Northrup ordered.

Slowly, she looked up. He stared at her, his stern expression turning to a charming smile as he grasped her shoulders and kissed her forehead.

"By God, Evelyn, you've grown into a pretty young thing."

The relief which accompanied Evelyn's realization that she was not to be thrown into the fiery pit erupted in a flood of tears, as she threw her arms about her uncle's neck. Clare smiled at the reunion and resumed her seat by the fire.

The earl gently unwrapped himself from his niece's embrace, eased her back on the chair, and sat down beside her. "Now, Evelyn, cease your tears, for they cannot save you from the lecture you deserve."

She sniffed, peeked into the earl's smiling eyes, then looked toward Clare, who urged her to heed her uncle. "And do stop behaving like a watering pot, or you shall indeed vex him beyond reason."

This sage advice had its desired effect. Northrup looked thankfully at Clare. It was obvious that she had a positive influence on the chit, he noted with relief, for it was becoming equally apparent that he would be hard put to handle her alone. For the next fifteen minutes, he held forth on Evelyn's thoughtless transgression, his stern words eliciting a series of meek and barely discernible responses.

"And, so, my dear," he finished, "I think you will concede how poorly you have behaved. You have caused much unhappiness and inconvenience to Miss Winchester, not to mention myself, your governess, and Nanny. Now, we shall return to Northrup Court, and you will answer to me," he said ominously, "if you should continue in your disobedient ways."

"But, Uncle," she gasped, "you cannot mean it. You cannot mean to exile me to the country! What about my comeout, Uncle? Why can we not remain in town for the Season?"

"Season?" Northrup's outrage was tinged with amusement. "You impudent miss. You dare to ask that of me, after what you have done?"

"Oh, Uncle, I simply must have my debut," she begged prettily. "Surely you could not deny me that? You could not send me to waste away at the Court, for that would be cruel. And Miss Winchester told me that you are not a monster."

"How very kind of her," he said, twinkling at Clare. She returned his look with a smile of her own and a shrug of her shoulders that suggested a reluctance to intercede further in family matters. He sighed and turned back to his niece. "Evelyn, supposing I were amenable to your request—I have not said that I am—but if I were, it is impossible for me to grant it at present, for I have no one to sponsor you. Needless to say, I shall never again trust you to that chucklehead, Merrow. I shall make every effort to find a suitable person and, next year, provided you behave, you shall have your Season, I promise you."

"Next year! Why, by then I shall be ancient. Oh, Uncle, you cannot be so hard." By this time, Evelyn's tears had reappeared. "I shall die, I cannot bear it!"

"Dash it, Evelyn, be reasonable," he demanded, raising his voice above the weeping that continued ever louder. The earl's face revealed a sudden, remarkable desire to return to the Peninsula and the single-minded rationality of men at war.

"Sir, if I may?" Clare interrupted quietly.

"Nay, ma'am, if you only *will*," he replied in desperation.

Clare crossed to Evelyn and, placing an arm around her, assisted the girl to her feet. "Evelyn, if you will be so kind as to leave us, I should like a word with your uncle."

Sniffling, Evelyn obeyed. Halfway across the room, she bobbed a curtsy, and fled upstairs.

"Shall we sit down, sir? I do hope that you will forgive my boldness."

"It is I, Miss Winchester, who must once again beg your pardon. After you have shown such kindness to that brat, I come into your drawing room and behave like a bounder. I daresay you are wishing the two of us at Jericho."

"Indeed no, sir, you mistake me. It is just that I could see that you and your niece could not deal together while she is having one of her crying fits. I should caution you, they seem to come on her rather easily." She smiled.

"I thank you for the warning, but I must confess that I am not surprised," he replied drily.

"It is a pity, however, that you cannot manage to bring her out this Season, as she is so set on it. Word of her escapade has not gotten out, and with her looks," she hinted, "I am convinced she would have no trouble in making an eligible connection."

"I quite agree, the girl is a beauty. Much as I would like to honor some lucky gentleman with the, er, care of my niece," he said, his eyes crinkling, "I could hardly entrust her to that governess, as I explained, so it would seem that my hands are tied."

Clare nodded in agreement. They sat quietly for some few moments, the silence strangely comfortable, as they mulled over the problem. The earl observed his hostess, who, in turn, seemed fascinated by a papier mâché box on the table beside her. Northrup noted with pleasure they way the sunlight, peeking through the curtain, struck golden lights in her brown hair. His eyes traveled to her full, pink lips, and he wondered for the first time in a long while . . .

"Sir," she began hesitantly, "I should not, of course, presume to speak for someone else or to intrude upon your family matters, but I have formed an affection for Evelyn during her stay and . . ."

The earl smiled. "My dear Miss Winchester, it is we who have intruded upon you. If you have some counsel you wish to impart concerning the guardianship of Evelyn, by all means, do so," he urged.

"Very well. I understood aright yesterday at Lady Emily's, your families have been acquainted for some years." Northrup nodded. "Well, it has occurred to me that, perhaps, you could prevail upon Lady Emily to sponsor Evelyn. She is one of the kindest people I know, indeed, she has been very kind to me. And I need not tell you that Evelyn could have no better entrée into town life."

The earl nodded again. "I agree, but unfortunately, that is impossible. The same idea came to be yesterday, after you left. Though I felt overbold in presuming on our long friendship, I finally broached the matter. Emily is not averse to the prospect, you understand, but her time is already committed to assisting in the comeout of her twin goddaughters. But for that, she told me, she would happily accept such a task."

"How unfortunate," Clare said sympathetically. "But, is there no one else, someone in the family, an aunt perhaps, to whom you might look?" The earl shook his head. "I do see your dilemma, then. Evelyn will simply have to wait. If you like, I shall be happy to try to reconcile her to these circumstances."

Northrup cleared his throat. "In fact, Miss Winchester, you might be of great assistance to myself and my niece, if you would be so good." Clare assured him that she would be pleased to lend whatever aid she might and, encouraged, he continued.

"As I said, Emily reluctantly declined my request, however, she did put forward an alternative." Watching her, he proceeded slowly. "She proposed that you bring out Evelyn. Indeed, she spoke extremely highly of you."

He did not have to wait long for Clare's response. She stared at him, her mouth open. "Surely, sir, you must be joking. Why I am hardly a suitable sponsor for your niece."

"I am well aware, ma'am, of the imposition, of the burden which I ask you to consider. Believe me, I would not be so brassbound if Emily had not urged me, and if I had not seen with my own eyes the authority that you are able to exert over Evelyn. As for your unsuitability"—he smiled—"I quite realize that I have no right to ask one so young herself to play fairy godmother to a green girl, and a willful one, at that. Again, I plead Emily's influence," he said in charming tones. Observing Clare's discomfort, he added, "Naturally, I shall understand if you refuse. In fact, I should not blame you in the least."

Clare shook her head. "It is not my age which makes me hesitate, for I am much older than you suppose."

Northrup grinned. "Miss Winchester, propriety precludes my asking how old you are, but you cannot convince me you are at your last prayers."

Clare flushed, and declared in a serious voice. "I am eight and twenty, sir."

"As old as that, ma'am?" The earl grinned mercilessly.

"You are quizzing me," Clare retorted, blushing a deeper pink. Dash the man, why should that look make her heart beat so? After all, had she not met many men in her youth? True, few were as handsome or as self-assured as Northrup, but many were of the finest families, gentlemen of the first stare. She had held her own with each of them. Why, she had danced with the Beau himself and never lost her composure, yet this man had only to look at her, and she felt like a young miss fresh from the country.

Northrup's smile vanished in the face of her displeasure, though a boyish twinkle remained in his eyes. "Forgive me, ma'am. I meant no offense, believe me. I find your honesty most refreshing."

"You are very kind. Much as I wish to help you, I fear I am not the best person for the responsibility you wish me to undertake." She could not explain to him the reason for her reluctance; after all, if he did not know of her youthful follies, and apparently he did not, why should she tell him? What puzzled her was why Lady Emily had put forward her name in the first place. Well, no matter, what was done was done. She must decline the earl's request as gracefully as possible, it was as simple as that.

"As to that, ma'am, I must disagree. If you choose to decline my petition, I shall not be put out, but pray, do not ask me to countenance such a disclaimer of your character. Lady Emily holds you in the highest regard, and I have seen how well you and Evelyn get on. And, Miss Winchester, you have yourself admitted a fondness for the girl. It is my opinion that you would make an admirable job of her comeout, and set her a good example into the bargain. Do you not think you might consider it? Both Evelyn and I would be most grateful."

Clare sighed. There just was no way to tactfully refuse the man and keep her own past and memories to herself at the same time. After all, her "transgressions" had hardly been serious, merely foolish, although some high sticklers had made no secret of their disapproval at the time. If truth be told, the prospect of once again moving among the ton, of the excitement of the Season, was not abhorrent to her. It might be an easy and practical way for her and Maude to re-enter society, as Lady Emily had suggested. Then, Evelyn, could not be forgotten; she would be thrilled to learn that her debut would not be put off.

"If you are certain in your choice, sir, I do not see how I can refuse."

The earl beamed. "Miss Winchester, how can I possibly express my gratitude?"

She returned his smile, though with a trifle less enthusiasm, for the next months would prove to be exhausting, more so, considering the character of her charge. She chuckled to herself. It was unlikely that Evelyn's willful nature and dodgery could best her. Past her prime she might be, but her own Season was not so very long ago that she had forgotten it. She was determined not to allow the girl to endanger her reputation.

"Please, sir, there is no need to thank me. I collect that Evelyn's gratitude will suffice for both of you," she said, laughing.

"On that score, I feel you must be right. Let us have her back so that we can give her the news. But first, I should like to arrange proper compensation for the services you have agreed to extend in our behalf—if such is possible."

Clare stiffened visibly. "Payment, sir?" she asked, arching a brow. "I have neither need nor desire for your money," she stated with cold finality.

Northrup, seeing at once that pursuit of the matter would serve only to alienate her, acquiesced. "Very well, Miss Winchester. As I have said, you are more than kind. My niece will need to be properly outfitted for her debut. You need but mention my name in the shops."

"As you wish, sir."

For the next half hour, they exchanged thoughts and comments on Clare's coming responsibility. They concluded that there was little likelihood that anyone would recognize Evelyn as the poor "parlormaid" from Madame Claudine's shop. It was decided that Evelyn would stay on at Edwardes Square. Although the earl kept an elegant town house in Grosvenor Square, he anticipated that estate matters would demand his attention over the next few weeks, necessitating his intermittent absence from London.

Evelyn's reaction was all that her two benefactors had predicted. It required some minutes for her exuberance to abate to the point at which Northrup could impart various caveats and instructions.

"You are to remember that Miss Winchester, besides being a friend, will, while I am away, take my place. You are to behave at all times as a proper young lady, and you will do just as Miss Winchester bids, without argument. Do you understand?"

"Why, yes, Uncle. I shall be the most obedient of girls,

you will see," she promised sweetly, her pretty face turned up to his.

"You had better be, brat, or you will find yourself in the suds with me *and* back at Northrup Court."

"Yes, Uncle, I shall do just as you say."

The earl bent down to place a kiss on her cheek. "Good. Tomorrow, I am off to the Court to settle a few matters, and shall return in about a fortnight. In the meantime, I shall have the town house made habitable and, when I return, I shall call upon you both. Assuming that I receive no bad reports from Miss Winchester, perhaps you would like to go driving in the park."

Evelyn and Clare both exhibited their pleasure at this promise. He then took Clare's hands in his and looked into her upturned face, his eyes sparkling. "Once again, Miss Winchester, you have my deepest gratitude. I am your servant, ma'am," he promised her, and departed.

The house seemed oddly empty without his presence. Strange that she should so soon have become accustomed to having him about. Clare gave herself a shake. Here she was, behaving like a green girl. Such foolishness! Why, the earl saw her only as a chaperon for his niece. There would be plenty of younger, prettier, and richer women to occupy his time. Oh yes, once word got round that the earl of Northrup had returned, there would be any number of mamas throwing their daughters at his head. And then there was Letitia Marlowe, his former love. Lady Emily had said that the woman was widowed. No doubt the unhappy loss of her husband had cured her of her selfish ways. If so, perhaps the flame between Northrup and Mrs. Marlowe could be rekindled.

Clare's ruminations were disrupted by Evelyn. "Oh, Miss Winchester, is this not the most divine development? Who would have thought that Northrup would turn out to be an angel instead of a devil? I cannot wait to go shopping. And just think, we shall attend the opera and go to routs and balls and the theatre and go riding in the park! All eyes will be upon us, for I am convinced that my uncle must be a prime whip. He will cut a dashing figure, indeed!"

Laughing at this nonstop chatter, Clare put her fingertips to her forehead. "I declare, you make my head spin."

"Oh, do forgive me, ma'am, for fatiguing you. But, do you not think him ever so handsome?" she asked impishly.

It was going to be a very long Season.

Four

The following weeks passed in a whirlwind of shopping. While Maude was often wearied by Evelyn's tirelessness and exuberance, she swallowed her complaints. On those few occasions when even Clare was frazzled enough to grumble, her aunt reminded her of the girl's connections.

She would then remind her aunt that it was Evelyn's comeout, not theirs, which was deserving of their attention. And as to her station, Clare could be heard to rejoin that they had once been used to mixing with many members of the peerage. Happily, this was the only point on which she and her aunt had come to cuffs of late, as arrangements for Evelyn's debut proved to be a pleasant diversion for all concerned.

Clare had grown used to her life of quiet domesticity and had all but forgotten the gay society of which she had once been a part. In the ensuing weeks, as she drilled Evelyn in matters of etiquette and recounted amusing anecdotes from nights spent dancing at Almack's, she found herself eager to return to the glittering world of the fashionables. She noticed that Maude, too, seemed happier than she had been in a long time.

Much time, it must be told, was taken up with shopping. Clare marveled at Evelyn's total disregard for her uncle's purse but, aside from occasionally rejecting out of hand an overpriced gown or unnecessary bauble, she kept her silence. After all, Northrup had provided carte blanche, and she was certain he would want his niece's appearance to do him justice. Clare's counsel was otherwise confined to assisting in the selection of appropriate gowns for a girl's initial appearance in London society.

It seemed that she soon had a wardrobe extensive enough to launch three girls onto the town. The clothespress in the sunny bedroom in Edwardes Square was quickly filled with demure ball gowns, morning, walking, carriage, and theatre dresses, frothy dressing gowns, caps, and nightshifts. Each dress was paired with a matching spencer or shawl of soft cashmere, silk, or crepe. Dozens of pairs of shoes were purchased, each embroidered or tinted in colors complementary to the dress which it accompanied. No ensemble was complete without hats, fans, and gloves, and these, too, Evelyn collected with a vengeance.

The shops in Bond and Oxford Streets were taken with ridiculous ease, and their frequent forays had been completed in the luxury of their own carriage. Two days after Northrup had departed for his country estate, Estelle had informed Clare that a footman awaited her pleasure in the foyer. She had descended to find a young man in spotless livery.

"Morning, Miss Winchester," he greeted her with a smile. "The earl of Northrup sent me, ma'am, to deliver that carriage and pair," he explained, jerking his head in the direction of the street.

"Carriage?" she echoed.

"The one as is drawn up in front, ma'am."

From the window, Clare could see a sprightly pair of perfectly matched chestnuts hitched to a shining barouche, its panels painted a warm brown. She turned to stare at the young man, her brow furrowed.

"The earl said they're for you, Miss Winchester, and I'm glad to be your groom, if you please, ma'am," he said with youthful pride. "My name is Hardy."

"For us? Impossible. I cannot accept such a thing."

"Begging your pardon, ma'am, the earl told me if you

was to say that, then I was to remind you as how you will be needing your own transportation, considerin' all the shopping and socializing you'll be doing, now that Miss Evelyn Hallisey is come to stay."

Clare considered a moment. If the carriage really was for Evelyn's benefit, she could hardly be so ill-mannered as to refuse it. "Very well," she conceded, "his lordship is very kind. But, while we can accommodate you, I am at a loss to know where we shall keep a carriage and team."

"Oh, that's no problem, ma'am. His lordship has made arrangements to stable them in the mews just down the street."

"I see. It would seem that the earl has thought of everything," she noted drily.

"Yes, ma'am." Hardy grinned proudly.

"Well, Hardy, you are welcome into our service. Estelle will show you to your quarters, and I shall let you know when you are needed."

"Thank you, Miss Winchester."

Evelyn had gone into raptures over the carriage, and Maude's excitement at once again having a private conveyance at her disposal could barely be contained.

The three were returning from a particularly expensive morning in Bond Street, shortly after Northrup's departure. Each was pleasantly exhausted, as she reflected on her purchases. Maude had managed to spend an entire quarter's allowance in the past days, and now she tittered happily over a new hat—an unusually absurd creation with ostrich plumes and lace. Evelyn was extolling the many virtues of the blue-velvet riding habit she had just ordered, picturing herself riding in the park.

Clare leaned back, contented, on the dark brown squabs and patted the large bandbox beside her. The contents were extravagant, but she had been unable to resist the high-waisted, cerise silk gown. Looking into the dressmaker's mirror, she had admired the tiny seed pearls sewn into a pretty seashell pattern at the neckline and sprinkled across the short sleeves and hem. Turning before the glass, she had seen how the delicate fabric fell in soft folds to her feet, which peeked out in silk slippers of a paler shade of rose.

Hardly a dress for a spinster, Clare thought wryly, but when she had seen it, she had ceased, for a moment, to think of herself as an ape leader left on the shelf. During the past week, as she waited for the alterations to be made, her change of heart had vanished, but, while she regretted the purchase, it had been too late to do anything about it. This morning, all that had changed once again. Feeling the cool silk brush against her legs, Clare shut her eyes and swayed as, unbidden, a man with bright blue eyes had waltzed her about the room.

As the carriage wheels spun toward Edwardes Square, she willed that image from her mind. She was getting addle-brained in her old age. What right had she to think that Northrup would even glance at her? No, she had her chance at love with Tobias Portman, and even he had spurned her, so why should a dashing man like the earl take notice of her existence? Clare sighed. Well, she would feel a diamond of the first water in that gown, even if no man looked her way.

Alighting at the house, Maude remarked on the profusion of crocuses and bright yellow daffodils, just beginning to raise their heads inside the wrought-iron gate. "Well, my dears, it seems that the winter has flown at last. Just feel that sun. Why, before you know it, our little garden will be all abloom, and we shall be attending the theatre, planning excursions to Margate and Lyme, watching balloon ascensions, and, oh, all manner of wonderful things!"

Evelyn linked her arm companionably through Clare's and Maude's, her step light and carefree. "Oh, yes, Miss Beauchamp, only think of the parties and balls," she added gaily. "Miss Winchester, I am on tenterhooks waiting for the Season to begin. All those beautiful clothes and nowhere to wear them. And where is Northrup? He promised to return soon to take us riding, and still we have no word of him."

"Now, Evelyn, before you know it, you will be dancing your way through all those pretty slippers you have bought." *And I,* she considered, *shall play chaperon and shall probably collapse from boredom.*

As she reassured her, Clare was sorting a small pile of mail. Evelyn and Maude were climbing the stairs to their rooms, when Clare called to them. Holding aloft a gilt-edged vellum envelope, she smiled. "Ladies, we have our first invitation."

Evelyn emitted a most unladylike, but very infectious whoop, as she scurried down the stairs and snatched the card from Clare's outstretched hand. Maude's descent was slower, due less to a more developed sense of propriety than it was to a partiality for ratafia creams and macaroons. She finally came to a rest, winded, between the two women and tried to peek over Evelyn's shoulder at the much anticipated piece of paper.

"What is it? Who is it from? Where are we invited? Oh! Will one of you not tell me?" she beseeched them.

Clare explained that they had been invited to Lady Castlereagh's the following week for a party to usher in the new Season. Maude's excitement proved to be a fair match for Evelyn's, and it was a few minutes before their initial euphoria abated to a level which permitted normal discourse.

"Oh, ma'am, I am transported. My first party of the Season. I am sure it will be very grand," Evelyn breathed.

"My, yes," Maude added. "Lady Emily always has given the loveliest parties. You could not ask for a more pleasant introduction to town life, I assure you."

Spring, in its capricious way, decreed the next day to be grey and dismal, but the mood inside the house in Edwardes Square remained cheerful, buoyed by anticipation of the dancing party two days off.

Maude, as had become her custom, was napping on the

lemon brocade chaise in her room. Evelyn was penning a voluminous letter relating her good fortune to a friend in the country, whose recent attack of measles had delayed her own planned comeout.

Clare sat contentedly in the drawing room working at her needlepoint, when Estelle announced Northrup. That gentleman, following close on the heels of the maid, was amused to see Clare fly to a small mirror which hung facing the doorway, where she stood adjusting the lace fichu at her neck and the beribboned cap which sat on her head. The thick carpet muffled his footsteps and it was not until his smiling reflection appeared in the glass that Clare was aware of his presence. Her fingers froze for a moment in their attempt to tame a corkscrew curl, and she flushed as she met his disarming gaze. Instantly, she spun around but, not realizing how close to her his lordship stood, she found herself smack up against him.

"Sir, please do excuse my clumsiness," she begged, a little flustered.

The earl, having grasped Clare's shoulders to prevent her stumbling, smiled down at her, then, as convention dictated, dropped his hands. He stepped back and bowed. "Not at all, Miss Winchester, the fault is entirely mine. I should not have taken advantage of you. I have long been accustomed to the rough company of soldiers and, to be frank, the sight of you at your mirror pleasured me. Pray forgive me," he apologized with a smile.

Her composure once more restored and her heart not untouched by this explanation, Clare motioned her guest to a seat.

"Sir," she admonished him with a laugh, "I think you meant only to shame me in my vanity."

"Never, ma'am," he replied. "It was not my intention to tease you."

"I see that you have not lost your easy address, sir."

"I am glad to learn of it, ma'am." He grinned.

Clare rose and tugged at the bellpull. "You will take tea?"

Northrup accepted as he looked across a vase of forsythia at his hostess. Damn strange that a woman could manage to look so captivating in a plain morning dress and dustcap, but there it was. Deciding it was wiser to steer his thoughts to a more mundane level, he inquired after his niece.

"I am pleased to report, sir, that Evelyn is doing famously, and we all are getting on quite well together. I am convinced that you will be very pleased, once you have the opportunity to get to know her, as we have."

Estelle entered in answer to her mistress's summons. "Tea, Estelle." Then, turning first to cast an inquiring glance at Northrup, "And please bid Miss Evelyn come down to join us, once you have brought the tea," she added, as he nodded his assent.

While they waited, Clare asked after the earl's affairs. Thinking she was merely making an attempt at polite conversation, the earl demurred.

"Kind of you to ask, Miss Winchester, but I think that women must find details of estate management most tedious."

"Believe me, sir, I should not be bored," Clare assured him. "My father always discussed the affairs of Caulfield Hall with me, as I had no brothers, and my mother, like so many of the ladies with whom you, apparently, are acquainted, found the subject deadly dull. If I may say so, my father derived some comfort from our discussions, and I should like to think that my opinions might have been of some small use to him." She stopped and gave a little laugh. "Good heavens, and you were wary of boring me! Please to ignore my reminiscences, sir. But, truly, I often miss my talks with Papa."

She looked a trifle wistful and Northrup, pleasantly surprised at her disclosure, hastened to reassure her. "Not a bit of it, Miss Winchester. It is refreshing to meet a woman who is capable of conversing on topics other than what is au courant in the world of fashion and how to make the most advantageous alliance in the marriage mart." There was an undercurrent of bitterness in his voice and a sardonic twist to his lips.

Clare gave a little laugh, but the arch of her brows betrayed the pique she felt at his indictment of her sex. "I fear, sir, that you are indulging in an unfair generalization. I must concede that some women may be as birdwitted as you have described. At the same time, however, there are many more who are intelligent and unselfish, and willing to converse on and take part in meaningful pursuits, if only permitted to do so."

The earl looked shamefaced. "My apologies, Miss Winchester, of course you are correct. I think I must have a rather jaundiced eye in the matter."

Clare reflected on the unhappy circumstances which she believed responsible for his cynicism and felt a twinge of sympathy, for she thought she understood how he felt. True, she had never really cared for Tobias, certainly not as the earl was said to have cared for Letitia Marlowe. Still, his repudiation of her had hurt all the same, coming as it did after society had all but turned its back on her. She gave her guest an understanding smile and urged him again to tell her of his activities since they had last met.

Given this opportunity, Northrup actually seemed eager to talk, and his enthusiasm was evident in his eyes and voice. "Devilish hard business, tending to an estate the size of mine, ma'am. Property's been managed quite well, I daresay—I have my late brother to thank for that—but, in the time since his death, some matters have, naturally, been neglected. I spent much of my time meeting and riding out with my tenants who, I must say, have been most patient during this time. But then, I can say with honesty, if not humility, that my family has always treated our tenants more fairly than many other landowners whom I could mention."

He continued in this vein for some minutes, Clare prompting him with nods and appropriate questions and comments.

He was still speaking thus when Estelle and Evelyn entered the room.

Evelyn made a demure curtsy to her uncle who, in turn, leaned down to place a kiss on her forehead.

"Uncle, I am so happy that you are returned. And I see that your leg is all healed, for you no longer have that horrid limp. Whatever has delayed you? We have expected you this past age and you have left us dangling, has he not, Miss Winchester? Are you lodged yet in Grosvenor Square? How long do you stay?"

Clare winced at the implication that she had awaited the earl's return with bated breath and hoped that he had more sense than to take the girl literally. He smiled and explained that estate matters had commanded more of his attention than he had anticipated and apologized for his tardiness.

"As for the town house, my dear, it's all right and tight. It is necessary for me to find another footman," he said, "as I have learned that Wilton has been buying low-quality feed for my cattle. The corn chandler who supplied him was generous enough to compensate him for the favor. Once I have found a suitable replacement, all will be complete. I plan to remain in town for the Season, but I expect my presence at the Court will be required more often than I should like."

"I hope that you will not be away from us too much," Evelyn replied diplomatically. "Uncle Evan, you have not forgotten our ride in the park, have you?"

"No, that is another reason for my visit—to ask you and Miss Winchester to accompany me to Hyde Park tomorrow afternoon."

Evelyn clapped her hands in delight. "Oh, but of course, we shall be happy to, shall we not, Miss Winchester?"

Clare smiled her agreement, then suggested that, if he were not otherwise engaged, he would be most welcome to dine that evening in Edwardes Square.

* * *

Northrup arrived rather early, declaring with easy honesty that he was yet unused to the custom of dining at eight when in town. Clare, dressed becomingly in soft aquamarine kerseymere, apologized and informed him that she would gladly have pushed supper forward to accommodate his routine. He expressed his gratitude, but conceded that he must readjust himself to town ritual, though for the life of him, he could not understand the reason to bring otherwise civilized folk to the point of starvation, before feeding them!

Clare laughed in agreement. "My aunt and I, as you know, sir, have lived quietly in town and, if truth be told, we generally dine at an earlier hour—a transgression which, were it generally known, would certainly shock all of the fashionables."

The earl returned her grin. "Ma'am, never doubt that your secret is safe with me."

The evening passed most pleasantly. A large part of it was commandeered by Evelyn, who insisted upon telling her captive uncle the details of each of her recent purchases. The earl heard all this with loving tolerance and, to his credit, even elicited additional revelations by interposing a question or two.

London's Season was just officially underway and that, together with unusually fine weather, brought out a large number of pleasure vehicles on the following day. Northrup's midnight blue barouche was pulled by a pair of high-stepping dapple greys. Clare reclined against the dove grey velvet seat and felt the carriage wheels rumbling over the pavement. She looked about her, then up ahead at Northrup. He sat relaxed, his shoulders straight, the ribbons clasped confidently in his left hand, and she admired his seemingly effortless ability to handle the team in the crowded streets.

They reached the entrance of the park at Hyde Park Corner and were soon rolling slowly along the Ladies' Mile in the company of dozens of other carriages of all shapes and sizes. The passengers of these conveyances were no less diverse.

Just ahead of them was a spanking new red curricle bearing an ebullient young man calling "What ho?" to friends and acquaintances near and far and clutching the reins unprofessionally close to his chest. Looking to her left, Clare chuckled inwardly, as she spied an aging matron in a tall green bonnet which accentuated her already considerable height. Beside this lady sat her quietly dressed husband, whose bored expression told the assembled company that he infinitely preferred the peace of his club.

Evelyn sat forward on the seat, looking eagerly about her and declaring that she had never seen so many fashionables gathered in one place before. Northrup was discreetly pointing out those persons of notoriety, explaining whether that distinction was derived from rank, wealth, or behavior.

"Do you see that man riding in the black carriage? The one seated beside the lady with the ridiculous bonnet?"

"Yes, Uncle, if you mean the gentleman with the beautiful chestnut hair."

"He is Lord Byron, Evelyn," the earl explained, as the man in question rolled his carriage up abreast of theirs. The two drivers slowed their horses to a smooth stop and nodded at one another. Examining him from the corner of her eye, Clare took in the poet's flawless complexion and the delicate, pale hands that held the ribbons.

He spoke first. "Northrup. I'd heard you were back. Good to see you after such a long time."

Northrup told him that he was lodged in Grosvenor Square and, seeing his soulful gaze fixed on Clare, introduced her and Evelyn, with something less than his usual grace. His acquaintanceship with Byron, though not close, did go back several years, prior to the latter's sojourn on the Continent. Never an admirer of the man's poetry, Northrup smiled as he heard Clare's complexion compared to a delicate species of garden flower.

Evelyn looked up at him adoringly and waited expectantly for a similar allusion to her charms. Alas, such was not forthcoming, though Byron declared himself enchanted as he bestowed a rare and scarcely noticeable smile on the girl. His companion seemed piqued at the loss of Byron's attentions and, with a practiced moue, pointed out that their horses were becoming restive.

"We must be off, I fear," he said, barely smiling once again. "Your servant," he assured the earl, and, turning for a last look at Clare, he inclined his head and drove off.

"It would seem that you have an admirer," the earl noted, as his horses resumed their pace in the procession.

"Oh, Uncle," Evelyn said, fluttering her lashes, "do you really think so? My, is he not handsome? And such a charming voice. Why, he is even more romantic than I had believed."

Her uncle was amused as he looked over one shoulder at his self-centered niece, and informed her gently, "My dear, I am afraid I was speaking of Miss Winchester."

Ever before the undisputed paragon within whatever set she happened to grace, the girl's jaw dropped with astonishment. "Miss Winchester? But, she is old!" At once realizing her pitiful lack of manners, she hastened to apologize to her friend. "Oh! Miss Winchester, I did not mean that he would not find you attractive just because you are old. Oh, my—that is, I mean to say . . ."

Clare kindly rescued the girl from her plight. "Not at all, Evelyn, I understand exactly what you meant. Your uncle, you see, is funning me." She laughed.

"You surprise me, Miss Winchester. I would not have thought you one of those artful females who fishes for compliments," the earl chimed in.

Clare accepted the jibe good-naturedly. "I meant, sir, that I am well-aware that Byron has a certain reputation which he must go to great lengths to uphold. His admiration of me, as you choose to call it, was nothing more than his natural inclination to attempt to charm the women he meets."

" 'Attempt,' Miss Winchester? Am I to understand that you were not transported by his words?"

Clare's response was couched in light laughter. "Truly, do you think me a green girl fresh from the schoolroom? His attention was rather pleasant; any female would be guilty of prevarication if she declared otherwise. But, transported, sir? I would have to believe that I am in the first blush of my youth, which, as we know, I am not," she reminded him, smiling at Evelyn, who flushed with embarrassment. "And then, I would need a fondness for fulsome compliments—another quality that I seem to lack."

The earl gave a low, appreciative chuckle. "My observation stands, ma'am."

The park was full of people, but not nearly as crowded as it would become once the Season had reached its height. Their circuit completed, they were just rounding the Serpentine and heading toward the gate, when Northrup remarked on the presence of Lady Octaviana Harper, a notorious gossip. Clare and Evelyn followed his gaze, which rested on a gaunt woman whose unnaturally pitch-black hair only emphasized the lines and creases of her face.

"Never say that is she, sir. I cannot credit it. Why, I do not think her hair was so black when I last saw her . . ." Suddenly hearing how her words sounded, Clare brought herself up short, but too late to forestall a hearty laugh from their escort.

"Indeed, ma'am, I should never lie to you. Lady Octaviana, The Harpy, as some call her, it is, and you are quite correct. I do believe that, unlike the rest of the human race, The Harpy's hair grows darker as her age advances. But, of course, no one dares quiz her about it, else she would have their reputation in tatters in a trice."

As they left the confines of the park, Clare reflected on the double standard ingrained in society and sighed. If Lady Octaviana could make so many people dance to her tune, perhaps she, Clare, would be left in peace.

* * *

"No!"

"But . . ."

"No! I will not discuss it, Evelyn. It is improper and . . ."

"But, Miss Winchester, all the girls paint."

"I do not care what the others do." Clare recited the ancient words spoken by mothers to their daughters. "I am concerned only with you. You are too young to use such artifice."

"Oh, what care I what people say! Anyway, it's not the same as it was when you were my age. Today, everyone does it. I didn't think you were so very prim, Miss Winchester."

"Evelyn, please." She tried another tack. "Your complexion and color are perfect, and most women would kill for lashes like yours. Let all the other girls paint, and you will have the satisfaction of knowing that you are the only true gem in a room full of paste."

After a moment's consideration, the girl decided the idea was very much to her liking and acquiesced. Unfortunately, that had been earlier in the day and now, when they were due at Lady Emily's in just forty minutes, she was in an even worse taking.

"Miss Winchester, I cannot indeed, I shall not, wear this gown. It makes me look an ape leader, an—an antidote! No one shall dance with me, and I shall die of shame."

This diatribe was emphasized with the stamping of a small foot, as Evelyn glared into her mirror and declared her social life ended before it had even begun.

Clare had been trying for the last half hour to convince the chit otherwise, so that she herself could dress for the ball, but to no avail. It became clear at this juncture that she was dangerously close to one of her bouts of tears, and Clare, apprehensive about her own reappearance in society, was hard put to deal with that behavior. She put down her own foot, figuratively speaking, and settled the matter.

"Well, my girl," she said with considerable severity, "if you do not want to wear that dress, which becomes you exceedingly by the way, you need not. Of course, you could always wear one of your others," she pointed to the pile of discarded gowns that littered the floor. "I should warn you, however, that if none of these will suit, or, if you decide against that lovely white crepe you have on, you will have to remain at home this evening." At this, Evelyn's eyes grew wide, and Clare aimed her leveler. "But Miss Beauchamp and I will tell you all about the party, since we are quite pleased with our dresses and," she finished pointedly, "shall be leaving within the half hour." She turned on her heel to go, and Evelyn's resentful concession that the crepe would have to do trailed after her.

As Molly helped her to dress, Clare wondered if she had ever been so vain. Yes, she admitted, she probably had been. But then, she remembered how painful had been her comedown, and she knew that, unlikely as the possibility was, she did not want that for Evelyn. She made a mental note to be more strict with her charge in future and gave herself over to Molly's solicitous ministrations.

Dealing with Evelyn's tantrum had left Clare with precious little time to spend on her toilette. Her gown, though simplicity itself, was striking, its style owing to its expert cut and delicious color. Designed in the popular high-waisted style, the pale apricot silk was tucked into cross pleatings across the bosom, enhancing her creamy skin. Tortoiseshell combs were pinned in her hair, which Molly had twisted into a riot of curls that framed her face in a most beguiling way.

Clare hesitated before the glass as she draped a cream-colored Norwich shawl over her arms. Surveying her appearance with what even the most discerning critic would have termed undeserved examination, she finally allowed herself a small smile of endorsement. *Well, I certainly won't set any hearts to fluttering, but the gown is lovely,* she decided, adjusting the shawl.

Upon his return to London, Northrup had found an invitation to the ball awaiting his notice, and he had offered to convey the ladies of Edwardes Square in his town coach. Clare and Evelyn descended the stairs to find him with Maude, hands clasped behind his back, his head inclined as he listened politely to her chatter.

Evelyn paused on the steps, awaiting her uncle's notice, so that her formal entrance could be afforded the attention which her youth told her it deserved. Clare, conscious of this aim, continued her descent with a smile and quietly observed their escort, who looked most attractive in ebony evening dress. Admiring his appearance, it occurred to her that the earl must have cut a dashing figure in his regimental colors. Her approach was announced by the rustle of her gown, and he turned to her, smiling broadly.

"Good evening, Miss Winchester." His gaze took in the figure that she had deemed only passable. "May I venture to say that you look remarkably charming in that confection?"

She almost found herself blushing but, after all, had she not once before remarked on his expert address? Not wishing to seem rude, however, she chose not to call him on his banter, rather dropping a small curtsy and thanking him for his kindness.

"Nay, ma'am, flattery may be a kindness. I observe and speak only the truth. You look lovely," he said simply.

An impatient cough from the vicinity of the stairs spared her having to respond and told all present that Evelyn could not be expected to wait forever for her share of the attention.

Northrup lifted his eyes and smiled with familial pride. "My dear, you are delightful. You put me in mind of a portrait of your grandmother, when she was about your age. You favor her, you know," he said with the slightest hint of melancholy in his voice.

Unwilling to be so easily won, Evelyn pressed him. "You

do not think this gown dowdy?" she asked, holding the dress out with a white-gloved hand.

"Dowdy?" the earl gasped with just the right amount of astonishment. "Evelyn, you could not look so in sackcloth and ashes, let alone that charming gown."

Evelyn shone with pleasure, and Clare worried that she might easily fall prey to the accomplished flirts whom she was bound to meet during the Season. At last convinced of her charms, Evelyn giggled and ran lightly down the remaining steps to drop a kiss on the cheek of her admirer.

"Oh, thank you, Uncle. I knew you would think so, for this gown is all the crack." She dimpled up at him coyly and turned to pick up her fan.

Northrup held open the door, and she and Maude preceded him into the carriage. Clare could not suppress a smirk of exasperation, which the earl was quick to catch.

"Miss Winchester, was that imp giving you the devil of the time, before I arrived?"

"Oh, no, sir," Clare drawled. "Why, did you not hear? That gown is all the crack!" The two laughed at this private joke as he handed her into the carriage.

It was clear that the Castlereagh staff had spent hours in the ballroom creating an atmosphere that was at once tasteful and exotic. Tall silk Chinese screens and potted topiaries had been placed with infinite care at appropriate intervals around the room, and flowers, straight from the hothouse, bloomed abundantly, filling the air with their light fragrance. Among the soft, green shelter of a stand of Norfolk Island pines stood assembled the orchestra that provided music for the evening's entertainment.

If Clare had been anxious, her fears soon were allayed by her gracious hostess, who welcomed her warmly and reacquainted her with a number of persons whom she had not seen in some time. To Clare's relief and great pleasure, those she met seemed genuinely happy to see her again, and if she detected a certain coolness from a few of the mamas present, she attributed it, without hesitation, to the undeniable charms of her charge. It would not have occurred to her that the more ambitious parents found her beauty and her attendance with the earl of Northrup more than a little upsetting.

Clare had been looking forward to renewing relations with her host, the viscount, but that gentleman's position as Foreign Secretary had once again called him unexpectedly from home. He and Lady Castlereagh, though childless, enjoyed a blissful marriage, unlike so many of their contemporaries. They were completely devoted to one another, and, to the amusement of her friends, Emily sometimes even accompanied her husband on his travels. This evening, she had decided against any of the more garish creations she had been known to wear in the past, and was radiant in a gold gown covered with a dark brown net overdress.

"I am so sorry to miss the viscount, Lady Emily," Clare said.

"No more than I, my dear, no more than I." Lady Emily sighed. "And doubtless he will not return until the small hours. Well, I shall bear up, I am sure. Now, tell me, are you enjoying your return to the beau monde?"

"Yes, I am. To own the truth, ma'am, I was all a-dither about coming here tonight, but I think that I was worried for nothing."

"Of course, Clare, just as I promised."

Maude passed in a rustle of green taffeta on the arm of a portly, kind-faced gentleman. "Lord Waterston." Lady Emily waved her fan in the direction of Maude's partner. "A bit garrulous, but a good sort, for all that."

The two watched as Evelyn tripped through the steps of a country dance with Northrup, her face aglow. Clare and Lady Emily were not the only observers. Two young gentlemen watched with open admiration and hurried to her side when the music stopped, begging the favor of a dance.

"It would seem that the Hallisey chit is already making a few ripples in our little pond," Lady Emily remarked as the young men nudged out the earl. "One hopes that this bit of success does not go to her head," she added sagely.

"Yes, that is a danger, particularly for one of her looks. I shall watch her carefully and see to it she does not take any toplofty notions into her head, for I assure you, Lady Emily, I take my responsibility to Evelyn and her uncle quite seriously."

"I am glad to hear it, ma'am."

Clare looked over her shoulder and into a pair of dancing eyes. "Sir," she smiled.

"Since, for the moment, it appears that my wayward niece is well cared for, may I request the pleasure of the next dance?"

Clare soon found herself expertly guided among the crush of dancers on the parquet floor. Much to her surprise and discomfort, she felt disconcerted by Northrup's nearness. His powerful body, brought close by the movements of the dance, seemed all at once overwhelming and irresistibly attractive. Fearful that he could detect her reaction, she looked about her at the other couples. A soft "ahem" brought her attention back to her partner.

"Forgive me, sir."

"Not at all, Miss Winchester, you seem to be enjoying the dance immensely. Are you sure you have need of my company?" he teased.

She laughed. "Certainly, my lord, for I can hardly dance alone, can I?" She felt relaxed now, but her eye was truly caught by two soldiers handsome in uniform, each partnering a pretty, gay miss. Both soldiers had that eagerness common to some men who have not yet seen battle and, like those who had gone before and others who would follow, both seemed pitifully young to face the horrors of war. The earl followed her gaze.

"I am told that Stephen and young Elmont are off to the Continent in a se'nnight."

Clare looked up into his eyes, which had suddenly gone

midnight blue, as they did when he was angry or thoughtful. "How awful," she sighed. The earl nodded in agreement. "How can they look so—so carefree? Surely, they are afraid. I think they must be shamming."

Northrup gave a little smile and looked at her intently. "You are very perceptive. To a great extent, you are correct. Those two young pups would sooner run naked through Hyde Park at five o'clock in the afternoon than concede their fears. They feel it their duty, you see, to conceal their true feelings from those about them, especially from the lovely young things with whom they are dancing. Then, too, the unknown thrill of war and the feelings of pride and responsibility which attend to the defense of one's country cannot be denied. Somehow," he finished sadly, "that—euphoria— vanishes quickly in the reality of war, and one becomes overwhelmingly aware of the futility and abomination of it all."

"I think I understand," she responded gently.

"Somehow, Miss Winchester, I knew you would. Pray forgive my maudlin wanderings."

She assured him that his words required no apology, as the dance ended and he escorted her back to her place.

Clare and Northrup stood on the perimeter of the ballroom chatting with Lady Emily and her twin goddaughters, Helen and Leah. They were as alike as twins could be—both pretty, plump, and possessed of effervescent personalities. Helen quite obviously had thrown her heart over the moon for the earl and seemed transported just to have him beside her. Presently, a handsome gentleman with burnished blond hair and a ready smile joined their little group.

"Why, Maximillian, how very delightful to see you."

"Lady Emily, you are lovely this evening." He turned to shake the earl's hand, and the two clapped one another on the shoulder enthusiastically.

"Northrup!"

"Newmarch!"

Introductions were made all around, as Northrup explained that he and Mr. Maximillian Newmarch were the oldest of friends. "It has been quite some time since we have seen each other. Max returned from the war about a year ago."

"Yes, heard you were back, old fellow. I'm just up from the country myself, thought I'd enjoy a bit of the Season." He looked at Clare with a very appreciative smile and didn't notice that in the last few moments, Leah, too, had fallen head over ears in love. "Your leg appears to have come along well. Filthy business all of it."

"To say the least of it, Max. But, let's not spoil the evening with talk of war." He gave Clare a sidelong sheepish smile. "Why not come along to Grosvenor Square tomorrow for luncheon, and we can bore one another with our tales?"

"Glad to."

The earl was just about to do his duty by the adoring Helen, when someone could be heard calling his name. Clare stood on her toes and peeked over his shoulder to see a middle-aged woman with a determined look waving a fan to pinpoint her location. The gesture was unnecessary, since her shrill voice and the flaming redhead smiling and waving at her side could have guided a blind and deaf man safely through a dark alley.

"My lord," Clare informed him with a grin, "I believe you are wanted."

He turned, smiled at the two women, and made his excuses to the ladies and Max. "With your pardon, Mrs. Denholm beckons," he drawled with a raised brow, and marched bravely across the room.

Lady Emily marked his departure with a shudder. " 'Mrs. Denholm beckons.' Mrs. Denholm has been beckoning since she first brought out that silly twit, Janine, four years ago. Odious woman. Can't tolerate her or her daughter. But then, there are some people one must invite to little gatherings, such as these. Oh well, I daresay Northrup can hold his own," she observed, as he and Janine took their places in the set then forming.

Newmarch, who had hardly taken his eyes off Clare, asked her to dance, and she happily consented. After he had reluctantly returned her at the end of the set, she stood a few moments alone, lost in thought. An affected male voice broke into her musings.

"My dear Miss Winchester—Clare. 'Pon my soul, it is you!"

Clare turned round to see a ruddy, full face crowned by the most carefully arranged curls and waves she had ever seen. Outrageously high shirt points were rivaled only by a neckcloth tied with amazing intricacy. She took in his pouter pigeon front decorated with fobs and chains and gave a little gasp.

"Tobias Portman!" she breathed, much less enthusiastic about the reunion than her old beau.

He clasped her two hands in his and beamed at her. She had to admit that he had changed little since last she had seen him, several years before. Quite a few pounds heavier, she noted, and, certainly, he had not had the blunt to afford such expensive fripperies when she had known him.

"You are as lovely as ever, I am sure. And set out in the first stare of fashion, too. You are, indeed, a picture, my dear."

Clare smirked, thinking that her appearance could not hold a candle to that of the dandy who now stood there ogling her with a quizzing glass and spouting empty compliments. She had long ago ceased being grieved over his rejection of her and realized that her feelings had been those of an innocent country miss easily overwhelmed by the attentions of a self-proclaimed man of the world. The emotions she had felt at his defection were really feelings of shame and, later, anger, at the knowledge that the man whom she had expected to sue for her hand had been naught but a spineless fortune hunter. She was later grateful that she had been prevented from marriage with Tobias, as she came to learn that a lifetime commitment, for her, would demand mutual respect and love between the two parties involved. She quickly became completely indifferent to thoughts of Tobias and, when she found that he had married the only child of a very wealthy landowner, she had been a bit surprised by his good fortune, but otherwise unmoved.

While Clare had no desire to see him again, she was cognizant of the proper behavior which society demanded of all its members and decided that Tobias probably should not be entirely blamed for the selfishness which came from his previously straitened circumstances. She managed a polite smile, which she could not know that Portman chose to interpret as a sign of encouragement, and asked, pointedly, after his wife.

Her former beau appeared properly saddened, as he informed her that dear Charlotte had been laid to rest just over a year ago. "Some insidious heart ailment, the doctors said. A tragedy, as you can well imagine," he said with a slow shake of his head. "I fear I still have not recovered from the loss."

She thought he looked remarkably healthy for one so stricken, but refrained from saying so, instead expressing her condolences for his sorrow.

He nodded gravely and soon changed the subject. He seemed to have completely forgotten the events that had separated them and regaled her, or so he thought, with details of the estate in Kent and town house in London, which had come to him upon his wife's demise. He, it seemed, had been left a wealthy widower—wealthy enough, in fact, to marry now where he pleased.

Clare listened as politely as she could, wishing all the while that Tobias would dissolve into the woodwork. The musicians, having just returned from a short interlude, were getting ready to begin a new round of playing. Northrup had finally disentangled himself from the tenacious Denholm women and had decided to request the pleasure of another dance from Miss Winchester. He had nearly crossed the room to the spot where he had deposited her some half hour earlier, when he noticed that she was not alone.

Unfortunately, he caught Clare at her most gracious, as she flashed a smile at one of Portman's bon mots. She was as unaware of the earl's intentions as he was of the extent of her civility. As she listened to Tobias prattle, she found it increasingly difficult to stifle a yawn. The dulcet sound of violins reached their ears and, as Clare could not conceive of a genteel way to decline his request, she reluctantly accompanied Portman onto the floor.

Northrup watched them closely, his lips curled in disgust, for he was acquainted with the fellow and found him a pompous, shallow boor. It never occurred to him that Clare had as much right as anyone else to enjoy the evening, nor did he know that she had been praying for just such an interruption as the earl's invitation to dance to deliver her from the egotistic tedium that was Tobias Portman.

I do believe, he thought, *that she's enjoying that fool's attentions. Women are all the same—a bit of fawning flattery can put them at one's mercy, no matter how they deny it. Well, they're welcome to one another, it's certainly of no significance to me.* But, for some reason then incomprehensible to him, he felt oddly put out. Turning on his heel, he decided to take his pleasure in the card room, where he spent the remainder of the evening losing each hand he played.

The earl and the three ladies regrouped much later for the return home. He and Clare were eager to escape the boredom that each had suffered silently since they had parted, and Evelyn chattered exuberantly with Maude, who was much taken with the attractive Lord Waterston.

Five

After the Castlereagh ball, the London Season took off with a rush, and the weather cooperated, as the days ripened quickly into one of the warmest springs in recent memory. The much-prized vouchers affording admission to that sanctum known as Almack's were bestowed on the ladies of Edwardes Square by their friend, Lady Castlereagh. It must not be supposed, however, that their entrée into that bastion of fashionable society was in any way dependent on their good graces with that worthy lady, for Evelyn's popularity was sufficient to assure her admission.

Life since Lady Emily's gathering had been filled with balls, routs, and card parties that lasted until the early-morning hours, carriage rides and walks in Hyde Park on fine afternoons, and teas and dinners given and attended, as each host or hostess tried to outdo the other. And there had been endless shopping and poring over the latest dress patterns to find just the right gown for Evelyn's comeout ball, now several days away.

If the pace seemed to Clare considerably more frenetic than it had been the first time around, she quickly adapted, even enjoyed it. She found that she derived much pleasure from her newfound responsibilities. If anyone recalled her past with distaste and wished to punish her for it once again, Clare was unaware of it, for she at last was able to confine her memories of those days to the distant recesses of her mind.

Lord Byron, naturally, was in attendance at many of the important entertainments to which they were invited, and there were but few occasions when the lame poet was not the center of attraction. He was possessed of what most readily described as a truly angelic countenance, as well as the body of an athlete, the latter partly the result of strict dieting.

Seeing him, women found it tragic that one of his incredible genius and beauty should be plagued by a deformity of his nether limb. The affliction, of course, prevented his dancing, and some wondered if his aversion to the waltz, its being a dance which one would have expected a gentleman of his romantic proclivities to champion, was genuine or the understandable result of his inability to participate in it. Clare had heard that, even amongst his most intimate friends, he was unable to discuss his problem without becoming agitated. Such a burden, she considered, for such a man, must be painful to bear. Perhaps that is why he so often seems melancholy.

At social gatherings, he would usually station himself in one place, sitting or standing in a carefully arranged pose, rousing himself infrequently, in an attempt to obviate attention to the awkwardness of his walk. His affliction for the nonce hidden, he could display his charms to their best advantage and, inevitably, he was to be seen surrounded by a coterie of admirers, male and female, as if he were holding a levee in his private rooms.

He had not forgotten his introduction to Clare and Evelyn in the park, but finding Clare an unmoved recipient of his favors, he had transferred them to the younger girl, lavishing attention and sweet speeches on her whenever they met.

Clare's assessment of him that day in Hyde Park was quite close to the mark. If the notice that he paid a lady was neither sincere nor singular, neither was it malicious. But, for a country-bred miss only recently freed from the schoolroom, to be complimented in her first Season by such a one as Lord Byron was the fulfillment of a fantasy.

Alas, Evelyn was just such a girl, and Clare feared that her young friend believed that the poet actually harbored a tendre for her. At first, Clare had thought it best to ignore the infatuation, hoping that it would burn out on its own. Finally, however, she decided she must speak.

"Evelyn, dear, I feel that we should discuss Lord Byron," she began.

The girl's eyes glowed as her hands flew to her breast. "Gladly, Miss Winchester! Have you read the copy of *The Giaour* that I gave you?" Without giving her time to answer, she went on, "Is it not wonderful?"

Clare raised a hand in protest. "Yes, Evelyn, I know," she interrupted. "I beg you will spare me your raptures, for I can recite the litany of Byron's virtues quite as easily as you can after these past weeks. And if I could not," she added drily, "I am convinced that he himself would be pleased to assist me."

"Miss Winchester! How can you be so insensitive?"

"Easily, dear, easily. Honestly, I, too, find him . . ."

"Irresistible?"

"Not quite. Charming is, I think, appropriate. And, of course, he is enormously talented. But, that is all, Evelyn."

"All? Why, he is . . ."

"Shallow?"

"Never say so!"

"But I do. Well," she considered, "perhaps that is a little harsh." She held up her hand to forestall additional comment. "But, dear, you must realize that he is a gentleman of easy charm, a man of the ton. I think he means no harm and I have nothing against him, but his behavior toward you—toward most women—is not genuine."

"Oh, Miss Winchester, I cannot believe you."

"I tell you it is true. It is said he collects locks of his admirers' hair, as Prinny collects snuffboxes. You must believe me, for your own good. Surely you cannot believe that his attentions toward you are extraordinary. Why, only see how he casts his spell over every other female about him. I have even heard a few rumors, vague, I admit, that he may marry soon." The stubborn set to Evelyn's chin showed that her words were unheeded. She sighed.

"Er, Evelyn, I am not at all convinced I ought to discuss this with you," she began, "but it seems that I have no alternative." She took a breath and hurried on. "There is a certain—lady—I shall not mention her name—who is inordinately attracted to Lord Byron." Uncertain how to continue, she paused a moment. "Well, dear, I must tell you that this, ah, lady's conduct toward him is, well, shocking. Why, she actually throws herself at his head. And in public! And, I hasten to add, in all fairness, that his behavior is no better, for he encouraged her at first, you see, and now that he is tired of her, he treats her quite badly. The entire affair is scandalous, so . . ."

"You are referring to Caroline Lamb, aren't you, Miss Winchester?"

Clare managed a nod, but could not help gaping. The girl had learned quite a lot during her short time in society.

"Yes, but his rejection of her is her own silly fault, is it not? She is hardly discreet, Miss Winchester, and probably deserves the censure she is receiving from him and the ton."

Clare was fast becoming desperate. Shutting her eyes, her fingertips to her forehead, she thought, *I am too old for this.* Clearly, the situation called for heavier artillery.

"Very well, Evelyn, I did not want to tell you this, but you have forced my hand. I have heard it said that he retires to bed with curl papers in his hair." The poor girl gasped, and Clare pressed on. "Some say he bites his nails, as well."

This tactic proved effective. When faced with Byron's flowery compliments the next night at the Honorable David Harcourt's crush, she had all she could do to stifle a laugh, remarking that, though his speeches were a delight, he must think her a nodcock if he believed she took him seriously. This was spoken with such charm and presence of manner, that Byron took no offense, rather slipping off to capture the heart of some other unsuspecting young lady.

The poet was not, however, the sole claimant for Evelyn's affections. Clare could be pleased to know that, unlike many of the solicitous mamas trying desperately to make their daughters successful in the marriage mart, Evelyn had no end of eligible suitors. And they called at all hours, every day. Clare often found herself unable to differentiate between Mr. Hoyt and the Viscount Brenmar, both of whom were fair, or between Mr. Whittier and Mr. Fleming. The latter two gentlemen shared an extraordinary passion for driving and were members of the exclusive Four-In-Hand Club. They were considered prime whips, but Clare had always considered theirs to be a fast set whose language could be downright vulgar, and Evelyn was under strict orders never to ride with either fellow.

Thus, the girl's desire to attend the Club's spring meeting grand parade had required no little amount of cajoling—dire predictions of her certain decline followed by the even more horrifying prospect of the sure diminishment of her standing in the ton—before Clare began to weaken. In this instance, she had thought it best to defer to Northrup, then seeing to some routine matters at the Court.

His reply had been prompt, thank heaven, for Evelyn had never ceased her pleading, and he gave his permission for the outing. Though he understood Clare's concern, he explained that the Club had changed for the better since its founding by the wild Barrymore brothers in the Regent's youth. Yes, it was true that they were occasionally inclined to mad pursuits, like taking over the reins from a stagecoach driver in mid-journey, but Evelyn naturally would never be subjected to such a lark. "The Club's rules," he wrote, "prohibit reckless driving, and I think you both will find the parade entertaining. Unfortunately, I shall not return in time to take you, but you may attend, provided you can find a suitable escort." He had gone on to recommend Newmarch's services, remarking that since that fellow had himself once been a member of the Four-In-Hand, he probably was planning to attend.

Happily, Newmarch was glad to accept. On the appointed day, the three found themselves waiting impatiently at the starting point in Cavendish Square just before noon, amidst a crush of others who had begun to gather some time before. Actually, Clare had been rather curious about this self-proclaimed spectacle. What should one expect from a group of irresponsible, wealthy young men whose sole collective interest lay in their carriages and cattle? She found herself pleasantly surprised.

Presently, a horn bleated, signaling the whips to form ranks. After a few minutes of carriage jostling, the leader cracked his whip crying, "Bang-up for Salt-Hill!" The procession began to pass, greeted by loud approval from the crowd, and soon escalated to a brisk trot. The drivers were proudly seated in carriages polished to a sparkle and expertly guided through the packed street the handsomest horseflesh she had ever seen. Some of the drivers even sported neck-cloths tied in the Mail Coach style, with one end of the scarf spread out and tucked into their waistbands. Max was pleased to provide them with a commentary of the various kinds of equipages and explained that they were bound for the Windmill Inn in the village of Salt-Hill. Clare was a bit less impressed when he mentioned the considerable amounts of port which would be consumed with dinner before the carriages turned (doubtless with somewhat less agility) for home. After the procession was out of sight, the three, declaring a collective desire for a refreshing ice, headed for Gunter's.

The next morning, Clare was seated at her desk in the window of her bedroom. She had just gone over the menu for the next few days with Mrs. Musgrave and now sat, ostensibly going over the household accounts, but actually gazing out of the window, her mind distracted by the view.

Clare's room overlooked the square, a situation which in another noisier or more fashionable part of town would have been to the detriment of the average sleeper. Her square, however, situated in Kensington and hard by Hyde Park and the Whig stronghold of Holland House, did not boast of the residence of any of the more boisterous members of the beau monde. The view was, by now, filled with the myriad colors and fragrances of a variety of spring flowers, which grew in the large fenced garden in the center of the square, tumbled from window boxes, and fringed the edges of the mellow brick walk set into an orderly herringbone pattern.

Sitting, chin in hand, idly watching a butterfly pay its morning calls, Clare had no idea of the charming picture she presented. She was clothed in a white-lawn morning dress sprinkled with pink rosebuds. As the butterfly flitted off to keep an engagement in the garden next door and a pair of peevish starlings began to racket about in the gutter above her head, Clare was roused from her reverie. She shook her head and berated herself, not for the first time that spring, for her decision to move her desk to the window. Smiling, she resolutely turned her attention once more to the neglected papers lying before her.

Her concentration became so fixed that she did not hear the knock of a visitor at the front door just a short while later. A soft tap on her bedroom door preceded Estelle, who announced the arrival of a caller.

"Well, Estelle, you had better call Miss Evelyn, I suppose," she said, assuming it to be yet another of the girl's many callers. "And do, please, tell her not to dawdle, for I must finish these accounts. Tell her caller that I shall be down directly to keep him company until she is presentable. Which one is it, by the way?"

Her maid looked puzzled. "No, ma'am," she said with a

shake of her head, "it's not for Miss Evelyn the gentleman's come, but for you."

It could not be said that Clare had wanted for callers these last few weeks for, in fact, she had been entertained by several gentlemen whose company she found diverting. Though she had not formed an attachment to any of them, she did particularly enjoy the company of Maximillian Newmarch. The mild surprise she registered at Estelle's disclosure arose from the fact that her callers were so vastly outnumbered by Evelyn's.

It became apparent that the maid was not going to expound on her news without more encouragement from Clare. "Who is here, Estelle?" she prodded with somewhat more patience than she felt.

"It's Mr. Tobias Portman, miss."

Tobias. Clare groaned. Apart from two or three bothersome calls, she had seen nothing of him recently and was heartily glad of it. But now, she was convinced, he had returned for the express purpose of ruining an otherwise lovely day.

Still dismayed as she entered the drawing room a few minutes later, she had to choke back an unmannerly giggle of disbelief. Tobias was a true harbinger of spring. He was encased in a neatly cut coat of robin's-egg blue embellished with brass buttons nearly the size of saucers. Clare glanced at his middle, which had always been rather plump, and wondered if he were wearing a Cumberland corset, for his waistcoat, a taffeta concoction of pink-and-white diagonal stripes, appeared close to bursting, as did his bright yellow nankeen unmentionables. Blinded by the glare, Clare blinked as he twirled a tasselled cane, and found herself speechless. Interpreting her silence as awe in the face of a veritable tulip of the ton, Tobias smiled with smug satisfaction and greeted her effusively.

She could only assume that the voice she heard came from somewhere within the voluminous, complicated folds of his neckcloth, which all but enveloped his mouth. Swallowing a laugh and mentally comparing his clownish exhibitionism to the simple tailoring that Northrup favored, she extended her hand and bade her guest to take a seat. As she watched him ease his bulk into a fragile rosewood chair, she wondered how in the world she had ever believed herself to be fond of such a ludicrous popinjay?

"My dear, you are looking very well and so happy," Portman intoned with some surprise, as if this condition, reached as it had been without his aid, were only somewhat short of miraculous.

"Tobias, how good of you to call," she managed.

"Tut, my dear, came as soon as I returned to town. Did you think I would not? What man alive is there who could ignore your charms?"

"Tobias, really, I beg you will cease such flummery."

"Flummery! My word, not a bit of it, Clare. I am injured to learn that you would think so." He extracted an exquisite snuffbox from his waistcoat pocket and flicked it open. "Why, do you think that I should waste my time on one who could not do me proud?"

Clare detested snuff. "I can recall, Tobias, another time when you paid me such compliments. I cannot help but think that your feelings now are no more sincere than they were then." Clare was aghast at her own lack of subtlety, but now she had no reason, and even less desire, to court his good opinion.

Unfortunately, like many arrogant people, Tobias was impossible to insult. "How can you say so, Clare? Surely you know that I have ever held you in the deepest, the highest esteem." Waving a handkerchief in the direction of her arched eyebrows, he continued. "No, no, I see what you are thinking—that I deserted you—but you are wrong. I thought I made it quite clear at the time that my, er, departure was completely beyond my control and, indeed, my personal, er, desires. But, of course, reason dictates that one must always be mindful of one's, er, circumstances, financial circumstances, that is. In any event," he finished, apparently rather pleased with his apologia, "my—circumstances as you must know, are now much improved and I have the luxury to, shall I say, follow my heart."

And not someone else's purse, Clare thought scathingly.

"Tobias," she interrupted, "I feel I must tell you, in all kindness and honesty, that your heart, in this case, is misplaced."

True to form, Tobias did not so much as flinch at this disclosure. "Now, now my dear, I understand that your head has been turned by all the attention you've no doubt been receiving of late. But allow me, if you will, to know what is good for you. After all, I have known you these many years. Once the novelty of the Season has worn off, I am convinced that you will view me with greater favor."

Clare delivered a sharp set-down designed to discourage any such intentions, at the same time explaining, in the plainest words possible, that she would not permit him or anyone else to know what was good for her. Her words once again were wasted. Tobias merely nodded sagely and said in injured tones that she, naturally, had the right of it, and he, of course, would never presume or force his attentions on any female, after which concession, he remained, gossiping idly, until Clare feared she would never be rid of him.

They were still sitting thus when the earl of Northrup was announced. Clare thought she had never before been so glad to hear anyone's name. Her relief must have shown in the face she turned up to greet her newest visitor, for he grinned in a most conspiratorial way, as he bowed over her hand. His tailoring was quiet in its elegance, from the creamy pearl buttons on his waistcoat to his impeccable riding boots.

"Miss Winchester," he said after acknowledging Portman, "forgive me, but you appear to be a trifle fatigued this fine morning."

She instantly caught the telltale glint in his eye and, feeling rather like a naughty schoolgirl, shot back a surreptitious look of thanks. Before she could reply, however, Tobias cut in.

"Here now, old man, Clare—ah, Miss Winchester, that is, is quite well, I can assure you. Why, I have just now been telling her that she is in unusually good looks."

Northrup's raised brows seemed to ask if Tobias Portman's pronouncements were always endorsed by the Almighty, as Clare, desirous of avoiding any friction, hastened to admit that she did feel a bit tired.

"Humph. No doubt all that socializing you've been doing," he pontificated. "It don't do to go dancing the waltz all night and then expect others to come dancing attendance upon you the next day." He smirked at what he felt was a particularly deft quip, then noticed a muscle twitch in Northrup's jaw. Raising his considerable form from the chair and advising Clare to take herself off for a nap, he turned to his rival and waited for him to follow suit. "Well, Northrup?" he finally asked, "as you have pointed out, Miss Winchester is fatigued. Shall we walk out together?"

Ignoring the broad hint, Northrup allowed a small smile. "You are too kind, Portman, but you need not wait for me." He paused maddeningly, as Tobias reddened, before adding, "I should like to see my niece, Evelyn."

"Oh, yes, of course, your niece," Tobias conceded. The two men exchanged curt bows, and Clare followed her old beau out of the drawing room.

The front door clicked shut and she returned to find Northrup, his back to her as he faced the window. She stood for a moment unconsciously admiring the way his tan coat lay so smoothly across his broad shoulders, and soon realized that they were shaking with suppressed laughter. No longer able to contain her own amusement she virtually collapsed into a chair and gave way to unrepentant mirth. She was immediately joined by the earl, who took the chair opposite and said that he could not remember when he had last seen anything so entertaining.

Clare raised her head, daubing tear-stained cheeks with a handkerchief. "I declare, sir," she said, trying to regain her composure, "you have saved me from a most tiresome morning. I thank you, for, truly, I saw no way in which to extricate myself save outright rudeness."

"I quite understand, ma'am, for how could you possibly *see* anything with the Sun King himself blinding you? Pink-and-white stripes! Gad, the man should be shot!"

At this, they both dissolved once again into peals of laughter. The first to recover, Northrup eyed his hostess's bubbling countenance with appreciation. "Miss Winchester, you are bewitching when you laugh. I wonder that clod Portman had not sense enough to put you in such high spirits."

Clare was at first taken aback at his remark and uncertain how she should answer it. She decided that the doyennes of society could not possibly have devised an effective means of dealing with such devastating charm as that displayed by the earl. Looking at him mischievously, she dimpled. "But, my lord, Mr. Portman *did* put me in these high spirits!"

They were still enjoying this irony when Evelyn entered. She flitted between Clare and Northrup graciously, bestowing light kisses on each, before coming to light on a chair beside her now "dearest uncle."

"If you have come to take us out, Uncle, I fear you are doomed to disappointment, since we are spoken for. Miss Winchester and I are to go riding with Mr. Hoyt at five o'clock."

Northrup smiled. "That is delightful, my dear," he said, casting a sympathetic glance toward Clare. "I would have been happy to take you riding, myself, but I am already promised to another female for this afternoon."

Evelyn appeared surprised to hear this, and the earl paused to regard her with some amusement, finally adding that the female was a bay mare he was considering buying from Captain Markham. Clare very slowly expelled a breath she had not realized she had been holding, as Evelyn squealed.

"Oh, Uncle, shall I ride her?"

"We shall see, Evelyn. But remember, you shall have to 'rusticate in the country' to do so, for I mean to keep her at the Court."

Evelyn did not seem as averse to this prospect as might be imagined but, nevertheless, decided not to pursue the matter. For a while, conversation centered around the Northrup stables, which she generously pronounced second to none in the county. Northrup explained that, happily, he had more time to spend on leisurely pursuits, such as acquiring new cattle, now that things finally had been put to rights in his town house.

"It was not until yesterday that I was able to find a suitable footman, and that, I confess, was at the expense of Lord Ashby. But, my new man seems most qualified, and I am pleased with him."

"Would his name be Edward Reynolds, sir?" Clare inquired.

The earl blinked. "It would, Miss Winchester. Do I understand you to say that you are acquainted with the fellow?" he asked with a smile.

"No, not I, but Molly Burton, my abigail, knows him. I understand that Lord Ashby, his former master, was a hard man to serve, and I am glad to learn that Reynolds will be working for someone more kindhearted."

"Thank you. I think that he and I shall get on well together. And now, if I may be permitted to change the subject, are you ladies quite ready for Evelyn's ball on Friday night?"

Evelyn avowed her anticipation. He nodded. "I am rather looking forward to your formal presentation, Evelyn. May I hope that you will honor me with the first dance?"

"Of course, Uncle. I shall be only too pleased."

The would-be recipient of her favors suppressed a smile. "You are all kindness, my dear. On the subject of dances, perhaps Miss Winchester would also be good enough to keep her first waltz . . ."

Maude bustled in, apologizing for her tardiness. "If that silly girl," she explained, referring to the hapless Estelle, "had but told me you were here, your lordship, I should have been down much sooner."

Northrup's visit ended soon after, and, extracting a promise from Evelyn not to keep them waiting on Friday, he departed.

Tobias called again the next day to invite Clare to attend a production of *Hamlet*. She recollected that the theatre had never held any fascination for him and suspected that for him, like so many others of his class, it was more an excuse for a social gathering than a cultural event. Doubtless he would be decked like a man milliner for the occasion and she would be obliged to endure his patronizing manner, as he pretended to intimacy with every fashionable present. It was with relief that she was able to cry off, as she had attended the performance only two nights before with Mr. Newmarch.

He harumphed, conveying both pique and surprise at this information. "A pity, m'dear," he intoned.

"Yes, well, I am sorry to disappoint you, Tobias."

"Me! The loss, I fear, is entirely yours, Clare. Newmarch is a right enough fellow, I suppose, in his way," he acknowledged grudgingly. "But then, you know, I cannot but find him dull, especially in matters sartorial. His appearance cannot have done you credit, I am convinced, and one must be ever mindful to appear at one's best when one goes into society." He wagged a finger for emphasis, and a heavy perfume permeated the air. "Perhaps I should do the chap a service and recommend him to my tailor." Clare nearly laughed aloud at the thought of Max, ever tasteful in his dress, tricked out in Tobias's style.

"And I will venture to say that you learned nothing from the play in his company. Did he explain the action to you, as the story progressed?" Clare was forced to admit that Newmarch had uttered barely a syllable while the actors were onstage. "Just as I thought! Terribly remiss of him. The fellow obviously is lacking in many of the necessary refinements. I cannot think," he puffed, "how he expected a woman to understand Hamlet's dilemma if he did not take the trouble to explain it to you. Really, m'dear, it was shortsighted of you not to wait for me to offer my escort to the play, for you would have enjoyed a much more enlightened evening."

Clare shut her eyes in exasperation and informed him that she had been quite capable of following the plot on her own and had found the evening quite pleasant.

"Newmarch has no grasp of the man's role as teacher, as mentor . . ."

"Tobias, I have the headache."

"Naturally you do, Clare. All that thinking, don't you know. A woman ought not to exert herself in such intellectual pursuits. They are much too taxing for you. Newmarch should have . . ."

"I *think* I shall take myself to my room, where I *think* I must lie down as soon as possible. That is, if you don't consider such a conclusion beyond my feeble intellectual capacity!"

"Not at all. Why should I? It is just such matters which are a woman's province. That is what I have been saying, is it not? Indeed, you should calm yourself, Clare. Like all members of your sex, you are becoming agitated by a little well-meant criticism."

Despite her limited mental faculties, it would not have taken her an uncommon length of time to decide just which object within easy reach could be sacrificed to throw at him. Thus, it was fortunate that he was able to accomplish so speedy and well-timed an exit.

Incredibly, Tobias returned the next day and asked to take her driving. Her sense of humor was such that Clare had by then been able to laugh at his prejudice, yet she had no desire to spend any time in his company. Her kind nature and the fine weather both conspired against her, however, and she found herself accepting his offer, provided he had her back in Edwardes Square in an hour—for, beyond that she knew, her amiability could not be stretched.

Tobias was not the best of drivers, his reflexes being too slow to avoid entirely the ruts and bumps in the road to the park. The carriage was well sprung but, even so, Clare began to wonder if she should have partaken of such a hearty midday meal. His repeated "Sorry, m'dear's" had become as irritating as his ineptitude until, at last, she snapped, "For pity's sake, Tobias, I'm not an accomplished whip, myself, but even I know that one is supposed to try to avoid the obstacles in the road, not take them head-on!"

"Now, that is unkind, Clare. A fellow cannot be expected to miss each and every one. I think that I can hold up my head amongst the better drivers in town."

Picturing a city full of drivers such as he, she choked back a retort. The man had a horrid hand with his horses, and nothing she could say would alter that fact. She considered what the members of the Four-In-Hand would say to his claim! Thinking of their reaction, she was wearing a most becoming grin as they finally rolled onto the gravel-lined way of Hyde Park.

Northrup and Newmarch had just turned their horses into the mainstream of traffic when they spied the couple in front of them. Newmarch gave an appreciative chuckle. "Hullo, look at that! Clare Winchester and that wantwit, Tobias Portman."

His companion saw no humor in the scene. "What the deuce is she doing with him? I thought she had more sense. Looks as if she's enjoying herself, too."

"Well, there's no law against her having a good time, is there? Though I admit I cannot see how she is managing it in this instance. Chap is an uncommon clod with the ribbons, though, ain't he? Ought to be attending more to his team than to Clare, uh, Miss Winchester. Still, I can't say I can fault him for that."

Northrup, watching them with a disgusted look on his face, did not seem to hear his friend. "What say, Evan, shall we join them? Something tells me she may be grateful for the intrusion."

"I say, Clare, ain't that Bentmore there? I'll just head over that way, I want to speak to him about putting me up for Boodles."

"No, Tobias, you can't just barge through the traffic like this. Don't! Oh! Look out!"

The oddsmakers at Watier's never would have taken the bet, but there was another equally ham-fisted driver residing in London. It was not enough for fate, capricious in its mischief, that the two simply occupied the same town, but the same park as well and, worst of all, at the same time. Tobias began to make his ill-judged way into the path ahead, without heed to cross-traffic, when his peer in a bright yellow curricle came up fast from the way to his left and attempted a turn into the same road. In the seconds which followed, horses reared and whinnied, drivers yelled, ladies screamed, and gravel shot through the air, as teams and mounts were pulled this way and that in a concerted effort to avoid catastrophe.

Mercifully, horses and people escaped serious injury to all but their sensibilities. It might even be said that the animals took the whole stupid incident in better temper than did their passengers and riders. Several of the vehicles were less fortunate. Few knew who had been responsible for the accident and, in the first rush of shock, the one or two who might have accurately laid the blame were too shaken to take any decisive action against the perpetrators. Outraged drivers screamed at one another over damages inflicted in the mayhem. Charges of clumsy driving flew back and forth, as distressed ladies dug into their reticules for salts, and lapdogs yipped in excitement.

"Damn fool!"

"You peabrain! Are you blind?"

"Oh, Jason, take me home immediately!"

"Blast it, Calpurnia, how do you expect me to take us anywhere when we're minus a wheel? Didn't want to come here today, anyway, but, no, you insisted. This is all your fault!"

"Oh, God! Look at the red paint scraped all over the door. Damme, it's dented, too. Can't even make out the crest any longer. M'mother will have my head for this!"

Northrup and Newmarch made their way to Clare. Ironically, Tobias's carriage was still serviceable, though, like so many others, badly scratched. Having climbed down from his seat, he stood sputtering and gesticulating madly, as he surveyed the damage, Northrup jumped in beside Clare with Newmarch close behind.

"Clare!"

"Are you hurt?"

"O—oh, my. N-no, I believe I am alright." Northrup helped to right her on the seat from which she had all but toppled, and she looked dazedly about her before she spotted her bonnet crushed beyond repair beneath the hooves of the chestnut. She shuddered with the realization that it could just as easily have been she which had been trampled. "For a moment," she confessed, "I thought we should have been overturned."

"A bloody miracle you were not," Northrup growled ominously, though he held her hands very gently in his own, as his eyes examined her for any evidence of injury.

"Thank God you're unharmed," Newmarch added. "Awful to watch the thing happening and be powerless to stop it. Never seen such bad driving in all my days." As if they were of one mind, he and the earl both turned to glare at the culprit responsible for the mishap. For his part, Portman was engaged in a heated altercation with the driver of the yellow curricle, which also had emerged with little damage.

"Look at what you've done, you idiot!"

"I? You, sir!"

"Portman!" Northrup and Newmarch bellowed.

"Eh? What? Oh, Northrup. Newmarch. Just look at what he's done!"

Northrup vaulted from the carriage to stand beside him and, grabbing the lapels of his coat, fairly lifted Tobias off the ground. The words with which he described his unhappy victim were not commonly heard in genteel company and certainly never in the presence of ladies, as the terrified Tobias quickly pointed out, nodding (as best he could, since the earl had hold of the knot in his Oriental cravat) in Clare's direction. Northrup suddenly let go and the man fell against the carriage, rocking it precariously on its much-abused springs.

Newmarch called out from his place at Clare's side. "Here, Portman, have a care! Are you having another go at tipping the lady out of this wretched vehicle?"

Northrup advanced on him again. "I doubt it, Max. He seems much more interested in the condition of his blasted carriage. Tell me, Portman, when were you planning to see to Miss Winchester? *After* you had the damn thing repaired?"

"I . . ."

"Damn right, Portman," Max echoed. "Where's your sense, man? Just see how shaken the poor thing is."

"I . . ."

"And come to that, when were you going to see to your horses? With your permission, Miss Winchester, I'll help you down from this contraption and take a look at the beasts. By the grace of God, they're unharmed. You should be . . ."

"Drawn and quartered," Northrup finished for him. He still looked as if he wanted to strangle the man at his side. "Do you realize that you could have killed them and a number of people, Miss Winchester included, as well?"

"Me? But, I tell you, it was his fault," Tobias croaked, his face scarlet with fury, as he pointed at his accomplice.

"Me?" that fellow screeched in righteous indignation. "How dare . . ."

"Enough!" Northrup shouted again, commanding both

men to silence. He looked about them. "If you've any sense at all, Portman, which I take leave to doubt, you'll get out of here before people recall your part in this mess and spread the word. I would not want to be you," he advised ominously, "if that were to happen."

"Gad, you're right," he gasped, forgetting to deny his culpability. He made as if to climb back into the carriage, but was prevented by dint of Northrup's viselike grip on the back of his neck.

"Go near the lady, and you're a dead man."

"That's right. You'd probably return to Edwardes Square via the river to see if she and the horses can swim," Newmarch chimed in.

"How will she get home? She'll look a sight mounted with either of you, but, if that's how it has to be . . ."

"I shall drive her," Northrup explained. "You," he said pointedly, "may walk."

"Walk? That's my carriage, sir!"

"And God help those of us who must share the road with you. I cannot, in all good conscience, inflict you and your carriage together on the rest of humanity."

By this time, some of the luckier drivers had been able to extricate their vehicles and were making for the gates of the park.

"I say, Evan, that is a bit harsh. Fellow's rather shaken, after all, even if this was his own fault."

"Splendid. The exercise will do him good."

"Well, that's true, but human kindness and all that, you know."

"Max, the creature is a toad; human kindness has nothing to do with it."

"True . . ."

"Damn it, you can't talk about me as if I weren't here!"

"Shut up!" the two men chorused.

"My lord! Mr. Newmarch! The poor man truly cannot be expected to walk all the way home," Clare interjected. Much to her consternation, her hands still were trembling a bit, as she pressed them to her temples. The accident had left her with a filthy headache, and their arguing was only making it worse. "I beg of you, if *someone* would only take me home!"

Newmarch reddened. "Forgive me, Miss Winchester," Northrup said, much chastened. "I fear we are behaving as badly as he. Very well, Portman, since Miss Winchester wishes it, you may take my horse. But, I warn you, if any harm comes to the beast, it means your life." He helped Clare into the carriage, climbed in after her, and let the horses pull for a couple of paces. "Everything seems to be alright."

"Don't worry, Northrup, I'll go along with him. After you bring Miss Winchester home, you can meet me at his house."

Northrup nodded, turned the carriage about, and headed out of the park. They rode in silence for several minutes, then, unable to contain himself any longer, he spoke.

"Would you be good enough to tell me, Miss Winchester, how it is that you could be so foolish as to ride with that— sapskull?"

Her eyes first grew wide with surprise at his tone and the unfairness of his attack, then narrowed in anger. "I don't believe I need explain my actions to you, sir."

He stiffened visibly. "Do forgive my presumption, madam. You might, if you wish, put it down to a misplaced concern for your continued good health."

"At this very moment, my lord, I can do quite nicely without your sarcasm." They glared at one another for a moment, then both gave a shamefaced laugh.

"Forgive a beast his churlish manners, Miss Winchester? My timing was completely off."

"No, sir, the fault is mine. You came to my aid, and I am unmannerly enough to get up on my high ropes." She gave him an impish grin. "But I do not wish to be in your bad books, my lord, so I promise that tomorrow you may ring a royal peal over me. But, right now," her fingers went once again to her pounding head, "I should make a poor showing in a battle of words with you."

"You shall find me primed and ready in your drawing room at the appointed hour, ma'am," he returned amiably. "Your head aches abominably, doesn't it? If I'm not mistaken, lavender water is called for, is it not? I think if you go straight to bed, you'll feel more the thing in the morning."

"The morning? Oh, no, my lord. Evelyn and I are promised to the Snowcrofts'. A musical evening."

"Musical evening, indeed. The last thing you need now is to sit captive while some aging dowager murders Mozart all over again. It's bed for you," he said peremptorily, "and I'll brook no argument. I'd offer to escort Evelyn in your place, but I'm not so devoted an uncle that I would subject myself to this evening's er—entertainment. Besides, I'm sure Evelyn will be none the worse for crying off."

Clare was too miserable to cross swords with him again, and he continued to chat quietly, hoping to take her mind off her discomfort. "It is a goodly distance from Hyde Park to Portman's address, I believe."

She replied that she thought it was. "Good. I hope Max lectures the lout all the way on the proper care and handling of his cattle. It should prove to be quite a long journey."

They both laughed at this, Clare feeling oddly comforted by his high-handed decision making.

Six

Clare suffered no lasting ill effects from the mishap in the park. On the morning of the ball, she met Evelyn in the breakfast room and suggested that they plan to spend the day quietly in anticipation of the late night they would have.

Convention as well as considerations of size dictated that Evelyn's debut be held at Grosvenor Square. Little of the work required for such an enterprise had fallen on the shoulders of the bachelor, Northrup, for he had passed the entire campaign into the capable hands of a most willing Lady Emily and a veritable cadre of tradespeople.

That lady's staff was comprised of no less than half a dozen experts, including her own pastry chef to create the sweets. Further support was provided by workmen who had cleaned chandeliers and windows until they gleamed and applied a fresh coat of paint to the ballroom, a florist whose participation in the endeavor Clare decided must have provided him with at least a quarter's income, and the Season's most popular musicians. Residing alone, Northrup naturally employed a limited number of servants, so enlistments were found in the form of footmen, maids, and grooms, the latter to assist in handling the carriage traffic which would crowd the square. For his part, Northrup supervised his steward's selection of wines from Berry Brothers & Rudd in St. James's Street. Finally, invitations, tastefully engraved on the purest white stock, were chosen. In the addressing of these, the three ladies—Lady Emily, Clare, and Evelyn—spent an entire afternoon demonstrating the graceful penmanship painstakingly taught them by their respective governesses.

Observing all this effort, Clare could be seen to shake her head in disbelief and awe, certain that, had she been in charge, she would have bungled the arrangements by having the invitations printed with the wrong date or neglecting to hire an orchestra for the evening. Evelyn, however, seemed to view the proceedings as no less than was her due and remained remarkably calm.

Clare, Evelyn, and Molly arrived in Grosvenor Square late in the afternoon and were ushered to adjoining bedrooms. Clare had decided to dress first, feeling that the greater part of Molly's time and effort should be given to Evelyn's toilette. At length, Molly was satisfied with her mistress's appearance, decreeing that she was certain to be the loveliest lady at the ball. Clare laughingly denied what she described as a biased opinion, but declared herself pleased with the results of her maid's work.

She was beautiful in the cerise gown which shimmered as she moved and accentuated the soft, mature curves of her body. Her mother's jewels as well as her own all had been sacrificed to creditors when Marcus Winchester had met with hard times, so Clare felt fortunate that the gown, with its fanciful pattern of seed pearls, needed nothing else to recommend it. Her only other adornment was two pink camellias pinned to her hair. As Molly went off to tend to Evelyn, Clare took herself to the ballroom.

She had just a few moments to observe the setting before the first guests began to arrive. The ballroom, painted a rich, creamy white, was large, taking up more than half the floor. French doors which filled the far wall had been opened wide, and their white draperies swagged back to allow the fragrant breeze which came off the back garden to freshen the room. Flowers were everywhere. The orchestra was tuning up beneath a spangled canopy, and hundreds of candles, sparkling in their ornate chandeliers, cast the room into a twinkling fairyland glow.

"You are pleased with Emily's efforts, Miss Winchester?"

She had not heard the earl approach (so neither had she seen him pause in the doorway to observe her at his leisure), really, the man had the quietest footsteps in the kingdom. "My lord, the room is breathtaking."

He did not seem to hear her, however. Now that he could observe her closely, his eyes took her in appreciatively, his slow smile making his approval quite evident. "Miss Winchester, you are magnificent. That gown is perfect for you. No other woman could wear it."

"Ah, sir," she twinkled, "I fear you are in league with the milliner, for she, too, swore that this gown and I were fated to be together."

"Indeed no, ma'am, I must plead innocent of such a charge. But, if she will contrive to always dress you thus, I should be only too willing to pledge her my loyalty."

"Thank you, my lord."

"I collect that my niece has timed her appearance to achieve its maximum effect?" Clare's smile confirmed this. "Just so. Perhaps she has more of her mama in her than I had thought," the earl considered with a sardonic chuckle. She glanced up at him from the corner of her eye. Not for the first time, she wondered at the disdainful side of his nature which now and then showed itself. "I believe I hear our guests beginning to arrive. Shall we greet them?"

Clare placed her hand on his arm, and they climbed the three steps to the doorway of the ballroom, as the butler announced the first arrival. Before long, the room was crowded with people. It seemed to her that all of fashionable London had come out for the occasion, and she felt a rush of excitement.

The women, dowagers and innocent misses alike, epitomized the talents of the finest dressmakers in the city. Silver spangles, golden netting, lustrous silks and frothy muslins fanned out across the room in a diffusion of colors, like the vast palette of some titan artist. If this were not enough, most of the women were bedecked with priceless jewels. Rubies, sapphires, and diamonds, some clipped to earlobes, others nestled within carefully dressed locks, or resting upon ample bosoms, were kindled by the light from the candles and shot tiny flares across the room. The men, except for the occasional dandy whose outrageous costume would have put to the blush the most flagrant demi-rep (had she been permitted entrance), were more simply garbed, but no less elegant, in their formal evening wear or dress uniforms.

The orchestra was playing a spirited country piece, and the distinctive rustle of gowns mixed with the clap of hands and the tap of heels to provide a pleasant accompaniment for the music. Everyone was smiling, enlivened by the energetic music and self-assurance which comes with the knowledge that one is an undisputed part of the most privileged and fashionable company to be found. Silver-and-violet streamers, the colors complementary to those Evelyn would wear, decorated trays of champagne which footmen carried expertly through the crush of already thirsty guests. Soon, Maude arrived, clad in royal blue and looking, for once, quite blessedly ordinary.

Then, Evelyn made her debut on the arm of her uncle, who was clad in stunning black-and-white evening dress. Clare watched, touched, as he proudly presented her and led her out to the strains of a waltz. She was certain that she could detect one or two gasps of admiration and gave a sigh that was a mixture of relief and agreement. Her intuition and taste, thank God, had not failed her, for Evelyn was enchanting. She wore a delicate white net overdress which fell into a deeply scalloped hem over a silk slip in the softest shade of violet. The neckline was cut no lower than modesty would permit, but the dainty décolleté conveyed the merest whisper of maturity for which Evelyn had pleaded and Clare had finally countenanced. The loose, sheer net sleeves had the same scalloped edging as the hem, and she carried a posy of violets nestled amidst a riot of silver and violet ribbons. The gown was set off to perfection by a necklace of pearls with which Northrup had that day presented her. Deep affection was apparent in the warm look which niece and uncle exchanged as they danced across the floor.

When the dance ended, Evelyn was soon surrounded by friends. That this group was divided pretty equally between the two sexes was to her credit for, if her looks captivated the young men, her easy, open manner likewise charmed the young ladies of her set. Several minutes were spent in filling out her dance card, which somehow seemed too small to accommodate all of her admirers, and then she was off to join in a quadrille.

Northrup claimed Clare for the same dance, and they made a handsome couple, turning several heads as they moved about the room. Their dance ended, the earl led her to a chair. Once again, she found herself strongly affected by his elegant appearance. Her eyes aglow with pleasure, she cooled herself with her fan and marveled at how well the clothes set off his figure.

As he bowed his thanks for the dance, the diamonds, which seemed to have been sprinkled among the folds of his immaculate cravat, twinkled at her. He looked deeply at this woman of whom he still knew so little and seemed about to speak when they were joined by Newmarch and another gentleman.

Clare greeted Newmarch with a smile, hoping he could not detect her preference for the company of the earl. Northrup, for his part, acknowledged the intruders most civilly but, had anyone noticed the resentful glint in his eyes, they would never have guessed that he and Max were the best of friends.

The stranger was introduced by his friend, the ever-smiling Mr. Newmarch, as Ross Trevelyn, a Cornishman in town on business, and the two men monopolized Clare's attention with pleasant chatter and compliments. Newmarch soon led her onto the floor, as Trevelyn, who was as captivated by her charms as his friend, begged the next dance. Evan remained, conversing idly with his new acquaintance and silently cursing his old friend. That he found the topic of copper mines singularly dull was not evident in his strictly cultivated manner, and he managed to appear sincerely interested.

He was able to maintain this illusion for some minutes until, suddenly, he stood as if frozen, looking over his companion's shoulder. Trevelyn soon realized that he was, for all practical purposes, speaking to a man who was deaf. He turned to follow Northrup's fascinated gaze and grinned in appreciation at what he saw. His host, abstracted, murmured an excuse and walked off.

Nearly halfway across the ballroom stood an overweight matron wrapped in pink silk and too many jewels, her husband at her elbow. Beside them was a statuesque beauty whose laughter tinkled softly on the ears of those around her. Her raven hair shone like ebony polished to a high luster and a thick fringe of lashes bordered brilliant emerald green eyes and shadowed milk white skin. Her gown was of almond pink, so pale as to appear almost white. The soft fabric was of such a remarkably delicate weave that it seemed fashioned from moonbeams. The woman's attention appeared to be fixed on those two with whom she was talking, but, in reality, she was keenly aware of the other people around her, one in particular, and her graceful gestures and carefully modulated tones were as studied as those of any lady who had ever trod the boards.

"Letitia."

She turned slowly and prettily, feigning surprise, a dainty silver-filigree fan stopped in midair. Playing her role as the consummate artist she was, she smiled a slow, captivating smile. "Northrup," she purred.

He bowed over her outstretched hand and raised his sober

countenance to her lovely face. He seemed in no hurry to do more than look at her, as she returned a look of calm triumph.

The matron's eyes fairly bulged. "My, my of course. I had quite forgotten that you two were once, ah, acquainted," she tittered.

"Pearl!" her husband hissed, nudging her ribs with his elbow.

"Whatever are you about, Frederick?" she persisted maliciously, as the couple in question moved off. "Why just a short while ago, I saw him fairly making calves' eyes at that Winchester upstart. This should set the cat among the pigeons, I tell you."

Her husband shook his head in confusion and asked his wife if she would not care to sit down, where, he thought to himself, she might have less opportunity to gossip. Why that cat Letitia Marlowe should want to sink her claws back into Northrup after all this time was beyond him. Why not leave the poor chap alone? And besides, he too had seen the earl dancing with Clare and had thought they made rather a nice couple. Well, he would never understand women, nor men for that matter, for wasn't Northrup looking like one in thrall to the Sirens' song?

They stood alone in the seclusion of some palms. "It has been a long time, Letitia."

Her laughter tinkled out again. "La, Northrup, how unoriginal. You disappoint me. And how unkind, to remind a lady of the passage of time. Have I become such a hag that you scowl at me so?" she pouted.

His face had indeed blackened, and her sally made him only more serious. "You are as enchanting as ever. No—more so, I think, as well you know." He paused. Then, "But you always did, Letitia."

Her good humor nearly restored, she teased him. "You always used to call me Letty. You were the only person I ever allowed to do so, you know."

"Once, you made me think I had such a right. As I have said, much time has passed."

She made a pretty little moue, not at all dismayed by the stiffness of his manner. "Oh, let us not talk of the past. You could not have known that I just came back to town, so when I heard of your niece's ball, I was convinced that you would not wish my lack of an invitation to keep me away. That is so, is it not? Are you not glad to see me?"

The pause he allowed before answering seemed to her interminable. At last, he said simply, "Of course I am." If his smile did not extend to his eyes, if, in fact, his eyes suggested more pain than pleasure, she did not, or would not, notice.

"Splendid. As I have said, I am just arrived in town, you know, and I hope that I may depend upon you to help me to get reestablished." He inclined his head gravely. "Oh, listen! I do believe they are going to play a waltz, and I do so love to waltz," she said gaily. She laid a white-gloved hand on his arm, and said provocatively, "Are you not going to ask me to dance?"

Clare had just been returned to her seat by a dashing captain of the Hussars, when Newmarch approached. "Miss Winchester, did I neglect to tell you how very lovely you look?" Generally, she bridled at such talk, but the friendship of the amiable Newmarch had become rather special to her, and, since he seemed sincere, she smiled sweetly and teased him.

"Mr. Newmarch, one day such talk will land you at the altar."

He looked at her warmly. "I have it on good authority that these worthy gentlemen are about to play a waltz. Will you honor me, ma'am, or has that cad Northrup already spoken for you?"

Clare hesitated. She had not seen the earl since Newmarch had claimed his first dance with her a full half an hour ago. She had hoped . . . But then, the earl probably had forgotten mentioning the waltz to her several days before. The first strains of the music were just beginning to float out over the ballroom, and a few couples already had moved onto the floor.

Newmarch's eyes had never left her face, and now he apologized for being so outspoken. "Please forgive me, Miss Winchester, I never thought to bring you to the blush, only Northrup . . ."

Clare turned a dazzling smile on him. "Not at all, sir, and I should love to dance with you."

He was an excellent partner, and soon she became lost in the music. Evelyn, looking very happy, floated by in the arms of a laughing young man.

"Are you enjoying the ball?"

"Ever so much. Tell me honestly, Mr. Newmarch, can you imagine life without the waltz?"

"No, I cannot. It is an excellent way for two people to become better acquainted, don't you agree? And do you not think you could call me Max—Clare?" he asked softly.

"Yes—Max, if you prefer."

"I do."

They danced for a while in companionable silence, caught up in the exhilaration which filled the room. "Good God!" she heard him mutter under his breath.

"Oh my, did I miss a step?"

"What? Oh! Not a bit of it, Clare. Just something I saw. Do forgive me."

She looked about her, but found nothing which could have occasioned this outburst. Since his familiar smile had returned, however, she dismissed the incident.

Not so Lady Emily. As her tall, handsome husband led her off the floor, he inclined his head as if to hear better and asked, "What's that, dearest? Did you say something about a cat?"

"Be sure that I did, Robert. Only see." She directed his

attention with a barely discernible flick of her fan and an unmistakable snapping of her eyes.

"Ah. Is that Letitia Marlowe with Northrup?"

"Just so, my love," his wife confirmed, steel in her voice. "And looking for all the world like a cat licking the cream from her whiskers. Brazen saucebox! How dare she? Only see how she throws herself at his head," she remarked, watching Letitia cling to Northrup's arm. "And just when I thought that he and Clare Winchester might be . . . Oh well, I must hope that he has the good sense not to fall under her spell again."

Newmarch had brought Clare to a convenient sofa, where they sat catching their breath and exclaiming over the accomplishment of the musicians. Northrup passed them but a short distance away, the beautiful brunette still attached to his arm. He did not notice their presence.

"Heavens, isn't she lovely, that lady with Northrup. Do you know who she is?" Clare inquired through a definite tightening in her chest. When her companion failed to respond, she turned to see the same frown she had noticed a few minutes earlier. "Why Mr. Newm—Max, whatever is the matter?"

"Letitia Marlowe," he replied in a low, even voice, answering both of her questions simultaneously.

"Oh," she said simply as the constriction in her breast worsened. She was spared contriving further comment by the timely appearance of one of her father's old cronies begging the pleasure of a dance. Thinking only to escape, but without knowing why it was she felt the need to do so, she gave him a winning smile and, excusing herself to Max, accepted the gentleman's invitation.

Clare awoke the next morning feeling unrested and out of sorts. She had slept but fitfully, and the sudden turn in the weather courted her mood as she lay listening to the relentless pounding of the rain against her window.

Really, she chided herself, she had no reason and less right to feel distressed at the reappearance of Letitia Marlowe in the earl of Northrup's life. But, there, she did, and now she must come to terms with it and put him from her mind. Her life was far more exciting than it had been in some time, so what right had she to complain? Keep on like this, she warned herself, and you will end up a bitter old tabby. She kicked off the covers in a fit of resolution and jumped from the bed, determined to enjoy the Season and all its festivities. She did not need the earl, she decided. Max was very attentive and would be there to help her pass the time.

It would have surprised Clare to learn that the gentleman uppermost in her thoughts had passed an even more restless night than she. Northrup had sat for hours beside an open window in his library in Grosvenor Square, the gas lamp unlit, and heedless of the rising breeze which blew in off the Thames, alerting the town to the coming storm.

His glass once again empty, he reached absently for the crystal decanter of port which stood at his elbow and realized that it, too, was dry. He looked at the glass cynically, as if seeing in it something or someone which no one else could detect. "Damn her," he muttered for perhaps the hundredth time that long night.

A long while later, Northrup took himself slowly off to bed, but the oblivion he had hoped for eluded him. It was nearly dawn before the heavy raindrops began their tranquilizing rhythm and his eyes closed, finally, in sleep.

The round of parties and theatre-going continued unabated. Northrup did not make himself a stranger to Edwardes Square. His estates well in hand, he remained in town, often taking them riding or joining them for tea.

Though they remained quite amicable, their relationship

had undergone a subtle but definite change, of which the earl was not unaware. Clare was as obliging as ever in her duties toward Evelyn and, certainly, all that was polite toward him, but that earlier open friendliness which they had known was gone. She seemed to him somehow distant, reserved, as if telling him that she did not wish their relationship to progress. Letitia, however, behaved in quite the opposite way, always available and always charming.

Clare tried to remain aloof to the earl. If her heart faltered when he looked at her in a certain way handing her down from his carriage or leading her through the steps of a dance, she blamed that traitorous reaction on what she chose to call her overactive imagination. For his part, Northrup could be seen with Letitia at his side at most every ball or crush which they attended.

Clare and Evelyn had spent the morning shopping and had just stepped into their carriage in Bond Street, when Northrup pulled up his team alongside theirs. Evelyn and Letitia had met at the ball, so he introduced the two older women. Clare smiled in acknowledgment, as Evelyn, exhibiting none of her usual exuberance, merely nodded and murmured an offhand pleasantry.

Letitia raised a haughty brow at what she chose to perceive as a slight from her escort's niece, but quickly recovered herself and smiled smugly as she hugged his arm. She was dressed in light blue lawn sprigged in forget-me-nots, which also trimmed her straw hat. A wall of bandboxes testified to several hours of serious shopping, and Clare was momentarily surprised at Northrup's apparent participation in such an enterprise.

She eyed Clare with a sly smirk. "Miss Winchester. Oh, yes, I believe Northrup may have mentioned you. Ah, of course, you are the woman who is helping to bring out Evelyn." Leaning over for a closer look at the girl, she smiled and continued sweetly, "My dear, you had all the young bucks after you at your ball. I can well understand, Miss

Winchester, why Northrup wanted a mature woman, some-one—with time on her hands, for such a responsibility. One must exhibit a stabilizing influence when playing gooseberry for such a delightful miss. How good of you."

Clare had the feeling that she had just been likened to an old, faithful dog and knew also that this was exactly how Letitia wanted her to feel. She decided to laugh aside this rudeness, thereby forestalling any obligation which the earl might feel to intervene. In truth, she wanted to strangle the wretched creature with the satin ribbons on her bonnet.

Finding her attempt to offend so easily thwarted, Letitia giggled, "I find it so much more productive to have a gen-tleman's opinion when I shop."

"And it is this man's opinion that several matters await his attention at home," the earl interrupted grimly. "If you will excuse us, ladies, I shall call this afternoon. With your permission?"

"Miss Winchester, I think she is quite the rudest woman I have ever met," Evelyn remarked after they had driven off.

"Well, dear, perhaps she is just tired from all her shop-ping," her companion suggested drily. "And speaking of tired, Evelyn, you are looking quite fagged yourself. Are you well?"

"Quite well, thank you," she replied, and lapsed into si-lence.

Clare grew pensive. The girl had been behaving rather oddly of late, and she was at a loss to understand the reason. Evelyn's debut had been an unqualified success and most functions were considered incomplete without her lively presence. What was more, she had turned down two perfectly acceptable offers. Her uncle had dutifully advised her of the merits of the gentlemen and all that they could provide her but, beyond that, had applied no pressure, and she had quickly declined the proposals.

When Northrup arrived that afternoon, Evelyn was in her bedroom. He exchanged greetings with Newmarch, who was just taking his leave of Clare. "I trust I am not intruding, Miss Winchester?" he asked with what had almost become typical formality.

"Not at all, sir, why should you think so?"

"Newmarch," he stated testily. "You seem to be spending an uncommonly great deal of time with him. I saw you together on Friday last, at the opera." When she did not reply, he said more pointedly, "But, perhaps, you were too . . . occupied to have noticed me."

"On the contrary, I did see you—with Mrs. Marlowe."

There was a long pause, during which he stood scowling and twisting his heavy signet ring, as Clare fussed over a bowl of flowers. The arrangement entirely ruined, she sighed and looked at him shyly. Hoping she sounded offhand, she asked, "If you saw us, why then did you not speak?"

"Well, ma'am, why did not you?"

Suddenly aware of the foolishness of their behavior, they lapsed into embarrassed laughter.

"Oh, my, I am afraid we must sound like a pair of silly children."

"Not you, certainly, Miss Winchester," he assured her gallantly. "The fault was entirely mine. But you are correct in another respect, I should have spoken to you first." He looked warmly into her eyes. "Perhaps you would care for a walk in the Green Park? It is but a short carriage ride from here, and such a beautiful day is too fine to waste indoors."

"That would be very enjoyable, but I think we shall be unable to convince Evelyn to join us."

"I had no intention of inviting her, Miss Winchester. At any rate, it is about my niece that I wish to speak with you."

The path they chose was quiet and not heavily trafficked, and Clare expressed her preference for the tranquil, uncomplicated walks of Green Park over the busier, more contrived grounds of the popular Hyde Park.

"I would agree with you, ma'am, even if I were not loath

to come to cuffs with you again. I find that I like you much better when you are smiling at me."

He gestured at a man not far away and sneered. "Miss Winchester, do you notice that fellow's complexion, his coloring I mean?"

"Yes. He seems to have spent some time in the sun." He shook his head. "No, perhaps not." She giggled. "Now you call my attention to it, his color is a bit, well, peculiar. And, my, he's quite dandified, isn't he?" she observed as the man walked past.

"Honor points for you, ma'am." She felt the muscles in his arm tighten under her hand. "A Bond Street Beau, if ever I've seen one. Rich, idle, and useless. That coloring, you see, comes from the ocher he's rubbed on his skin."

Clare looked puzzled. "You know, now that I consider the matter, I think I have seen a few others like him. But, whyever should he do such a thing?"

"To appear as you first thought him, as if he'd spent much time in the sun, fighting on the Continent. Others wear big gilt spurs on their Hessians to imitate cavalry officers."

"That's despicable!" she gasped.

"Indeed."

She could see the disgust in his eyes. "A far cry from the chaps we talked of at Emily's ball, eh?"

"And from you," she answered softly.

He gave a slight smile. "I'd love to knock him on his empty head, but I doubt he's worth the effort."

Clare considered her own past deceptions and blushed.

"Miss Winchester?"

"It's nothing, sir, only shame for such hypocrisy." He patted her hand, and she wondered if he would hate her as much if he knew that her past was not as incorrupt as he believed.

Clare lowered her eyes and changed the subject. "I, too, would like to discuss Evelyn with you."

He smiled again and led her toward a bench in the shade of a spreading tree. "Yes, tell me, how is the Season going?"

"Well, I think, but have you noticed that Evelyn has been—oh, rather quiet of late?"

"Yes, I have, and I had hoped that you might be able to enlighten me."

She shook her head. "I wish that I could. Actually, it is difficult even to put one's finger on just what is amiss. She is physically well and as biddable as—well, as ever Evelyn ever is," she explained with a smile. "And, yet, she is not herself."

"Do you suppose that she has been disappointed by some young man?"

"Oh, I think not. She has any number of beaux at her feet and, of late, she seems to be taking less interest in them."

Northrup nodded his understanding and said thoughtfully, "Perhaps a change of scenery?"

"Where would you take her, sir?"

"Well, I suppose to the country. To Northrup Court."

"Do you think she will go?"

"Ma'am," he smiled, "do you think I shall give her a choice? It is for her own good, after all. All this merrymaking very like has exhausted her. A week or two in the country should do much to restore her vitality. And, if I may be so bold, you could do with a respite from chasing after the minx all these weeks."

"Truly, sir, I have enjoyed it, for the most part. I shall miss her while she is away."

"But, Miss Winchester, that is not necessary. I should like you to join us."

"How very kind of you to think of me, my lord, but I am afraid . . ."

He raised a hand in protest and smiled. "Miss Winchester, are we ever to be at daggers drawn? I expect to meet such opposition in my niece, but not in you," he chided. "All the proprieties will be observed I promise you. My old nanny still resides at the Court, and there is a vast number of servants."

Clare accepted his teasing with good humor. "Very well, I shall be most happy to come with you to the country."

Although prepared to do battle with Evelyn, to their amazement, she found the idea most agreeable. The earl generously extended the invitation to include Maude, but after making an oblique reference to a gentleman called Mr. Langley, she begged off, blaming previous engagements. There seemed no point in delaying their departure now that all were agreed, so it was decided to leave for Gloucestershire early the next morning.

Letitia sat in Octaviana Harper's drawing room drinking tea amidst a circle of women. She had been galled by Northrup's brusque reaction to her slight of Clare and by his intention to call later in Edwardes Square. That irritation had quickly been replaced by a seething, albeit well-concealed, rage when, once out of Clare and Evelyn's earshot, he had rung a peal over her head for her poor behavior. Her cheeks still burned at the thought of the set-down he had delivered her.

Conversation around the tea table soon turned to the Season and those maidens deemed Incomparables and those Doomed to Failure.

"The Foster girl has little to recommend her but a handsome dowry. Plain as a pikestaff she is."

"How true, Beryl, but she's prettily behaved, and that fortune will no doubt land her one of the oldest titles in the kingdom."

"Now the Hallisey chit is something else again. A diamond of the first water and a dowry as well, you know."

Letitia's ears pricked. "Yes, she is indeed lovely. But that woman who follows after her! Is she anybody? She certainly behaves as if she were the darling of the ton."

"Why, my dear," Lady Octaviana chimed in, "don't you remember her? We called her The Changeable Rose." She leaned forward as if confiding in her listeners. "She painted, you know. Of course, many of us do, but her efforts were clumsy and too noticeable. And such gowns as she was used to wear! Not to mention the Argyle Rooms and the Cyprians Ball. Miss Clare Winchester was quite popular during her own Season, until her father lost all of his money, and then, of course, the ton decided it would no longer countenance her, er, unusual behavior."

There was a collective nodding of heads and clucking of tongues behind lips pursed into self-righteous smirks. Like most people, Letitia despised her hostess, knowing that if she were absent, The Harpy could just as readily be feeding off of her reputation. But she was much too careful to offend the old gossip by word, deed, or neglect of her boring teas. She sat back now with a sly smile and listened very closely.

"Her behavior might have been considered, shall I say, quaint, had her circumstances been different. But, after all, what one might call amusing in a girl with the very best expectations can only be viewed by the ton as an inexcusable breach of etiquette in one whose pockets are practically to let."

Several of the women recalled the story and all now joined in repeating everything they could recollect or, failing that, all they could enlarge upon or invent. One pointed out that the passage of time, together with the support of Lady Emily and Northrup, put paid to anyone's desire to dredge up Clare's past.

"Still," an unsuccessful mama put in, "she pretends to be above reproach, as if she had a rightful place in the beau monde! It is just too bad!"

The journey to Northrup Court in the Cotswolds was long and tiring. They departed London before six the following morning, and, despite the added daylight hours generously provided by the summer, the last rays of sun were fading into twilight before they arrived in Gloucestershire.

Anticipating the long trip, Clare had brought along a copy of *Castle Rackrent* by Maria Edgeworth to help pass the time. The book lay unread in her lap, however, as she found it impossible to keep her eyes from the beautiful countryside through which they passed.

The day was fair, and the earl chose to ride alongside the carriage, thus leaving more room inside for the ladies and Molly. They drove at a brisk clip, and, as recent rainfall had washed the dust from the roads, they were able to ride with the windows open to the fresh air.

On first hearing of their intended sojourn, Molly's eyes had clouded over, and she wondered why her mistress should wish to go haring off to the country leaving particular friends like Mr. Newmarch.

"Mr. Newmarch, Molly, or Mr. Reynolds?" Clare had teased with a laugh. On her knees rummaging through a drawer for the mate to a glove, she had expected her maid to answer in kind. Met with silence, she looked over her shoulder to find her brushing away a tear with the back of one hand.

"What is it? Goose! I was but teasing, I thought you knew that!"

"Oh, miss. It's just that, working for his lordship, Edward, Mr. Reynolds, is much happier, and the earl is paying him a fair wage." She flushed prettily. "Yesterday, he took me walking and bought me a posy from a street vendor. And, now, he thinks he can put some money aside . . ." She blushed furiously.

"But, then, whatever is the matter? This all sounds wonderful."

"Yes, but now if we go off to the country, he may forget me," she cried woefully. "He has mentioned a pretty under-house parlormaid in Grosvenor Square with blond hair and . . ."

"My, my, so things are as serious as all that, are they?" Clare asked softly. "Well, then, suppose I promise you that your Edward will not be tempted by this fair-haired female?"

"Oh, miss, how can you do that?" Clearly, Molly had little faith that her mistress could accomplish such a feat.

"Well, I had hoped to surprise you, but I see that is much less important than making you easy. His lordship mentioned that your Mr. Reynolds is to accompany him to Gloucestershire, so, you see, the two of you will not be separated after all!"

Molly's reaction had been all that Clare could have wished and, throughout the journey, her thoughts were on the carriage which followed carrying their baggage, a new saddle purchased by the earl and, of course, Mr. Reynolds.

Clare smiled across at Evelyn and decided that they had brought them their own little echo of London's clamor. The girl had begun chattering after they had passed the first toll house and, even now, showed little sign of fatigue. She was more animated than she had been in days, regaling them with anecdotes of her Gloucestershire childhood and details of the neighborhood. Even Molly, usually driven near distraction by what she called Evelyn's babbling, was generously disposed to indulgence.

They took luncheon at The George in West Wycombe and a while later, the carriage turned off the main road and onto a gravel drive which wound through a vast parkland and, at length, rolled to a stop before the wide stone steps of Northrup Court.

Seven

Despite her resolution of the previous night to rise early and inspect her surroundings, Clare did not stir until almost ten-thirty the next day. She lay for a few moments in a pleasant haze of confusion, uncertain where she was or what had wakened her. After finishing the previous night's supper, she had been so tired that her examination of her bedroom had begun and ended with the assurance that it contained a place for her to sleep. Now, she stretched and took a leisurely look about her.

The room was a little longer than it was wide. Glistening casement windows filled almost the entire wall to her right, while the other walls were papered with tiny roses. The mantel of the fireplace to her left was painted the same cream color as the woodwork. Drawn up to the hearth, now filled with a crowd of daisies, was a low marquetry tea table which held a couple of leather-bound volumes. On either side of the table stood a shamelessly unstylish overstuffed chair and a chintz-covered chaise longue beckoning the room's occupant on a cold winter day. A door in the far corner opened into the dressing room, which, she noticed when she had washed last night, contained an old armoire, its polished wood carved in a linenfold pattern. In front of the bed, near the windows, stood a rosewood desk.

She sighed contentedly and snuggled deeper into the drift of feather pillows. *Such a pretty room, and it is so quiet here, I shall surely enjoy this rest,* she thought with relish. A frown creased her brow. What, then had roused her? Surely not those delightful birds playing just outside her window.

Clip! Clip! Clip!

She realized she had heard that noise before. She crossed the soft carpet and, kneeling in the deep satin-striped window seat, pushed wide the casement window, which had been left ajar.

The Cotswold Hills rose in the near distance, as if standing sentinel over the expansive Northrup holdings. Off to her left was a verdant deer park. A fragile-looking folly of white latticework stood just beyond its boundary, promising to afford its occupants a cool pleasant view both of the timid creatures within the park to the west and the formal gardens laid out to the east.

Resting her folded arms on the windowsill and her chin on her hands, Clare sat admiring the charm and serenity of the moment. The stench and smoke of London were gone, and she breathed deeply. Ah, surely, that was the unmistakable fragrance of roses. She looked down. Just beneath her window was a large rose garden. It was obviously the product of someone's lavish attention for, even from here, she could see that it contained blooms of every imaginable hue, size, and shape. The light summer breeze carried their heady perfume toward the house and, as the pale yellow gauze curtains fluttered, she took in the fragrance again.

Looking about her, she saw what had awakened her. Directly ahead and close by her window stood, or, more accurately, bent, an aged gardener carefully and expertly wielding a pair of hedge clippers.

Clip! Clip! Clip!

Good heavens, she thought, *when at home, I scarcely notice the fishmongers screaming in the streets, but here I am disturbed by the slightest of sounds!*

She pulled her wrapper more closely around her. Idly watching the man, she wondered at first at the particular slowness of his work among the shrubbery, in fact, the loving care with which he seemed to perform such a mundane task. The shrub on which the gardener worked stood in the foreground and was some five and one half feet tall, which was to say, somewhat shorter than he. Looking closer, her eyes widened in surprise, for this was no ordinary shrubbery.

As the old man stepped aside, he revealed a very large and very arrogant rooster, his beak open in command. A topiary garden! To the rooster's left, an elephant of magnificent proportions balanced precariously on one foot, his trunk extended skyward. "He must be nine feet tall!" Clare breathed. A rabbit, long ears askew, cavorted on the grass beside a round, ridiculous pig. She laughed aloud and clapped her hands in delight. Her very own menagerie!

The gardener looked up and, smiling, touched his cap. "Morning, miss."

Forgetting her appearance, Clare waved back, grinning. "Good morning. Are these your friends?" she called back gaily.

"Aye, that they are, miss," he said with pride. "Quite old friends, too, some of them."

Clare could easily understand that many of the shrubs must indeed be old. Their very size and shape told of many years of loving dedication, not to mention imagination, which produced the frolicsome antics now displayed for her pleasure.

"They are wonderful. I commend you on your skill."

"Thank you, miss," the man replied, beaming.

Molly entered, bearing a breakfast tray. "Well, miss, finally awake, I see," she teased.

Clare laughed. "Had I known so many friends awaited me, I should never have been such a slugabed!" Smugly pleased with her maid's puzzled look, she motioned to the window. The gardener had gone back to work and was painstakingly trimming a carrot that the rabbit grasped in one greedy paw.

"Oh, have you ever seen the like?"

They sat companionably, both enjoying the view as they devoured Clare's breakfast.

A short while later, dressed in mint green lawn, Clare remarked that if she didn't make an appearance soon, the others would think her forever lost to the spell of Orpheus.

"You're too late. His lordship rode out very early this morning, and Miss Evelyn has gone off visiting somewhere."

"Oh. Well then, I shall go for a walk in these lovely gardens."

"Miss, if you're going out, you should take a hat. The sun, you know," she advised, extracting a floppy straw gypsy hat from a bandbox.

"Very well, Molly, I shall *take* a hat." The item dangling by its wide green satin ribbons from one extended arm, she headed once more for the door.

"I don't suppose I could also convince you to wear your gloves?"

"You are quite right. You cannot convince me," Clare replied, her eyes twinkling, and ran from the room.

The grounds of the Court extended far beyond what could be seen from Clare's window, much too far to explore on foot. She hoped to have the opportunity to ride during her stay, but it had been so long since she had done so, and she was a little concerned lest she make a fool of herself. She considered. Perhaps Northrup would take her on a tour in his carriage. In either event, for the present, she would have to content herself with looking at what was close to hand, and this she did eagerly.

The day was warm and the sun bright. She went first to the topiary garden, where she spoke again with its caretaker whose name, she learned, was Sampson. After that, she took a closer look at the rose garden, another part of Sampson's domain, noting a large variety of tea roses, which she knew had to have been imported from the Far East. Clare could see the terraced lawn and, to the right, several men working busily in the orchard. Even from this distance, it was clear that there were a vast number of trees, quite sufficient, she estimated, to satisfy the needs at the Court, as well as providing amply for the tenants, with enough fruit remaining to bring to market.

Considering all the attention the grounds received and the perfection with which they were laid out, Clare had at first worried if she were committing some faux pas by walking there at all. Perhaps the whole thing is meant to be viewed from a distance, she wondered, seen, but not, somehow, appreciated, like some of the great houses of which she had heard. At her old home, Caulfield Hall, such had not been the case. The property, though certainly not as large or as grand as this, had been well worn by the inhabitants of the house, she recollected with a touch of sadness. Her apprehensions were allayed early on in her stroll, however, as one of the gardeners cheerfully directed her to various areas of interest and beauty.

"These gardens was made to be enjoyed, miss," he assured her. "That's what them at the Court have always wanted. If you walk just over that way"—he gestured with a grimy hand which clutched a small and faded clump of pansies—"you'll see a path. Follow that, and it will take you through the best parts of the gardens."

Taking his direction, she continued her ramble. The path did, indeed, wind its desultory way through the grounds. Breathing deeply, she stopped now and then to look at an unconventional, yet curiously striking arrangement or combination of flowers and decorative shrubbery. The discovery of an occasional bench placed conveniently near the path, or concealed among the plantings from the casual observer, gave further testimony to the gardener's words.

Eventually, she left the path and climbed a small rise capped by a natural stand of trees. Just farther on, she came to a rustic stone pond partially shaded by a huge willow. She had then been walking for quite some time and gratefully sat down by the glittering pool, where goldfish flitted back and forth. Clare trailed her fingers idly in the clear, cool water and stretched out full length in the grass, dreaming unbidden thoughts of the earl.

A shadow suddenly darkened the pond. Clare raised her head, screening her eyes with one hand, expecting to see a wayward cloud across the sun, and looked up into Northrup's laughing eyes. Flushing a deep crimson, she hoped that she had not been thinking aloud! *I must look a pretty picture,* she considered wryly, *sprawled on the grass like a hoyden.* As she picked up her hat, tossed carelessly on the ground, he reached out a hand to help her to her feet. Rising, she brushed off her skirt and looked up at him with a smile that, she knew, did nothing to hide her awkward position.

"Have you been here long, sir?" she asked drily.

"A few minutes. I did not want to disturb your reverie. One of the gardeners gave me your direction. Have you enjoyed your walk?"

"Yes, I have. This is most peaceful," she said, waving her hand toward the fishpond.

"Thank you, I have always felt so. My father had it constructed for my mother shortly after they were married. I've come from the back of the house. Sampson tells me you are quite taken with his handiwork."

"Oh, yes. I must say that the view from my window is utterly charming."

He made a small bow and smiled. "Good. I had hoped you would find it so."

Clare lowered her eyes, happy that he had given thought to what might please her. She looked up again and smiled. "The topiaries are delightful!"

Northrup laughed. "I quite agree. Kit and I spent many happy childhood hours playing hide-and-seek and stalking animals in our little 'zoo.' "

"And the roses certainly are among the finest I have ever seen."

"Oh, the roses! I nearly forgot," he said, extending a perfect deep pink bloom that had just begun to open its petals.

Smiling with pleasure, Clare took the flower. "Thank you, my lord, it is beautiful."

He nodded. "Yes, and it is, I think, exactly the color of the gown you wore to Evelyn's ball. That is what made me pluck it. A very lovely gown, if I neglected to say so at the time, Miss Winchester."

"Oh, you remembered."

He was regarding her closely. "Of course I remembered," was all that he replied, and that rather brusquely. They stood looking at one another, neither saying a word. Letitia, Clare thought, would have uttered something captivating in a circumstance such as this. Doubtless the earl finds this exchange quite tame. *He probably is already wishing he had taken* her *to the country instead of you.* Northrup gave her his arm and they strolled leisurely.

"What is that little building to our right?"

"The lavender house. Hasn't been used since my mother died. She used to prepare lavender oil and water for the whole estate. I daresay you must be hungry after your little expedition. Shall we go in to lunch?"

Evelyn had returned by this time, and the three partook of a delicious luncheon of cold meats, Double Gloucester cheese, and raspberry tarts, as she told them all the details of her morning. She had taken the dogs for a run in the park and then ridden her horse, Trinket, to the nearby Crowley estate, only to find that its occupants were away from home and not expected for a few more days.

Her uncle interrupted at her mention of riding. "You took a groom with you, I trust, Evelyn?"

"Of course, Uncle Evan. Jackson accompanied me," she replied, her eyes wide and innocent at the absurdity of his question.

"Oh, yes, of course," her uncle echoed, amused sarcasm edging his voice.

Clare smiled into her glass of lemonade. She had learned that the imaginative Miss Merrow had lately been employed as companion to a kind, albeit eccentric, old woman in another district. "It seems that the old girl believes her house is haunted by a wicked cavalier," Northrup had explained. "It is not, but her children would do all they can to humor her—doubtless her considerable fortune accounts for their solicitous attention. In any event, when I heard of the position, through a neighbor, I knew immediately that she and Merrow should deal extremely well together." Prompted by the roguish gleam in his eye, Clare had been unable to keep from laughing.

Her host told Clare that he wished her to meet his old nurse, Nanny Somerset. Evelyn began to make an excuse about checking on one of the dogs, suspecting that he might have picked up a thorn during their morning ramble, but her uncle forestalled her.

"Nanny reminded me this morning that you have one more tongue-lashing coming for your thoughtless escapade, my girl, and you might as well have done with it. I'll have one of the grooms see to the dog."

Nanny sat in an airy chamber, whose windows were open to the warm summer day and a view of a sparkling lake. The room was filled with mementoes of her life with the Hallisey family. One table held nearly a dozen miniatures, most of them representing her two male charges. Cherubic faces grinned up at Clare, one dark and devilish, the other more fair and open. This pictorial history covered different stages of their lives. One grouping included a smiling young man, whom Clare took to be Christopher, standing next to a fragile-looking blonde, obviously his wife, and beside this stood a rendering of Evelyn. The most recent painting of the earl depicted him in his regimentals. While the man in that picture was indisputably handsome, the artist had caught a faraway look in his eyes and a subtle, barely noticeable twist to his lips which told of deep, unspoken feelings.

Several crudely wrought wooden figures stood on a table which also held some seashells and oddly colored stones which the children had collected on holidays and exploratory walks in the country. A sampler stitched by a balking Evelyn had been lovingly framed and hung by the door, and a vase of yellow roses perfumed the air, giving testimony to Northrup's earlier visit.

When they entered, Nanny's fingers were busily tatting an intricate piece of lace. The old woman laid aside her work and greeted them. She and Northrup smiled warmly at one another, and a deep, mutual regard was plain. Clare was introduced and happily received as Nanny's bright eyes examined her with unabashed frankness.

For the next five minutes, the three visitors sat quietly as Evelyn, for what she dearly hoped was the last time, had her failings recounted in the most severe tones. Her penance finished and the girl once more properly contrite, she sat meekly for a time, then begged leave to go. That granted and as Northrup's attention was required in the stables, the two left together.

If Clare had been uneasy wondering what she and the old retainer would converse about, her discomfort was short-lived. They soon were talking with the ease of a long-established relationship, and Clare found herself quite taken with the woman's outspoken, honest ways.

She remarked on the treasures which filled the room. "Yes, child, they are—that is, this family is—my whole life. I came here so many years ago. My husband, Jamie, and our babe had been carried off by the fever, and I had to find work."

"Oh, Nanny, I am so very sorry."

The woman smiled across at her. "Now, that is so very long ago and time has deadened the pain. I can remember them now with happiness—something I was unable to do for many long, lonely years. But, finally, I had my boys, as I have always called them, to keep me quite busy. I tell you, once Christopher, Kit, was born," she laughed, "those two rascals gave me little time to dwell on my sorrows."

She spoke lovingly of "her boys" for some time, relating their pranks and achievements, their good qualities and bad. Eventually, she told Clare the story of Northrup's heartbreak at the loss of his Letitia to another.

"Not that he ever spoke of it, mind, for he never said a word, just went off and bought his colors. Christopher agreed to take his place at his father's side, for the old earl was still alive at the time, and then he was off.

"Naturally, I—the whole family in fact—was actually pleased that he didn't marry that spoiled creature, but, my dear, at such a cost." The old woman's tone was decidedly bitter, and they sat in silence for a few moments. She soon regained her usual happy frame of mind, however, and turned her bright eyes once more toward her visitor. "And what of you, dear? You must tell me all about yourself."

Clare respectfully provided the good woman with the usual biographical details, omitting the more unhappy parts of her history.

Nanny listened patiently and, when Clare had finished, looked at her shrewdly. "Good heavens, Miss Winchester, Evan has told me all *that*. You cannot convince me that a woman as attractive as you are has led such a singularly dull existence."

Clare blushed, uncertain how to reply.

"Now, don't go all missish on me, I'd not gammon you. It's true. Pretty you are not, but you are a handsome woman, as well you must know. Now, tell me, why are you unmarried?"

Clare blinked, completely at a loss as to how to deal with such intrusive candor. Looking across at her, however, she knew that malice had never found room in that kind heart and that her confessions would not be repeated. Indeed, she found she wanted to talk to her of her past, and almost before she realized it, Clare was telling Nanny all about herself.

* * *

The next morning, the earl asked Clare to accompany him to the stables. When they arrived, he requested that she wait outside, and a moment later returned, leading a bay mare.

"Miss Winchester, meet Aphrodite."

Clare stroked the soft, warm nose which nuzzled her arm and laughed with glee. "Aphrodite! She is beautiful, sir, what a perfect name."

"It seems to suit her."

She circled the animal slowly, surveying her points. "I would say you have a prime bit of horseflesh here, though, of course, I am no judge. Is this the horse you bought from Captain Markham?"

"She is, and, I quite agree, I got the better end of the bargain in this beast," he replied, stroking the horse's neck. "She's a high stepper and a bit spirited. Do you think you can handle her?"

"I?" Clare's face lit up. "Oh, I should love to try!"

"Good. If you would like to join me for a gallop, I shall wait while you change."

"I shall be back in a trice."

She changed from her morning dress to a tailored riding habit of emerald green trimmed with heavy black braiding. The garment dated back several seasons and was rather worn, but Clare noted with relief that its style had held up well enough. True to her word, she was back at the stable in short order.

Northrup complimented her on her appearance and promptness, then helped her to mount. The saddle, she noticed, was brand-new, and since Evelyn had already ridden out, she realized that he must have purchased it for her use. He apparently sensed her thoughts and, as she settled herself, expressed the hope that she would not find the stiff, new leather too uncomfortable.

"Indeed, no, my lord. You are most thoughtful."

Northrup had mounted his stallion, Triton. "Not at all, ma'am," he said briskly, "just practical. It has been some time since you have ridden? Then, if you will follow me, I think today we might confine our excursion to the first half of the deer park—until you feel at your ease on horseback again."

Clare had been a good horsewoman, and she was more than a little pleased to find that it all came back to her quickly, so that she did not disgrace herself. Thereafter, the earl and she rode out together often, occasionally accompanied by Evelyn. They toured a good deal of the Hallisey estate, though by no means all of it, for the family holdings were vast, and Clare met several of the tenants. Some of them contributed to the area's industry by weaving or working various crafts in their homes, and all of them appeared to hold their landlord in esteem.

Clare never tired of the scenery, declaring the Cotswolds the most beautiful country she had ever seen. One sunny day, the three shared a picnic on the grassy banks of the Severn. She thought she had never seen her host so at ease, and attributed this to his happiness at being home again after so many years. True, he was an elegant man of the town, who took as much pleasure in the beau monde as it did in him, but it was plain that he was in his element and truly happy here in Gloucestershire.

She looked across at him now and sighed contentedly. Heedless of the damage the grass would do to his buckskins, he reclined lazily beside her, his back molded to the gently sloping trunk of an old tree. One leg was carelessly stretched full length upon the ground, the other bent at the knee to support a hand which absently grasped a mug of ale. His eyes were closed and a peaceful half smile rested at the corners of his mouth. A light breeze came off the river and ruffled his hair and the simple fold of his collar, which he had begged leave earlier to unbutton, à la the style affected by Byron, else, and at this he had grinned, the heat surely would overcome his still-frail constitution.

Clare was weaving wildflowers into a dainty wreath, an accomplishment of sorts she had thought left behind and since forgotten in what seemed a long ago childhood. Evelyn rose and yawned, declaring that the warm sun was near to putting her off to sleep.

"Umm," the earl put in, "I have been trying to stir myself this past half hour to test my old skill at skipping stones on the water, but I concede that the mere thought of the effort daunts me," he said placidly, eyes still shut.

His niece laughed. "You, Uncle? Skipping stones?"

"I would have you understand, brat, that unlike Athena, who sprang to life fully grown and fitted out, I was not born into this adult and, I hasten to add, utterly irresistible frame. Your father and I spent many hours here at the river. Of course, most of the time we were supposed to be tending to our chores." His smile broadened at the recollection, and he chuckled softly.

"You had chores, Uncle?" she asked, finding the prospect of a young, disobedient uncle most astonishing.

"Yes, we did. Not all of us lead the life of leisure that you enjoy! At any rate, more often than not, disagreeable chores and a sunny day such as this"—he waved his arm expansively, sloshing the ale in his mug—"invariably brought Kit and me here to the river where, also invariably, I bested your father at stone skipping. The loser did the other's work. So, you see, our chores did get done—er, in our own good time!" he finished with a disarming laugh.

"What a conniver you were!"

"Naturally, child." He was the very image of innocence. "Unfortunately, it was not very long before Kit caught on to why I always suggested the river as the testing ground to see who would do our work!"

They all three laughed at this bit of mischief. Evelyn announced her intention to go wading and asked if anyone cared to accompany her. Northrup opened one eye and sipped at what remained of his ale.

"You jest, Evelyn. As you can see, my youth has flown, and I find myself completely and blessedly incapable of such strenuous exercise. And Miss Winchester is engaged in creating a floral masterpiece, though very likely you do not grasp the magnitude of her effort at this moment," he explained drily. "Only watch how skillfully she intertwines that daisy in her garland."

"It is so gratifying to know that true art is recognized. I fear I cannot tear myself from my work!" Clare exclaimed in mock-grave tones. He bowed his head in acknowledgment.

"Oh, you two! Very well, I shall go wading alone. I can only hope that I do not fall in."

"Good God, take care that you do not," the earl cautioned, "for I am certain that I could not rouse myself to rescue such a troublesome bit of a girl."

She scampered off with a giggle, and Clare, looking at the now completed wreath in her hands, thought that the day must have some kind of magic in it, for it seemed they had all returned to their childhoods.

"Miss Winchester." He regarded her with a grin that always made her heart tilt. "I must inform you that if you expect me to wear that decoration, you are all about in your head. I have not fallen so far back into my boyhood as that," he laughed, as if reading her thoughts.

"You, sir?" Her brows arched, and she grinned, quite unaware of how delightful she looked. "I must tell you that this—masterpiece"—she held the circle aloft dramatically— "is not for you, but for a certain beautiful female . . ."

"So be it," he said, reaching out and placing the flowers on her hair. "There."

"Oh—I—" she stammered. "I meant it for Aphrodite, you know," she explained shyly, gesturing to where the horse stood munching clover.

"A pity, for I prefer it just where it is. But, if that is your wish." He shrugged and removed the wreath and walked over to Aphrodite. The flowers repeatedly fell off her head and, after much debate, it was decided to loop them over one large ear, where they hung drunkenly, giving her a decidedly saucy air. He shrugged again. "As you like."

A veil seemed to have dropped down over his eyes, and she was uncertain what had caused this sudden change in his behavior.

Riding back to the Court, Clare noticed that his tenants seemed well provided for, particularly so in comparison to some of the hovels she had seen on the ride from London. She said as much, and Northrup explained that many of the cottages were new, having been completely rebuilt within the past several years.

"I take my responsibility to those who are dependent on us seriously, Miss Winchester. There are some landowners who do not. Their lands are disgraceful and their tenants unhappy. But, our people have always been hardworking, honest, and loyal. They deserve to be treated fairly, to have decent housing. You see, I feel it is their right. Relations between this family and those who live on our lands have never been anything but good and, as long as I am alive, that is how they will remain."

His dark mood had vanished and Clare found herself warming even more toward this man who took such care with those whose well-being rested in his power. Thinking of that power, she was once again reminded of the vast gulf which stretched between her and the earl. Probably his recollection of that difference had prompted the earlier change in his manner. To be sure, she came of good family, but Northrup had wealth, position, and influence, in addition to a title that went back many generations. *No, I must cease these flights of fancy,* she told herself. *Just because he has not mentioned Letitia Marlowe since we arrived, just because he has been so very kind to me* . . . She shook her head as if that would free it of such thoughts. He turned to

her, flashing a smile, and pointed out a cluster of recon-
structed outbuildings. She willed herself to give a formal
smile and a small nod.

"Yes, my lord, most impressive," she said with great civility.

Neither heard the other's dejected sigh.

They sat in the drawing room one sultry night after dinner,
Northrup reading the newspaper and Clare working at her
needlepoint. They had lapsed into an amiable silence, as Evelyn played a romantic sonata on the piano. Clare paused in
her work, trying, in the light of her candle, to decide between
two shades of yellow for the flower she was about to stitch.
Raising her eyes from her canvas, she was surprised to meet
Northrup's gaze.

He leaned back in a nearby wing chair, his legs stretched
out before him and crossed at the ankles. One elbow was
propped on the arm of the chair and a long finger rested
lightly on the cleft just below his lips. His right hand, extended casually on the other arm of the chair, held a glass
of Madeira. The newspaper lay forgotten on the floor. He
was watching her with frank intent from under half-closed
eyelids, and she was disconcerted to find that his gaze did
not waver when their eyes met. She stared back, almost as
if in a trance. Suddenly, the music stopped, and the spell was
broken.

"Oh, Uncle, I have the most splendid idea!"

Northrup exhaled deeply and gave a slow smile. "Dare I
ask for details, Evelyn?"

"But naturally, Uncle. I think we should have a dinner
party. Would that not be wonderful? We could give it in honor
of the Crowleys' return to the neighborhood."

"My dear child, as I understand it, they have been gone
only a fortnight."

"Yes, I know, but now they are *back*, for I saw Peter only

this afternoon, and I should like to have a party above all things."

"So, you saw the Crowley boy, did you? A find lad." Northrup considered. Evelyn was looking a bit more like herself this evening, he saw, and doubtless she was missing the busy London scene. "Very well, Evelyn, you shall have your dinner party. But not, I think, to welcome back our good neighbors, rather to reacquaint ourselves with them. We have been neglectful of our duties, I fear."

"Oh, Uncle, thank you. Miss Winchester, you will help me, won't you, for I have never planned such an event."

"I shall be happy to."

The earl smiled. "You are most kind, Miss Winchester. I do seem to recall, however, that this was supposed to be a rest for you from the demands of our little wretch."

A smile and a light wave of her hand indicated that Clare did not feel in the least put upon. Evelyn ran off to her room to retrieve a menu that, with incredible foresight, she had already begun to compile. Gresham entered on her heels to request his lordship's attention to a small household matter, and the two men withdrew for a few minutes to the library.

Clare felt the need of some air, for the room had become decidedly close, and she wandered out through the French doors and onto the terrace. A breeze had come up and the moon was waning and the stars hung temptingly, like brilliants, in the sky. "Here you are," said a deep voice from the doorway.

Turning, she looked into the earl's eyes. "My lord."

"Must you call me that? Can you not call me Evan? Or even Northrup, I suppose. Everyone does."

"I prefer Evan."

"I should like you to call me that, Clare."

The breeze blew a loose curl across her cheek, and he gently restored it to its place. "Your hair is like silk," he said softly. His fingers rested on her hair and his eyes bored into

hers. It seemed that hours passed, then, he drew nearer.
"Clare—"

"Uncle Evan! How many may I invite?"

Northrup laughed softly and shook his head. "One might
wonder who is guardian to whom," he commented wryly.

The dinner party the following week was a success thanks
largely to Clare's skillful planning, for Evelyn was unused
to managing such affairs and frequently asked her mentor's
advice and assistance. At Northrup's request, this official
reopening of the house was restricted to a fairly small number, with the promise of a grand ball in the old style at the
holidays. Invitations were accordingly sent to and accepted
by the vicar, the Truesdales, and the Crowleys, all living
within easy distance of the Court.

The vicar, Mr. Thayer, a tiny, white wisp of a man with a
strong jovial voice which belied his frail appearance, was
the first to arrive. As he greeted Clare, she thought with
amused surprise that his sermons from the pulpit must be
particularly commanding, coming as they did, from so im-
probable a speaker. Heartily pleased with the earl's return to
England and the resumption of entertainment at the Court,
he expressed his feelings by pumping his host's hand with
vigor until that gentleman thought it might fall off.

"So good to have you back among us, my lord," he
boomed. "I've always said a Gloucestershire man is never
truly happy anywhere else but in his home country. Not but
what your good brother was anything less than a fine man-
ager for the estate, you know, but this is where you belong,
my boy, and I know you will not mind my saying so."

The Truesdales came during this effusive speech. They
were three: Mr. Lionel Truesdale, a large shaggy man with
a toothy grin, his wife Bettina, a charming woman with
fluffy, grey hair, a friendly manner, and a small, rather
squeaky voice, not unpleasant to the ear, and their daughter,

Katherine, Kitty to her friends, who, doubtless, were numerous. The girl, about seventeen, was blessed with enormous green eyes, soft, flaxen hair, and a tiny pink sugarplum of a mouth. It was she, Clare had been informed, laid low by measles, with whom Evelyn had corresponded during her weeks in London. Naturally, the two girls had met frequently since Evelyn's return to the country, with Kitty eager to hear, firsthand, every detail and bit of gossip from her friend's vast experience in the Metropolis. Now, she went into raptures over Evelyn's blue-sprigged muslin, which she declared very au courant.

When the Crowleys made their appearance a short while later, it could not be said that they were not all that was correct and amiable, but they seemed to somehow stand apart from their neighbors.

This demeanor did not, however, extend to their son, Peter. He was a handsome young man of probably nineteen years, with a cheerful smile ever ready to his lips. He greeted Northrup warmly and, with the easy manner of an older brother, teased the laughing Kitty, who responded in kind. This accomplished, they all made their way to the drawing room. Peter turned his attention to Evelyn and, since they had fallen slightly behind the others, there was no one to see the fleeting look of affection which passed between them.

The food was well prepared, and the diners ate their way through a succession of grouse soup, lobster patties, woodcock, a hot joint, and two kinds of tart. Betwixt these offerings, they nibbled on pickles, candied orange chips, and jellies. Finally, they adjourned to the drawing room, where, somewhat to Clare's surprise, the senior Crowleys and Truesdales engaged in a most congenial game of whist.

Evelyn and Kitty played the piano, Mr. Thayer and Peter at their sides, as all four sang a selection of popular songs. They were soon joined by Northrup and Clare, who found themselves unable to resist the lilting tunes. In any event, the enthusiasm and ringing voices of the singers, most notably that of Mr. Thayer, had made their efforts at conversation futile.

The two girls sat at the keyboard with sparkling eyes and gay smiles. Northrup stood at Kitty's side, and Clare could not help but notice the way he smiled down at her, as well as the charming manner in which the girl returned his look. Was it possible that this was where the earl's affections lay, with the delightful and young Kitty Truesdale? After all, their families were well acquainted and their estates within easy distance. It seemed to Clare quite logical. But no, she could not envision Northrup wed to a girl still practically in the schoolroom. *Why, he would be bored to death in a month. Wouldn't he?* She looked at Kitty's golden head bent over the piano and sighed. There was much to be said for youth. Clare looked up into Northrup's eyes. He grinned broadly, as his deep voice rolled into the next verse of the song. At the moment, he could not have looked less like a prospective suitor. She grinned back at him and raised her voice to match his, willing the image of him and Kitty from her mind.

Evelyn suggested they play a light, romantic air, and all agreed. She and Peter, unaware they were being observed by Clare, were exchanging a warm, meaningful look as they sang the sentimental lyrics to one another. It was quite plain that they had a tendre for one another, and Clare finally understood the reason for Evelyn's listlessness in town. She wondered if anyone else had seen what she had, but a quick look at the vicar and the earl revealed them both to be fully engrossed in the music.

The atmosphere at Northrup Court was much changed two days later. Clare and Northrup had ridden out early, but Evelyn had declined an invitation to accompany them. He had not yet come up from the stables and Clare, on her way to change from her riding habit, heard the sounds of soft crying coming from Evelyn's room. She tapped on the door several times and finally let herself in. The girl lay across the bed, sobbing into her pillow.

"Evelyn, what is amiss? Whatever has happened?"

Evelyn only cried the harder and it took some time before she was able to confess, between shuddering sobs, her love for Peter and his for her.

"But that is wonderful Evelyn. Peter seems to be a fine, unexceptionable, young man. I liked him very much. But, why do you cry? Is it because you think your uncle will not countenance the match? Why, he appeared well disposed to him. Is there any reason why he would object to your marriage?"

Evelyn pushed a tear-soaked curl from her eyes and shook her head violently. "Of course not!" she declared, amazed that Clare could doubt Peter's eligibility. "Why, all those prancing dandies and fine lords in London cannot compare to Peter. Before I went to town, I thought perhaps what I felt for him was just admiration, but I know now that isn't true. I love him. I do. He is all that is wonderful. Do you not agree?"

"Most definitely, Evelyn," Clare replied with a reassuring smile.

"Oh! It is too awful!"

"Dear, please, tell me what is wrong."

"His parents! They say that it was agreed years ago, when Peter and Kitty were still in their cradles, that they would marry. Their mothers grew up together."

"I see. So, his parents know of your feelings for one another?"

"Yes, for Peter spoke to them yesterday. Oh, he knew of their plans before, but he never really believed that they would remain steadfast in their desire. But, they have! They told him he must abide by their wishes and Kitty by her parents'."

"Oh, dear. Well, and what has Kitty to say about this?"

Clare asked, guessing that the girl's feelings might be else-where.

"Kitty likes Peter well enough. Naturally. But, she does not love him. She says her parents' plans are foolish, and that she will not go along with them, but I know they will force her to. She wants to go to London next Season and is looking forward to it ever so much. Of course, I have told her how dull and pointless the life of the ton is," she explained with a world-weary sigh, "but she does not listen. She says that I am too besotted by Peter to enjoy such a gay life. In truth, she is right, for I found that I did not care a fig for any of that without him."

Clare decided it would be unkind to remind Evelyn of how eagerly she had taken part in the first few weeks of the Season, how relentless had been her pursuit of her London comeout. How much better it was that the girl had a taste of the beau monde and concluded on her own how best to lead a happy life. But, now, what to do? She was at a loss to solve this dilemma. At last, she had promised her to speak with her uncle. Perhaps he could think of some way to bring these two young people together.

After supper, Evelyn told Northrup her story. At the girl's request, Clare had joined them and sat quietly, not wishing to intrude. Northrup did not express much surprise at his niece's disclosure, and was, in fact, pleased with her choice. But he was taken aback at the obstacle placed in the path of the would-be lovers.

"Dash it! So that is why the Crowleys seemed so distant the other night. Indeed, I never remember their being anything but friendly and open. Evidently, they knew then which way the wind was blowing. Well, Clare, what think you of this pickle? I'm damned if I'll have my niece rejected out of hand in this manner," he declared protectively.

"My lord—Evan—I believe this is no passing fancy on Evelyn's part, and from what she says of the young man, he harbors the same feelings. It would be a shame to see them kept apart." She shook her head sadly. "Is there nought you can do?" Evelyn echoed this question in a thin, desperate voice.

"I can but speak with his parents, and I shall do so, of course. But, Evelyn dear, you must understand that I can only try to change their minds. Ambrose has always been a reasonable sort—wish I could say the same of Marion. In the end, my dear, the decision must be theirs, and we must, perforce, abide by it. I have to admit that, from what you have told me, I do not hold out a great deal of hope. I shall be shut up with my agent on already delayed business most of tomorrow, but be assured that I shall call upon the Crowleys as soon as I have finished." He patted Evelyn's wet cheek with a loving hand and smiled. "I promise you that I shall do my very best to convince them that they are wrong—diplomatically—and that their son could have no better or more loving wife than my sweet niece."

Evelyn wept quietly, protesting that his mission was a hopeless one, as Clare, uttering soothing words, escorted her to bed.

Clare was arranging a bowl of white roses in the conservatory the next afternoon. She was especially fond of this room. The outer wall was almost entirely glass, giving onto a view of the park, and huge double doors led to the terraced lawn. Thunderheads had assembled in the sky, waiting completion of their numbers to pour out their fury in the storm which had threatened to loose since early morning.

The usually bright, sunny room now was steeped in ominous shades and thunder grumbled impatiently in the near distance, as Clare lit the lamp at her elbow. Recalling their discussion of the previous evening, she sighed heavily. She did not hold out much hope for a happy resolution to the problem, though, naturally, she had not admitted that to Evelyn. Such a pity that the two young people might not be allowed to marry.

Her thoughts wandered back to that night on the starlit

terrace. She was utterly confused by Evan's behavior toward her. As well, she found it hard to deal with her reaction, for, even now as she remembered the incident, her heart beat wildly.

This confusion had not lessened in the intervening days, for the incident had not been repeated, and he had offered her no explanation for his behavior. Obviously, he had been about to say something more, when Evelyn interrupted him. But what? She knew that he felt completely at his ease with her, for he often spoke of his plans and estate problems. Perhaps that was it. No, she discarded the idea as quickly as it had come to her. He surely had not behaved like a man who wished to discuss something about his estates.

Then she recalled Letitia and the feelings he had once had for her. The woman's beauty could not be denied, and now that she was free once more, it was not unreasonable that Northrup's passion for her might have been reawakened. Certainly, Letitia's feelings for him were no mystery, but could Northrup see that? Perhaps, a little afraid that she might reject him again, he had sought reassurance of his charms with another woman. In truth, however, Clare did not think him a man to trifle with a lady's affections. She sighed.

She inserted the last rose into the crystal bowl and paused. She had not seen Evelyn since last night and assumed she had slept late and kept to her room, preferring to be alone with her thoughts. It was now gone four, however, and she wondered if the girl might not be ready for company. But, Evelyn's room was empty, and a passing maid informed Clare that she had ridden out early that morning.

Clare felt she might have gone riding to clear the cobwebs from her head. Still, it was odd that she had not yet returned. She made her way to the stable, where Stemple, the head groom, told her that Evelyn had called for Trinket to be saddled and, contrary to his earnest pleas, had insisted on riding out alone. He had wanted to advise the master, he said, but had been told that he was closeted with his agent and not to be disturbed except in case of emergency.

"Well, much as I know his lordship did not want Miss Evelyn to go without a groom, miss, she had done so many a time and, to be fair, she is an excellent horsewoman. So, you see, though I knew the lass was wrong, I wasn't sure it was urgent enough to disturb the earl." He cast a knowing eye skyward. "But, she is not back yet, miss, and I know now that I was wrong not to tell his lordship. I was just about to send a man to find her."

Clearly, the fellow was concerned both for Evelyn and for his position, and Clare assured him that he was not to be blamed. Evelyn had ridden off in the direction of the Crowley home. Her mind worked feverishly. She did not think Evelyn was stupid enough to run off to Gretna Green and be married over the anvil, but she was less certain that she was not desperate enough to allow herself to be compromised, and thus force a marriage with Peter.

Ordering Aphrodite to be saddled, she hurried back to the house to change her clothes. Passing the library on her way out, she hesitated. Should she inform the earl? Her suspicions were yet unconfirmed, and she dearly hoped they would not be. She would wait. Perhaps her concern was all for nought. She declined the groom's services and, as she rode off, told him that if she had not returned within an hour, to inform his lordship.

Clare rode off in the direction of some run-down, abandoned houses in the quarter of the estate which had not yet received Northrup's attention. A likely place for two would-be lovers to have a tryst, she decided. Seams of lightning creased the sky. She passed no one on the way and a high wind came up and heavy raindrops began to fall, impairing her vision. Clare was quickly soaked to the skin. A deserted cottage loomed ahead in the darkness and she urged Aphrodite forward. Once she neared the house, it became plain that no one was there, for no light glowed from inside and

there were no horses in the shelter of the lean-to. Thunder
and lightning tore through the skies. By this time, the rain
had become torrential, already forming puddles in the track.
Clare had neither the desire to keep Aphrodite abroad in such
weather, nor the will to continue her search in the downpour.
In any case, she could not see more than a few feet ahead
of her, so she could not possibly hope to spot Evelyn and
Peter.

She reined in Aphrodite and tethered her under the lean-to
for, though ramshackle, it still offered adequate shelter. Rummaging in some refuse, she ferreted out a few old rags and
was able to remove most of the rain from the frightened
animal's coat. The old, simple latch gave easily under the
weight of her shoulder, and she let herself into the house.
Looking about her at the deserted room, Clare was grateful
to find some logs left by the hearth and immediately set to
making a fire. Her habit was soaked, quite ruined, she noticed
with dismay, and she shivered with cold as she added more
kindling to the fire.

Stemple had no intention of waiting out the hour pro-
scribed by Clare before reporting to the earl. He was convinced that he was in that gentleman's black books already
and now, in this blasted rain, he thought grimly, and both
ladies out in the storm, there was no telling what would befall
them—or him.

The poor man's fears had not been unfounded. Upon hearing the news, Northrup had bellowed and demanded of the
fellow the reason for his employ, if not to accompany the
women of the house on their rides. His usual fair-mindedness
returned quickly, however.

"Naturally, it was not entirely your fault, Stemple, for
Miss Winchester in her own misguided way was trying to
spare me concern. But that niece of mine!" he bellowed
again. "That undisciplined brat will be the death of us all—
most probably Miss Winchester, chasing after her in this
weather. Aphrodite could bolt. She could lose her way . . ."

He passed a hand over his brow, his eyes as dark as the storm-shaded sky. "If anything has happened to her . . ."

Stemple was anxious to allay his master's fears. "Aye, sir, but Miss Winchester has a good head on her shoulders. No doubt, she took shelter somewhere once the rain became so heavy."

On her way back from the kitchen, Nanny, arrested by the commotion, had entered the library in time to hear the last of this exchange. "Master Evan, never say that Clare is out somewhere in this awful weather?"

"I wish I could not, Nanny, but 'tis true. She rode out a short while ago looking for that wretched child," he replied, struggling to maintain his composure.

Nanny gasped. "Good God! Are you telling me that Evelyn is up to her tricks again?"

"That she is. And this time, she has gone too far."

He heard a gasp and looked up to see a drenched Evelyn standing in a large puddle in the doorway, her face stricken.

"Thank heaven you are alright, child," Nanny breathed, her hand to her heart.

The earl glared. "Do not be too hasty, ma'am," he told her.

"Oh, Uncle Evan, I am so sorry. I never thought that . . ."

"Silence! Your thoughtlessness has reached its limit. Miss Winchester is at this moment out there"—he pointed to the rain-lashed windows angrily—"looking for you. Get to your room and do not dare to leave it. I shall deal with you when I return!"

"But, Uncle, Peter is just outside and soaking wet!"

"Damn Peter! Nanny will tend to him! Now, get out of my sight!"

The girl ran from the room, sobbing, and Nanny bustled out to see to Peter.

"Stemple, saddle Triton. I shall be at the stable directly." So saying, he took the stairs two at a time to collect a cloak.

* * *

The rain and wind pounded mercilessly on the cottage roof, which leaked in several places, effectively muzzling any other sounds. Clad only in her lace-edged chemise, and pantalettes and stockings, Clare presented a tempting picture, leaning toward the sweet-smelling applewood fire, as she tried to dry her hair.

"Thank God you are safe!"

Startled, Clare whirled around, clutching her dress to her breast and, wide-eyed, cried, "My lord!"

Her hair hung about her shoulders, and the firelight in the darkened room brought out amber lights in the damp, soft waves, turning her skin a rosy pink.

Northrup's usually shining boots were clouded with spattered mud and, as he crossed the room, he threw off his sodden cloak revealing the shirt and trousers which clung to his body. He shivered, and the shirt immediately joined the outer garment in a widening pool of water on the rough wooden floor. His first thought had been only thankfulness that she was safe but, as he extended his hands to the welcome warmth of the fire, he was all at once aware of her appearance.

He stood still, his eyes running slowly over her body that the rumpled dress did so little to conceal, and then he looked deeply into her eyes. "My God, Clare, but you are beautiful." His voice was low and soft, and he took a few slow steps toward her.

Clare felt the attraction as much as he, for he looked more appealing now than he ever had in his faultless finery, but she knew that she must not forget herself. She swallowed, moving off to his left and backward toward the hearth. "Evan—my lord—please," she whispered.

"No, 'Evan,' remember?"

"I came out to find Evelyn, but . . ."

"I know. She and Peter are safe at the Court," he explained, as he smiled and bent down to kiss her lightly.

She tried to move away, but he grasped her shoulders gently. "Don't run away from me, Clare."

"Evan, I . . ."

"Hush." His cool lips moved to her eyes, her forehead, her cheeks and, finally, again to her lips, which he took with abandon. Placing his hands above her elbows, he gently pushed her arms about his neck where, she found, they felt most comfortable and natural.

Evan's eyes caressed her. "You are beautiful," he murmured again. She looked up at him. "My little one, you have driven me to distraction these last weeks."

"I?" she asked in surprise.

"You," he pronounced. "Do you not know that I love you, Clare?" She shook her head. "No, of course you do not, for, fool that I am, I did not realize it myself for a long time." His hands caressed her body slowly, running over the soft contours of her hips. His lips moved to her neck and burned a slow path to her breasts. She trembled with pleasure as he lowered her gently to the tattered rag rug in front of the blazing fire and kissed her, exploring her mouth with hunger.

Clare touched his bare shoulders, hesitatingly. "Is something wrong, my love?" he teased. She found herself blushing furiously again and shook her head. "What, then?"

"It is just that I have ever—admired your broad shoulders," she replied, her eyes lowered.

"And do you still?"

"Oh, yes, indeed," she assured him with a broad smile.

"Good," he said, and laughed lightly, returning his attention to the hollow of her throat.

"Oh, Evan, we must not, truly we mustn't," she protested breathlessly.

He smiled down at her, his fingers flirting expertly with the satin ribbons of her chemise. "Indeed, Clare? Do you wish me to stop?" he asked, nuzzling the soft, warm spot he had just exposed.

"Oh—oh! Yes."

Northrup raised his head and cocked a rakish eyebrow. "You are quite certain? You have no—doubts about the matter?"

Clare shook her head stoically and wondered if he could feel her heart pounding.

"Very well, my dear," he sighed with mock resignation. "I shall stop—if you do." She looked at him, bewildered. "If you will but remove your lovely fingers from my hair and stop holding me—quite so fast," he said unwrapping her other hand from around his shoulder and placing a lingering kiss on the palm.

Clare blinked up at him in surprise. "Oh! I did not realize . . ."

His eyes twinkled with pleasure. "Ah, but I did, love." His voice was low and throaty. "I did." He held her fast and brushed away a damp tendril of hair. Clare moaned softly and entwined her arms tightly about him once more, as he kissed her again. The weight of his long, hard body pressed intimately to hers was delicious. She could think of nothing, want nothing, but his wonderful nearness.

The storm outside had run its course and Clare and Northrup, hearing the sound of hoofbeats, jumped up from the floor. She looked to him. "Oh, Evan, what shall we do?"

"I'll see to it, don't worry." He strode to the door and stepped outside into the cool air. Clare began frantically pulling on the rest of her damp clothes and, a few moments later, he returned.

"One of my tenants. He was passing by, saw the horses and the smoke from the chimney, and was going to look in to find out who was in here. I told him that I and a friend"— he grinned at her conspiratorially—"took shelter here from the rain and sent him on his way." He paused and looked at her lovingly. "We had best go, love."

They smiled warmly at one another and, after several last kisses, hand in hand, left the cottage.

Thanks to Clare's intervention, Northrup was not so hard

on Evelyn as he had threatened. The girl had thrown herself into Clare's arms, crying with relief at her safe return and, tearfully, told her story.

Having spent a long and restless night, she had risen at first light. Poor Evelyn believed that her uncle's mission to the Crowleys was doomed and, if so, that she and Peter would not be permitted to meet, as they once had. Determined to see him alone, she rode to Crowley House, where she wakened Peter by tossing some pebbles against his window.

They had spent the day deeply engrossed in innocent conversation and avowals of undying love, losing track of time until the blackening sky and sinister rolls of thunder obtruded upon their solitude. At Peter's urging, they had headed for the Court but, though they gave the horses their heads, they were caught in the storm a mile from home and thoroughly drenched.

The still-shaken girl finished her tale with profuse apologies to all and gratitude that Clare had survived the adventure unharmed. Northrup suggested that, exhausted as they all were, they get an early night's rest. "I shall think on an appropriate punishment, Evelyn, and will talk with you further tomorrow," he had promised.

A low fever kept Clare to her bed the next morning and confined her to the environs of her room for two days after that. An habitually busy nature had always made her a difficult patient, but her temperament in this instance was nearly despondent. Awakening the day following the events in the cottage, she was informed of Northrup's having been called unexpectedly to London by his man of affairs. Upon hearing this news, she fell back upon the pillows and sighed. She had thought of the last few days before their scheduled return as filled with tête-à-têtes, passionate kisses, and declarations of everlasting devotion, but, instead, her lover was to be far away in London, while she lay abed in Gloucestershire.

Molly, the bearer of these ill tidings, had received further

instruction from his lordship. "He said to tell you and Miss
Evelyn to pack up your things and follow him, miss, because
he expects he won't be back for some time. I'll get started
with your clothes."

Clare brightened but, when she tried to rise, her head began to pound and a dull, ominous ache spread through her
limbs. Responding to Molly's summons, Nanny bustled in a
moment later, all concern.

"A fever," she pronounced with gravity. "Well, I'm not a
bit surprised, dear, after that foolish mischief yesterday. You
should have left Evelyn to her own resources; it would have
served her right. A good scare and a thorough soaking were
no more than she deserved and no doubt would have done
more good than harm, that's my considered opinion."

Still clucking her disapproval, the old woman shot direc-
tions at Molly, who longed to tell her that she was quite
capable of caring for her mistress without any help. Tucking
another blanket about Clare's now shivering form, she shook
her head sadly. "Well, miss, it's for certain you won't be
doing any traveling today, or very like for a day or two more,
either, else you'll catch your death, you will."

"That's right," Nanny chimed in.

"Oh, Nanny, really I do not feel so bad as all that. This
is nothing more than a chill, I assure you. I shall wrap myself
warmly in the coach and perhaps a hot brick or two and
I . . ." Clare's voice dwindled off, for even she knew she was
being foolish.

"You are not to leave that bed, miss, and that's the end of
it," Nanny interrupted sternly. Molly stood at her side nodding in silence.

Clare groaned as her feeble protests went unheard and, finally, she capitulated. In truth, her eyes felt as if they would
burn out of their sockets, and her head ached abominably.
Molly crossed to the window and drew the draperies against
the clean, glaring light of the rain-polished sun. Returning to
sit on the edge of the bed, she patted her hand sympathetically.

"I'll bring you some toast and tea in a bit, but try to sleep now."

She and Nanny left the bedchamber, shutting the door softly behind them. Two or three days! How could she bear it? She lay there, recalling the incidents that had so changed her life.

She and Evan had ridden back in silence, each content simply to bask in the mutual love they had, at last, acknowledged. Almost at their destination, Evan had drawn their horses side by side into a verdant copse, where he leaned over and kissed Clare as deeply and lovingly as ever he had in the cottage.

"Evan . . ."

"Yes, Clare?" One finger raised her chin, lifting her face to his, and she saw that same roguish gleam in his eyes as he tried and failed to prevent his lips from turning into an irresistibly sensuous smile. "Is there something amiss, my love?" he teased.

Sighing in blissful resignation, she answered his smile with her own. "Nothing that I can think of," she replied, caressing his cheek and reaching up to kiss him.

His hand played and tangled aimlessly in her unbound curls. "Did I tell you that you must never pin up your hair again? Or wear those blasted caps?" His voice was a bare whisper in her ear.

"I believe you failed to mention it, my lord. And, if you please, remove your hand from my hair, for I must already look a fright." She grinned and did what she could to put her appearance to rights. "What will they say at the Court, seeing me like this?"

His eyes raked her slowly. "You look," he began, and then shook his head, as if uncertain how to continue. "You look quite extraordinary. If I were not a gentlemen—no, that is not right, for I fear that I am not—if you were not a lady, my dear, I should bemoan our lack of a blanket," he said, looking at the lush but sodden green grass beneath the trees, "which, alas, prevents my showing you just how lovely you are. And damn what they will say at the Court!"

Clare looked him straight in the eye, as she spoke with mock solemnity. "I should tell you, sir, that lurking somewhere in my distant past is an aunt whose wanton reputation as one of the king's favorites was of no little embarrassment to her poor family. I think perhaps her niece ought to leave before she manages to overcome several subsequent generations of proper, ladylike conduct." So saying, she urged Aphrodite to a gallop and, laughing gaily, was off, followed by an equally merry Northrup.

Clare sniffed, missing the earl desperately. Two or three days was an eternity. She turned the pillow and rested her cheek on the cool fabric. The earl. *Just think of it,* she mused, *me, Clare Winchester, and a peer of the realm. Well,* she considered, *my own lineage is above reproach (barring that wayward aunt,* she thought, grinning), *although there is Father. But Northrup already knows about him, so that can't signify.* Suddenly, her heavy lids shot open.

He may know about Father, but, he doesn't know about me, about my silly behavior in the past. What would he say? Clare kicked away the covers in which she had become entangled as she worried this problem. *My past,* she told herself, *was nothing but the ill-considered behavior of a careless, indiscreet miss. I realize that now. And Northrup will realize it, too. Why probably, we shall laugh ourselves silly over it. Yes, I shall tell him when I get back to London,* she decided, and fell at last into a fevered sleep.

Eight

On the sunny afternoon of his third day in London, Northrup was departing his club, having enjoyed a light luncheon of cold fowl in the company of an old comrade. His business, concerning some of the investments in Evelyn's inheritance, had been concluded more speedily than he had expected, and he was left on his own until his niece and Clare arrived in town. As he stepped into the street, a smart curricle pulled up beside him at the curb.

"Good afternoon, Northrup." Letitia peeked out with a surprisingly cold stare on such a warm day, from under a dainty orchid parasol with a deep edging of white lace.

"Letitia. Good day to you, Sterne."

The older, sober-faced gentleman who sat at her side was less than pleased to keep his horses standing while his lady exchanged pleasantries with this young, handsome peer, who also happened to possess a valiant war record. He managed, through a sort of bravery of his own, to nod civilly.

"How nice to see you again. You have been from town?" she asked sweetly.

The earl inclined his head, concealing a smile at her poor attempt to make him believe that she had forgotten his whereabouts. Letitia knew full well that he had been in the country, and with whom, for she had taken no trouble to disguise her displeasure when he had apprised her of his plans before leaving for the Court.

"Your charming niece, she has returned with you?"

"Not yet, Letitia. Miss Winchester took a chill, I am afraid, and their departure was, naturally, delayed," he explained, relating to her the details he had received only late the day before via a hastily sent missive from Nanny. "I expect them in a day or so."

Letitia's green eyes glittered maliciously in the shade of her parasol, but her voice remained (at least to her companion who had been the grateful recipient of her attention these last weeks) deceptively sweet. "A chill? My heavens, how very unfortunate. And surprising, too, considering that one would think Miss Winchester definitely more at home in the dull quiet of the country than amidst the gay life we so enjoy here in town." Before Northrup had the chance to give her a proper set-down, she continued. "But, my dear Northrup, your preoccupation with your niece's companion," she rejoined with undue emphasis on the last word, "explains your otherwise unforgivable lack of memory, of course!"

"I very much fear that you have left me behind, madam," he said evenly. "What, may one ask, have I forgotten?"

"And still you do not recall!" she chided him with a pretty moue. "Why, today is my birthday."

"Ah, but of course. My felicitations, Letitia. Indeed"—he cocked a brow—"my memory does fail me. How many years is it?"

She flushed an unbecoming shade of crimson, but controlled an equally unbecoming retort which rose easily to her pretty, full lips. "Heartless beast! How can you roast a lady so?"

Satisfied that his barb had found its intended mark, Northrup bowed. "You are quite right, Letitia, my deepest apologies. Pray forgive me."

"I should not do so, you know," she pouted as her escort mumbled something about the rag manners of the younger generation. "But I shall, provided you attend my birthday party this evening. I shall expect you at eight-thirty," she directed him with a distinct note of triumph in her voice.

Left without a polite alternative, he nodded his acquiescence, and the curricle drove off. He turned down the street in the opposite direction, much less pleased with the world than he had been a few minutes earlier.

Lights were burning in every window of Letitia's fashionable house in Bruton Street, and soft music emanated from the upstairs ballroom as Northrup handed his hat and cape to the butler. The clock in the foyer finished chiming nine and Northrup allowed a small smile at the contrary streak in his nature which had prompted him to arrive thirty minutes later than the hour appointed by his hostess. The truth of it was that he had wanted to avoid her for as long as possible, for, though he had given her no reason to hope, he dreaded the Cheltenham tragedy she might enact when told of his intention to wed Clare.

The realization of his feelings for Clare had been of no little amazement to him. Despite his responsibility to beget an heir, he'd had no real intention of marrying. Letitia had given him his fill of devious women, and he had thought never to find someone he could both love and trust. Then Clare had come along. Kind and charming and genuine, she had never put on airs, never tried to trap him, and he knew her ready wit would ensure that their partnership would never be dull. He laughed at himself for he had yet to broach the subject of marriage with the object of his plans. Recalling with delight her responses to him at home, he knew that she shared his feelings. Still, the woman was so damned independent, there was no telling what she might—or might not—do. Well, he promised himself this would be one time when he would brook no dispute. Clare Winchester was going to marry him if he had to carry her to the altar.

Northrup's amusement at this prospect faded as the butler ushered him upstairs. He declined the servant's offer to announce him to the other guests and paused in the doorway.

Absently tapping the box that contained Letitia's birthday gift, he surveyed the room. The crowd was not terribly large, he reckoned, some two dozen, counting Letitia and himself. A grin spread slowly over his face, as he scanned the company and finally became aware of the obvious—an inordinate number of the guests were men—the cream of the ton, too, so Northrup noted, and those females in attendance clearly were inferior to Letitia in looks! *Ah well,* he thought as he set a course across the room, *at least the evening shall be diverting.*

Letitia was seated amongst a coterie of admirers and, though she observed his arrival from the corner of her eye, she pretended not to notice him for some few moments. At last, she chose to recognize him and, in a loud tone blithely ordered the others to clear a path to her side for her "dear Northrup." He disliked being singled out in such a manner, but he bowed neatly and greeted her.

"Northrup, how kind of you to come to my little party. And on such short notice, too."

"Happy birthday, Letitia."

Taking the beribboned package which he extended, Letitia fluttered her lashes in a most beguiling manner. "A gift, too? Why, Northrup, you spoil me, indeed you do, for I should have been quite content with just your presence, you know."

The remaining stragglers soon disbursed as it became clear that their lady's charms were focused on the earl. She untied the ribbons slowly and deliberately, smiling at him all the while, and removed from its swathing of violet satin, an antique silk fan painted with plump, sanctimonious looking cherubs. She waved the fan languidly and gave a little smirk. "How very—quaint," she remarked, eyeing the pious choir of little beings. "Am I to take this as a commentary on my moral character?" she teased him.

"Madam," he answered drily, "I should never so presume. Rather, I thought you would admire the craftsmanship of the piece."

She looked at the fan askance and made a quick recovery. "Oh, but I do, er, of course. It is charmant. And now, are you not going to ask me to dance, my dear?"

As they danced, she made a couple of broad allusions to their future. With nothing yet settled between himself and Clare, Northrup initially decided to sidestep those remarks, but, when she referred to an upcoming dinner party to which she obviously assumed he would accompany her, he knew he could no longer remain silent.

"Letitia, I am afraid I shall be unable to escort you to His Grace's, next week."

"Unable? Whyever not?"

"I am already committed elsewhere."

"Indeed?" she asked, her brows arched. "Ah, well, no matter. I daresay Sterne or Baron Wychwood will be only too pleased to accompany me. I trust that you have no previous engagements for Saturday next. Lady Ellerby is giving a ball which I should hate to miss."

Clearly, his salvation lay in his admission of his love for Clare. Letitia was watching him expectantly, awaiting confirmation of her plans.

"Well?" she persisted, as the music ended and still he had failed to give the correct reply.

"Letitia, there is something I must explain to you. I shall not be accompanying you to Lady Ellerby's ball or to any other events of the Season." He paused. "You see, there is someone else."

To say that Letitia was taken aback would be considerably understating the case, for rejection by a member of the male sex was something completely new, and her silence as they stood facing one another, was threatening. Her lips were set in a hard, uncompromising line. In a trice, however, she had regained her poise and forced a hollow laugh.

"A poor joke, my dear. If you choose not to go to Lady Ellerby's, that is quite alright, for I know you find her a dead bore, but such extremes as these are unnecessary, I assure you." She tapped him playfully on the cheek with her fan.

"You mistake the situation, Letitia. I am in love with Clare Winchester." His gentle, sober tone was in marked contrast to her feigned banter.

She paled. "Northrup, if this is your ungentlemanly way of repaying me for marrying Tom, I think it is entirely too bad of you. Why, that was all years ago," she uttered in a strained whisper, suddenly uncaring of the mention of the passing of time. He gave an almost imperceptible shake of his head. Schooled from early childhood to hide her fierce temper from the opposite sex, Letitia had been an apt pupil, for few suspected her true nature. At this moment, however, she was finding it nearly impossible to control a rapidly rising hysteria.

"Letitia, I am convinced that you will soon forget any unhappiness which I may have caused you, for you have any number of the finest gentlemen in London at your feet," he said, sweeping the crowd with a movement of his arm.

Her mind worked quickly. Gazing up at him, her hand resting lightly on his arm, her attitude was one of honest and unselfish concern. "My feelings are not important, Northrup. It is your kind nature, indeed, your *happiness* which is uppermost in my thoughts."

"Pray, have no worry on my account, madam. I dare to hope that Miss Winchester will accept my suit."

Ah, so he did intend to marry the creature. She nodded grimly. "Yes, I have no doubt she will." Northrup raised a haughty brow in question and she continued. "Northrup, I fear that I must be frank with you. May we confer privately?"

"Letitia, there is nothing to discuss."

"Ah, my lord, but there is," she insisted. Puzzled, he bowed stiffly and followed her into the library.

She posed prettily in an intimate, dimly lit alcove and gestured for him to take the seat beside her. "Northrup," she began. "I think you must know of my feelings, my deep affection for you." Her eyes were focused on her hands, folded demurely in her lap, and she very nearly managed a blush. "I had, of course, hoped that the circumstances of such a declaration as the one that you have just made would have been—shall I say, different." The earl's blank stare gave her no encouragement, and she heaved a dramatic sigh and went on. "Well, at the very least, I intend to do my best to ensure that you will not be hurt."

"You are all kindness, Letitia," he drawled. "However, you need not trouble yourself, as I mentioned, I am convinced that I shall not be unhappy."

"Nor deceived?"

"What do you mean?"

"Naturally, you do not know. I was convinced that you did not, and I thought you could remain ignorant of the sordid facts. I admit that, at first, I was concerned about Evelyn, after all, she has become so very dear to me, but she was so often in your good company that I determined not to worry. But now, oh dear, how shall I say this?"

"Letitia, what the devil are you talking about?"

"I am afraid that I am speaking of Miss Winchester, my lord. There are some details about her past which you have a right to know," she said sweetly.

His eyes bored into her. "Be careful, Letitia."

"I called her Miss Winchester, but she was once known by another name. The Changeable Rose, she was called, for it seems that is what she was. She painted, you see. Oh, she was almost notorious in her Season. You were on the Continent then with your regiment, so I suppose you could not have known. And that was not all. She wore the most daring of gowns, hardly appropriate for a young woman. Why, even I, an established matron, should not dare to appear in public arrayed as she was." If all of this, related in tones most shocked and affected, were not enough, she was hardly above embellishment.

"Do you know that she was even seen alone, unchaperoned,

you understand," she explained redundantly, "with some of the wilder young bucks of the town. Then, of course, there was her visit to the Cyprians Ball and all manner of unseemly places. Her actions were considerably less than proper or discreet. *People talked,* my dear. Why, there was even one, dare I call him a gentleman, who hinted—well, no matter, he has since gone to his rest, I hear. But, you must understand, there is no knowing what really took place on those occasions. The ton, needless to say, was shocked.

"It was only with your entrée and the support of *dear* Lady Emily that she was once again allowed into our circle. You may well understand my trepidation, then, when I learned that this coming—nay, I feel duty-bound to say, fast and vulgar, female was allowed the care of your lovely and impressionable niece." She paused for effect, then went on.

"And the worst of it is her fortune, or, the lack of one. Oh, do you not see, my darling? Everyone else does. Why, simply everyone has remarked on the way she has twisted you about her finger. It's common knowledge that Clare Winchester is dangling after your money and your title. She has said as much, I am told. I expect she believes that we should have to accept her then. As, of course, we would Northrup. For your sake," she ended sympathetically. "Although God knows if the ton would be so magnanimous. Forgive me, dearest, but why else should she be willing to take on the comeout of a young, though I hasten to add, dear, miss whom she does not even know?"

"Letitia, I warn you, I will not hear . . ."

"Only please hear me out, for it is only your welfare which concerns me. I must tell you that there have been a good many smirks and jokes and, for all I know, wagers in the clubs. Naturally, no one has the nerve to quiz you to your face, and I have told all who dared to laugh in my presence that your attentions to such a common sort of person could result only from your generous, kind nature, nothing more.

But, good God, Northrup, none of us expected you would be so foolish as to fall into the trap of this creature."

He sat as one turned to stone. "You say that you expect her to accept your proposal. Well, but of course she will, for that has been her plan all along! Why, if she had not succeeded with you, she would have had Tobias Portman and Maximillian Newmarch to fall back on, for I am convinced that it is for just such a contingency that she has been cultivating them, although they would be a poor substitute for you. It would, of course, have been preferable for her to deceive either of them, though I have the greatest regard for Max, than for her to humiliate you. Oh, dearest, how can you be so blind?"

"As I recall, Letitia, the last woman who served me so ill was you. How can I know that this is not more of your treachery?"

She had the grace to blush, but had been prepared for his question. Casting down her eyes, she barely whispered in a broken voice, "Ah, you are cruel to remind me, but so right. For many years I have regretted my foolishness. And I know you can never forgive me." She stole a look at him, but his face gave her no reply.

"Oh, my dearest, if you only knew how many times I have wished I had my choice to make again." He did not gainsay her, and she pressed her advantage. "I was so young and silly, but I am wiser now and older." She allowed a self-deprecatory twist to her lips. "Now, I know better, although it is too late for me. But you, at least, must be happy, I am determined on that! Miss Winchester is no schoolroom miss, either. She knows quite well what she wants—your title, your fortune, and your position. And she knows just what she is doing, I promise you. Her age and maturity cannot pardon her, as I had hoped they would pardon me, one day, in your eyes."

Could it be true? Northrup's thoughts collided madly, his pride too damaged to allow him to reason clearly, making him susceptible to Letitia's tale. Clare had seemed content with her situation, and he had detected no hint of the grasping nature so typical of many women of his circle. But that would have been part of her plan, would it not, to play the innocent, the poor, unassuming female whom he would wish to protect, to provide for, by offering her his hand and all the wealth and power which went with it. He recalled that Clare had never had many kind words for Tobias Portman, but that was easily attributed to her need to play them off, one against the other. And Max!

The earl had been pursued by enough females to be keenly aware of his attractions, and he wondered for a moment how it was that Clare could consider an alliance with someone like Portman. His clouded reason quickly explained that, for a woman such as Letitia described, money was of great importance, and Tobias certainly had plenty of that. She need only overlook his unhandsome appearance, which surely would not be difficult, given the size of the man's purse. His lack of a title and influence, however, might well be far greater obstacles. Poor Max was another matter. While he, too, could not boast of a title, his looks were infinitely more palatable than Portman's, he was quite well off, and had a greater place in society, albeit less than Northrup's. He knew that his old friend would be grateful to learn of this plot. Through the haze of his fevered brain, Northrup remembered that Max was out of town and thus blessedly safe from her vile scheming, at least for the present.

He was all at once aware of Letitia's hand resting gently on his. She looked at him with practiced innocence and fired her last shot. "Oh, my, could it be that you did know, after all? Here am I, needlessly concerned for your feelings and dear Evelyn's interests, while you have been aware of this all the time and did not find it of the least significance."

There was a long silence during which his eyes never left the candle flaming on the table at his knee. He disregarded her last comments. "You are certain of this?" His voice was low and betrayed none of the desperation that clutched at his heart. Her answering nod seemed almost sympathetic, as if she were reluctant to confirm what she knew would cause him pain.

He rose slowly and turned toward the door. Letitia hurried after him, not entirely sure that her narrative had produced sufficient effect. She placed a restraining hand on his forearm and begged him to look at her. His face masked a fury only barely held in check, a sensation emphasized by the powerful tension she felt, stonelike, under her fingertips. She looked at him apprehensively and, for just a second, thought that she detected an unspoken agony, before the midnight blue of his eyes became impenetrable. She fairly shuddered. Had she gone too far?

"Well?" His deep voice was a low, empty monotone. "Was there something else you thought I ought to know?"

"No. I . . . that is . . ."

"Be good enough to remove your hand. I have no need for your sympathy and even less desire for the company of your deceitful sex. I bid you good night."

Torn between incurring his wrath by further attempting to delay him, and the possibility that her last chance to sway him might be slipping away, she watched the door close behind him and cursed her helplessness. Had she destroyed his feelings for Clare, as she intended, or had she only driven him away from herself forever?

Northrup did not return to Grosvenor Square that night. He walked the damp streets for hours, failing to recognize or even see acquaintances met along the way. Nearing the neighborhood of the Seven Dials, he would have been trampled by the hooves of a startled hackney team, but for the extraordinary reflexes and strength of the coachman.

" 'Ere, guv'nah, you awright, then?" the agitated driver asked, springing down from the box and rushing to his side. *Bloody fool,* the man thought, *walks smack into the path of me team and who's to blame? Me, Mick Barton, that's who. Ruddy toff! Gets hisself killed and I'm left to pay. And where*

*would I be then, I'd like to know, and the missus just brought
to bed with our fifth.*

"He'll be just fine, driver," said a sickening, sweet feminine voice. "Won't you, your lordship?"

His head filled with a common, cloying scent applied with much too generous a hand, Northrup found himself helped to his feel by a flaming redhead with a patented, artificial smile.

Some time later, an empty bottle of blue ruin tumbled noisily to rest under a well-worn, far from clean bed. "Make a fool of me, will you?" Northrup growled, as he bent again to the woman's lips. "Deceitful slut," he groaned.

"Your lordship, please! I ain't the lady who's made you so mad. I ain't! Please!"

His eyes at last focused on the poor creature and his head began to swim wretchedly. "Clare. Clare. Damn your eyes," he moaned, and fell onto his back and into insensibility.

Nine

Clare was so excited at having returned to London and once again being near her beloved that she found it difficult to sympathize with Evelyn's unwillingness to leave Gloucestershire. They had sent round a note to Grosvenor Square apprising the earl of their arrival and now sat in the drawing room.

Her maid's romance with Edward Reynolds had progressed faster than even she, Molly, had hoped, and she had shyly confided, whilst nursing her ailing mistress, that he seemed on the verge of proposing.

Maude was away visiting friends and Evelyn was curled up in the window seat, her head resting against the glass, as she gazed disinterestedly out into the street. Clare sighed. She had tried all the way in from the country to brighten her spirits, to no avail. She avoided mentioning Peter's name, rather describing a play recently opened at Covent Garden, which she declared herself all eagerness to attend. Thinking that the earl would not be averse to his money's being spent in such a noble effort, she even went so far as to suggest that, following their long absence from town, Evelyn must be impatient to see what new delectables awaited her in the shops. The girl managed just the merest requisite response, and Clare knew any further attempts to distract here would be fruitless. She had exchanged a telling, helpless look with Molly and lapsed into silence for the rest of the trip.

Clare looked first at Evelyn and then, accusingly, out the

window of the drawing room at the dreary day. She shook her head. Really, even the weather seemed to be working against her. A few minutes later, Evelyn turned and gave a little smile. "Dear Miss Winchester, I have been behaving like a perfect goose, and you have been ever so patient with me. I do apologize," she said with a soft voice.

"Not at all, dear. I entirely understand your feelings, you know."

"Yes, I do know, and I thank you for your understanding and, what's more, I promise to amend my mopish ways at once."

Clare was not a little surprised at this resolution and the look that she returned made that feeling plain.

"I dare say you must think I'm cracked, but I assure you that is not the case. At least"—she bit her lip with uncertainty—"I do not think that I am. You see, I believe that even if Uncle Evan tries to speak with the Crowleys, it will do no good. I am convinced that they mean to have Peter marry Kitty, and there is nothing that even Uncle Evan can do about it. And so, I suppose it is best that I am in London and he is in the country. Why, I have begun to forget him already."

A quivering chin and two or three stubborn tears gave the lie to this bravado, as Clare sat down in the window embrasure and put a comforting arm about her shoulders. "There, there, Evelyn."

Evelyn raised watery eyes to her friend and sniffed as she tried to smile. "I shall be alright. One does not really die of a broken heart, after all, no matter what the poets say."

Clare looked at the girl with more fondness than she had ever felt for her before. "No, Evelyn," she confirmed, "one does not." It was clear that she had not yet begun to forget Peter, but her determination was encouraging nonetheless.

"The earl of Northrup, ma'am."

Now that he was arrived, Clare suddenly felt rather shy. But for the discussion (as she wryly termed it) with Evelyn the night before he left the Court, she had not seen Evan, and was at a loss as to how she should behave. She had no word of him, as she thought that she might, and, for a time, especially as she lay abed in the uncomfortable throes of fever and the more treacherous fits of boredom which accompany sickness, she wondered if he had run off in revulsion at her light-skirted behavior. At those times, she sternly reminded herself of his admission of love and of the fact that his own actions could be described by the objective observer, should such, God forbid, exist, as that of a rakeshame who had taken advantage of a woman in a helpless situation. She then declared herself a fool for expecting him to send a letter, when they had been separated for just a few days. Before you know it, she had chided herself, you'll become one of those tiresome females who expects a man to dance attendance on her every minute!

About to be faced with him at last, however, all her emotions came rushing back and she felt the color rising to her cheeks. With a mental shake, she fought down her anxiety and, as he crossed the threshold, she fairly beamed at him.

In all of her imaginings, Clare had envisioned a variety of reactions on Northrup's part when next they met. But, she was not prepared for the man who confronted her now, rage in his eyes and a sneer on his lips.

"Good day, Miss Winchester," he said in a harsh, clipped tone. "Evelyn, go to your room and pack. You are returning with me to Grosvenor Square, where you may finish out the Season."

Evelyn looked from him to Clare, who sat beside her as if frozen. She rose and crossed the room. "Uncle, what are you talking about? Is this a joke? Are you teasing me? If so, I am too dull to see the humor." As he shook his head in stern denial, she pleaded. "Why am I not to remain here in Edwardes Square with Miss Winchester and Miss Beauchamp? What have I done? I know I behaved badly at home, but surely here in town . . . Is this your way of punishing me?"

"You have done nothing amiss, child. You have conducted yourself with all propriety while you have been here, a fact which, given the circumstances, astonishes me. Now, do as I say. Pack your things, for I wish to quit this place as soon as possible."

Not knowing how to interpret his riddle or his mood, Evelyn stared at him in confusion and finally turned beseeching eyes to Clare.

"Do as your uncle says, Evelyn."

She blinked in surprise at her friend's seeming betrayal and, crying, fled the room.

Clare and Northrup stood facing one another for several moments, she numb with shock, he fighting to control his temper. At length, hoping that her voice did not betray her emotion and wishing that she could control the shaking of her hands, she spoke.

"Ev—my lord, I had not expected such behavior from you."

"Did you not?" he sneered.

"No," she retorted bravely, "I did not. Of course, it did occur to me that, upon reflection, you might have found my actions in the country to be . . ."

"Befitting those of a slut?" he supplied with a quickness which made the words more cruel.

Stung, she took a step backward. Closing her eyes against the tears that threatened to spill, she took a deep breath, resolved to deprive him of the satisfaction of seeing her cry. "That is very unjust."

He laughed, and his eyes mocked her. "You would think so. It must always seem unjust to have one's devious and carefully laid plans found out."

"What are you talking about?"

"Ah, you are a consummate actress, are you not? Amongst other things. A pity that your scheme has been uncovered."

"My lord, I beg you to enlighten me. What scheme? And why do you call me such names?" she pleaded, stricken.

"Do not try to gammon me; I am aware of what you are now, and I find those names most appropriate. But, perhaps, you prefer to be called by your other name. The Changeable Rose, is it not?"

Her hand leapt to her pounding heart and, for the first time in her life, Clare thought she might faint. "Dear God!"

"He, ma'am, will not help you. Did you truly believe that you could hide your shameless past forever? My God, woman, but you must have thought me a fool. Using Evelyn to get to me and using me, my name, to reestablish yourself in society. Such audacity!

"Oh, I admit, I was a willing dupe, actually believing you to be the sweet innocent you played at. I even fancied myself in love with you. Your behavior at the cottage was most convincing, but then, practice really does make perfect, does it not? I am sure that the shy, unwilling virgin is a role you have enacted before—evidently with as little success!"

"How dare you speak to me in such a manner? How dare you accuse me thus?" Outrage was beginning to overcome her hurt. For just a moment, she was sorely tempted to strike him but, somehow, she realized that such action would only reinforce his opinion of her. "I never thought to use Evelyn in any way, I . . ."

"Oh? Odd, isn't it, that yours are the only wishes she obeys. Witness her refusal to heed me just a few minutes ago. And why else, might I ask, did you agree to sponsor her in the first place?"

"I agreed, you will do me the courtesy to recall, because you begged me to. You will also remember that I told you at the time that I was not the proper person to do the job, but you were so eager to have her off your hands that you chose not to listen. And, sir," she finished, her voice, much to her dismay, beginning to rise, "perhaps the reason she does not heed you is because you bellow orders as if you were still in the army and have all the sensitivity of a soldier on the march!"

"You are hardly in a position to criticize my behavior, or anyone else's. Oh, you are clever. You knew that I had no idea what you meant when you referred to your being the wrong person to bring her out. If you'd had a modicum of decency, you would have told me. Even a lightskirt makes no secret of what she is." He looked down his patrician nose at her. "But then, a lightskirt does not usually have ideas above her station and, therefore, nothing to hide."

"You wrong me," she protested, not knowing of Letitia's lies. "You speak of indiscretions committed long ago. Foolish, yes, but those of a thoughtless, silly girl. I saw no reason at that time to tell a stranger of my youthful follies. Later, of course, I intended . . . But then, you see, I thought that you would understand and view them, as I have lately come to do, as harmless."

"Harmless?! Is that what you call your behavior, when you have the care of an innocent, impressionable, green girl? Everyone knew you for what you are. Everyone, that is, but I."

Her heart was broken, and she spoke in a strangled whisper. "Somehow, I believed it would not matter to you. Indeed"—she lifted her chin in defiance once more and said with some difficulty—"no one forced you to care for me. I had believed your behavior in the cottage sincere, for I could not believe you meant to take advantage of me. Just as I never intended to trick you."

"Cunning wench! Oh, I freely concede you blinded me. I am sure you planned to make your confession to me—just as soon as the banns were read. It is fortunate for me that I have friends who care enough for me to tell me of your deceit. No more of your lies. The Northrup title and fortune will never be yours."

"My God, do you truly think yourself such a catch, to prompt me to such despicable action?"

His lips curled in a mocking sneer. "Let us say that I think *you* did."

"I think you must be mad. Pray, leave my house at once,

for I cannot bear to look upon you any longer. I shall not make any further attempt to vindicate myself to you, for I see it is fruitless. I cannot think how I ever came to love such a heartless, cruel man."

"Be honest, ma'am, you did not love me; you care only for what I could have given you—respectability and money!"

"Respectability? I need none of you for that, my lord!"

"Ha!"

"And I thank heaven that I am not to be wed to one so puffed up by his own consequence."

"You mean, to one whose eyes have, at last, been opened. Work your wiles on another, for I'll have none of you. But, I warn you that Maximillian Newmarch is not fresh from the country and is no more likely to take the bait than I."

She blinked, further confused, and the thought flitted through her mind that he must be mad. "Max?"

"Aye, Max. Don't flutter those eyelashes at me! I would advise you to direct your efforts toward easier prey, like that ass, Portman. He . . ."

"Get out!"

"With pleasure." So saying, he strode from the room and nearly collided with Evelyn, who had just entered the hall, portmanteau in hand. "We shall send for the rest of your things, Evelyn. Let us go."

She stared at him. "Uncle, I do not want to go. I wish to remain here with Miss Winchester. Please mayn't I stay?"

"No!"

She turned pleading eyes to a trembling Clare. "Please, dear, do as your uncle bids you," she whispered desperately. She knew that she could neither keep back her tears nor cope with Evelyn's weeping, and she wished only that they would depart.

The girl threw her arms about her friend and kissed her, then, retrieving her bag, ran sobbing from the house. Without a word, without even a look, Northrup followed her into the square, and the carriage tore away as if making its escape from the very gates of hell.

Molly, who had heard Northrup's voice thundering from the drawing room and Evelyn's tearful race up the stairs, had followed the girl to her bedroom, wondering what harebrained scrape she had gotten herself into this time. Gleaning no information from her (for, indeed, poor Evelyn had none to give), save that she must immediately quit Edwardes Square, Molly had to content herself with drying tears and assisting in the gathering of myried possessions. That finished, she crossed to Clare's bedroom and sat on the edge of the bed to wait. It can be imagined, as she listened to the indecipherable sounds reverberating from downstairs, that Molly was sorely tempted to rush to her mistress's defense.

Later, as she cradled her sobbing lady in her arms, her own face wet with tears of sympathy, she listened patiently, as Clare choked out the words describing her encounter with the earl.

"That dog!" Molly spit, her grey eyes glinting as she handed Clare yet another handkerchief. "How dare he use you so? His precious lordship should be flogged. Aye," she instructed the world at large, "all men should be flogged, the insensitive, selfish wretches!" The dark blue ribbons of her cap bobbed along with the vigorous nodding of her head. "Oh, if only I had him here, I swear I'd plant him a facer he'd not soon forget!"

Delivering such a set-down to the earl and all of his sex on behalf of all of her own was, unfortunately, not in her power, and so Molly's frustration and fury continued unabated. Thus it was quite justifiable to her, while utterly mystifying to poor Mr. Reynolds, that he should find his face soundly slapped when, the next afternoon in the seclusion of a copse of willows in Hyde Park, he should attempt to claim a kiss, a pleasure which had not been denied him in the recent past.

Never slow-witted, Mr. Reynolds wisely abandoned his

amorous intentions, but visions of her mistress's distress still filled Molly's head and she delivered a scorching diatribe, the cause of which her poor victim, clever though he thought himself to be, was at a loss to comprehend. To his credit and to Molly's relief, when she finally considered her behavior, his confusion was exceeded by his fond regard and demonstrated most admirably by a surreptitious smile, as he walked her slowly about the park until she had regained her normal temper.

She gazed up at him shyly, a hand to her lips. "Oh, Lord," she breathed, suddenly realizing her conduct. He smiled down at her.

"It's alright, dear. Would you care to tell me what has happened to turn you into such a harridan?"

She blushed. "No, Edward, I cannot, for it is someone else's secret, you see. Someone who has been most sorely used. But I am truly sorry that I slapped you. It was very wrong of me to treat you so."

He took her in his arms. "Although some of us can be bounders, Molly, my love, I promise you," he teased, rubbing his cheek gingerly, "I shall take the greatest care not to incur your wrath myself."

"Oh, Edward," she had sighed, before returning his kiss.

Maude did not return from her visit until the day after the dreadful scene. The crying had ceased by then, but it had been replaced by a most uncharacteristic pitiful, almost unnerving quiet, which even the imperceptive Maude was hard put not to notice.

She assumed that Evelyn had chosen to remain in the country. Clare was tempted to leave the woman in ignorance but, reasoning that she was bound to hear of the girl's presence in town, explained that it had been mutually decided that Evelyn would be better off in Grosvenor Square. Believing that their guest had been quite alright with them in Edwardes Square, Maude was inclined to press the point, until a glance at her niece's firmly set lips convinced her that further questions would be of little use. When questioned about her despondence, Clare gave an unconvincing wave of her hand and claimed her poor spirits were owing to a weakness left over from her fever and not cause for concern. Maude seemed willing to accept this explanation, but she paid little heed to Clare's minimizing of her condition. Though declining all of her aunt's suggestions, Clare could not but be touched by her solicitous attentions.

In the following days, she declined all invitations and remained at home, where, despite the passage of time, she found it impossible to pull herself out of her despair. It was not that she considered the prospect of not becoming Northrup's wife a deprivation, for had she not existed quite happily without him? It was not, she also lectured herself that she still loved him, for how could she feel anything but hatred for one who held her in such contempt? Had she been able to turn her angry passion into indifference, she might then have felt more at peace with herself, but, alas, she could not. His distaste, the cruel words he had so brutally spoken still tore at her, and she could no more stop hating him than she could leave off thinking of him.

When he returned to town, Maximillian Newmarch called on several occasions and was politely turned away. That Tobias Portman was subsequently admitted was due solely to Clare's having been passing through the hallway, as Estelle answered his knock.

Their discourse was not the sort upon which long and mutually gratifying and happy relationships are built. Clare was at first at a loss to account for her own behavior. Certainly, his attire was not unusually ludicrous. He, after all, surely looked no more nauseating in his lime green satin coat with sky-blue stripes than would the next man. Nor was his manner any more condescending than she had known it to be in the past. In short, on this otherwise unremarkable afternoon, Tobias was, to all appearances at least, no more nor less than ever he had been. She finally decided that her actions stemmed from an already wretched humor, a condition that required only Tobias to make it worse.

"Well, Clare, no doubt you have been remarking my absence lately," he began, as she somehow managed to curb her tongue. "Had to see to a trifling problem with my tenants. If my agent, Browning, were not so spineless, I would not have to waste my time dealing with those people, and I have so informed him. Only just imagine, if you will my dear, my consternation at traveling such a distance only to find that the 'grave problem' to which that fool alluded in his letters was merely the same complaint about the supposed need for new fencing and roofs that these wretched folk have been trying me with these last two years.

"As you might well expect, I again reminded them of their good fortune to have any sort of roof above their heads. I concede that there are, perhaps, one or two cottages which could stand a bit of repair"—his tone was that of one much injured—"but, my finances are such that an expenditure of that magnitude cannot even be contemplated until spring, at the earliest." He paused long enough to take out yet another beautiful snuffbox, the price of which, Clare assayed, could easily have repaired no less than half a dozen cottages.

"I need not tell you that Browning now understands how short-lived his position will be should he pester me with such matters again."

No, Clare thought drily, *you need not tell me, for I know only too well how insensitive and selfish you are,* and she frowned as she pictured the unfortunate tenants and the browbeaten Mr. Browning. For a moment, her mind wandered as she considered how unlike those people were to the contented tenants on the Northrup estates. She gave a little shake of her head, the better to banish him from her mind, and realized Tobias was addressing her.

"And what of you, Clare? I hardly need ask how you are, for you look a fright, I do not mind telling you. I take it the Hallisey brat has been running you to death. Really, Clare, a woman of your years cannot expect to keep such a pace without its telling in her appearance. I came to offer my escort to the assembly of Mrs. Aldgate on Friday, but 'tis plain you are not up to the occasion and, I must own, I almost hesitate to be seen in company with you until you are in better looks."

Only Tobias could have uttered such callous remarks without the subsequent realization that she whom he addressed would take offense. Clare eyed him contemptuously and stifled the sharp retort which rose to her lips. She wished to be rid of him as soon as possible and felt that a quarrel would serve only to prolong his stay, so she determined to be coldly uncommunicative and hoped that he would soon take himself off.

"Indeed, Tobias, I grieve that my appearance does not please you. I fear you cannot blame dear Evelyn, however, for she has removed to her uncle at Grosvenor Square. If I look poorly, it is the aftereffect of a slight, but stubborn chill and fever I suffered not long ago. Perhaps I should take myself off to bed. If you will excuse me . . ."

Of course, he ignored the hint. "A chill, you say? In faith, I never knew you to be sickly before. Such a weakness of the constitution will not do," he intoned cryptically. "Still, I can only be pleased, yes, very pleased indeed, that Northrup finally has seen fit to accept the responsibility of his own niece. It was hardly suitable for you to be so burdened."

"I must assure you," Clare interjected sternly, "that I did not consider Evelyn a burden to me."

"Of course you would not, my dear. You are too good to express such feelings. But I, of all people, know what a trial she was to you, and I alone recognize your relief at your newly regained freedom." Clare's resolve was eroding fast and, before she could make a further effort to remonstrate at his apparently intentional misunderstanding, he continued.

"I must confess, though I realize this should come as no revelation to you, my dear," he began, a patronizing, smug smile on his face, "that it is not entirely on your account that I rejoice in the girl's departure. Surely you know that she was too much in the way."

"Tobias, please, I . . ."

His grin broadened and he held up a hand to silence her. "Really, Clare, you are beyond the age at which coyness is considered charming. And then our long relationship, dare I say our understanding, both serve to make your diffidence unnecessary. Still, I am, after all, a man of experience, and I understand that a woman feels the need for some amount of wooing, no matter that the outcome be known to both parties at the outset. That is the reason for my gladness at the departure of little Evelyn. I am prepared, you see, to court you before our banns are called. I must tell you, however, that I do not intend to do the pretty overlong. But, there, I am persuaded that you are as eager as I for the wedding to take place, so we should be able to dispense with these posturings in, shall we say, four or five weeks?"

Clare had sat quietly during this address, her mouth agape, her head in a whirl at his audacity. Tobias took her silence for approbation and continued to smile, infinitely pleased with himself, his plans, and the world. She stared at him, wanting all at once to slap him and to laugh in his face. Amusement, so foreign to her these past days, won out and she fairly roared with laughter. ". . . mistaken, so mistaken . . ." were the only words he could distinguish from her mirth.

"What mistake? Who is mistaken? Good God, are you well? What do you mean? That fever must have addled your brain."

When she caught her breath, she saw the confusion in his face and managed to respond. "I am quite well, Tobias, I promise you. And I mean that we both are mistaken. Had anyone troubled to ask, I should have said that you had not the capability to astound me, but, there"—she nearly went off into giggles again—"I was wrong. You, sir, were even more mistaken in presuming that I should marry you."

"What's this? Ah, I see it now. My proposal was not passionate enough for you."

"Proposal? Presumption, sir!"

"Oh, well, as for that, we each know what we want, so what is the sense in pretending? You must know that I do not have the address of Byron, madam."

"Tobias, you do not have the address of flower pot, but that is beside the point." She stood before him, her fists clenched at her sides, both surprised and pleased at her nerve. He had brought all her agony and frustration to the surface, and she was, at last, furious.

"Impudent minx! How dare you?" he sputtered. "Who was willing, I say *was* willing to overlook all of your shortcomings? Who else do you think will have you? I think you must be mad to give up the chance to be my wife. Obviously, you have no conception of the size of my fortune . . ."

"Why, Tobias, I can but think that your fortune is of no great size if it cannot support improvements to your tenants' houses," she said acidly. "In any event"—she forestalled his rejoinder with a haughty wave of her hand—"I must tell you that all of your money only makes you rich, Tobias, it can never make you endurable! Any female might be glad to share your income, but few would be willing to pay the price of it!"

"What! Why, you jade!"

"Just so," she agreed, and inclined her head slightly, so that he could not see that this accusation had flown true. Clare was spared the effort of throwing him out, as he turned on his heel, vowed never to favor her with his company again, and quit the house.

"Thank God," she breathed, and sank back into her chair, exhausted but strangely, perversely, pleased by the encounter. At last, she was rid of him. She sat thoughtfully. *Is he correct? Will no one else have me? No*—she sighed—*I suppose not.*

Of a sudden, she was awakened to the futility and foolishness of her recent behavior. *This will never do,* she chided herself. *I have become a hermit because of the cruel actions of one small-minded man. Why, one might think that my happiness depended on him, that my very life revolved about the high-and-mighty earl of Northrup.* The realization that she had reacted in just such a manner was the source of no little embarrassment, and that disappointment in herself, in its turn, was the cause of a very healthy, very cathartic consternation.

Damn the man! Let him despise me, if that is his choice. I shall not perish for lack of his company, for I have my friends. It had occurred to her that he might make his opinion of her public, but Maude had never mentioned a hint of rumor, and dear Max still faithfully left his card several times a week. She knew that Northrup's silence was not borne of kindness. Rather, she suspected, it sprang from a desire to avoid the humiliation of admitting publicly that she had made a fool of him. *Well,* she decided, *I shall come out of this ridiculous seclusion and enjoy life as I choose and as best I can.* Considerably cheered by this resolution, she spent the next couple of hours wondering just how to put her new self into action.

Maude remarked on her improved looks later that day, when she returned from her round of calls.

"Yes, Aunt, I do feel completely recovered," she confirmed. "Oh, but I must tell you that Tobias Portman is quite at odds with our evaluation of my appearance," and she went on to tell her aunt of all that had transpired that morning. Clare was ready to be admonished for turning away so eligible a suitor but, to her surprise, the older woman smiled and said that if her niece did not wish to marry Tobias, she could think of no single reason why she should.

"Why, I am so happy to hear you say so, Aunt. I had thought that you—well, that is, he is quite well off, you know . . ."

Maude patted her hand. "That's quite alright, dear. I know what you are trying to say. In truth, a short time ago, I confess you would have been correct. After all, dear," she counseled, shaking her finger, "there is a good deal to be said of independence, even if the gentleman in question is not—well, not entirely what one might wish, and very little to be said of living poorly."

Clare looked puzzled, as her aunt, having delivered this shocking blow, sat back and folded her hands in her lap, a smug, secretive smile on her face. "I, too, have news," she declared, looking as if she would burst if Clare failed to ask for enlightenment. Her niece gladly obliged.

"Well, my dear, you know Mr. Langley, the wool merchant." Clare shook her head. "No, you do not, I suppose. But, if you had not been in the mopes these past weeks, you would, you know." Clare accepted this rebuke willingly, aware that all her thoughts of late had been focused on herself and, once again, mentally swore to mend her ways. "But, no matter, Clare, for you will like one another, I am certain. Indeed, you must, for we are to be married, Mr. Langley and I."

For the second time that day, Clare was completely surprised by unexpected marriage plans. "Married? But, Aunt, I had no idea! Oh, I am so happy for you," she cried, hugging a grinning Maude.

Maude laughed. "Thank you, dear, I had hoped you would be. And best of all, Edgar is extremely well off. Of course, I do realize he is in trade, but . . ."

"Oh, Aunt Maude. You are not—that is, you would not wed him because . . ."

"No, Clare. I would not wed Edgar if I did not care for him, and that," she assured her with a candid smile, "was a great surprise to me, I must confess!"

"I am truly glad."

"Yes," she resumed, "but the fact is that my husband-to-be is rich, and that is such a great relief to me. To us. Only think how our lives will change. You shall, naturally, make your home with Edgar and me. We have already discussed it, and he is entirely agreeable."

Clare shook her head, finding all of this more than a little difficult to take in. "You are all that is kind, Maude, truly. I thank you and Mr. Langley, too, for your kindness, but I shall remain her in Edwardes Square."

"Really, Clare, don't be a ninnyhammer. You cannot remain on your own alone, it just isn't done, dear. We can provide you with anything you could wish for. Anything at all. We both want you with us." Her niece still demurred, and they discussed the subject at some length. Finally, to please her aunt, Clare agreed to reconsider the matter.

The supper at Brooks's had been surprisingly uninspired, even the wine indifferent, especially for a gentleman dining alone and languidly casting about for diversion which, thus far, had eluded him. Having risen from his secluded table, the man would gladly have quit the place with no more than a civil nod to the dandy who now stood at his side bespeaking an all too recent intimacy with all too much port. The great fellow in pink, of necessity, spoke first.

"Well, Northrup. Dining alone, I see. You surprise me. Why, I should have thought you might be entertaining some lovely female in a private room at Grillon's."

"And you, Portman, surprise me. I should have considered you incapable of sight, much less thought in your present condition. Good God, man, have you no more sense than to go about town disguised as you are?" In a better mood, Northrup might have snickered at his own pun, the thrust of which was entirely lost on Tobias.

" 'Pon my soul, Northrup, you're the second person today I have had the pleasure of astonishing. Ha! But then, neither your opinion nor that of the Winchester female signify with me!"

Clare. Northrup's jaw tightened. To be truthful, of late, he had been no stranger to the wine decanter himself, though he had the breeding to keep to his own apartment when he was foxed, and he had begun to wonder if Letitia had been completely honest in what she had said about Clare. Clare had seemed truly bewildered by his accusations, and he, better than anyone else, knew how devious Letitia could be. And now, it appeared, this fool was annoying her again.

"What of Miss Winchester, Portman?"

He was too deeply into his cups to notice the odd spark in the other man's eyes. The color rose in Tobias's face, turning it a hideous shade of purple, ill matched to his coat. "What of her? I shall tell you, sir. She is, ever was, an ill-bred little minx. Cold and calculating with airs above her station. Here was I, willing to shut my eyes to all her faults, forget her past, and she refuses me, if you can believe it. Not only that, but insults me into the bargain. Insolent! Such language as I have never heard from the lips of a lady. Oh, but she readily admitted that my income appealed to her. She's a bold one, she is.

"Of course, I thought her to be quite mad to decline my excellent offer. Why would she do so, after all? Well, today, sir, I found out. The devil! She ain't mad, she's crafty. Hanging out for a better catch, though I don't know where she'll find one. Well if you've seen *The Times* today, you know what I'm speaking of. That aunt of hers has made herself quite a match. Caught that Langley fellow, the one with all the money in wool. You must know him. So that's it. Clare thinks with all that money behind her, she can't fail to leg-shackle herself to the most eligible, aye, the richest man she can find. You didn't fall into her trap, I see, too clever for her. 'Faith, after all these years, I should know what a devious little schemer she is, but I was willing to forgive that. Suppose she figures if that old woman can do so well for herself, her own prospects must be even better! Suppose she can always redouble her efforts with that fellow Newmarch. I've seen them together enough. Eh? Where are you going?"

Northrup did not hear him. *So, Letitia was right,* he thought as he departed the club. Climbing wearily into his carriage, he growled a direction to his driver and turned eyes half-closed with disgust out the window to the streets, dotted here and there with the eerie glow of gaslight.

Clare's change of heart and Maude's plans made the atmosphere in Edwardes Square both busy and a good deal more cheerful. There were arrangements to be made and a trousseau to buy and, if in her quieter moods, Clare discovered that her gay spirits were more forced than spontaneous, she refused to dwell any longer on the cause of her unhappiness.

She had yet to attend any public assembly, claiming a fatigue that would prevent her enjoyment of company. In fact, this excuse was not so very far removed from the truth. All the demands on her time, demands that Maude surrendered entirely to her niece's efficient management, left her quite tired at the end of each day. Mr. Langley became a frequent dinner guest, and Clare found him to be all that she could have wished for her aunt.

He was a kind-faced man of simple tastes and good humor, and Clare was amused at the change which had come over Maude since the advent of this gentleman. She seemed happier, indeed younger, than Clare had ever known her to be. In truth, her desires for what she termed "the little luxuries of life" never lessened, but Mr. Langley gladly indulged her, never arriving without a gift, which might have been a stunning ruby necklace or a length of the finest silk. Clare was seldom forgotten in his generosity and, despite her protests, was often the recipient of a small, but obviously expensive bauble, most recently a beautifully patterned shawl.

She could easily understand her aunt's attachment to this man and looked forward to their evenings together, when his joviality inevitably gave a true lift to her spirits. On numerous occasions, he pressed her to accept their invitation to make her home with them, but she declined. She had been too long her own mistress, she explained, and though she never said so, she did not wish to intrude on the happiness and privacy of her aunt and soon-to-be uncle. Finally, it seemed that Mr. Langley understood her feelings.

One evening, while waiting for Maude to join them for dinner, he broached the subject again. Quite aware that her repeated refusals could easily be interpreted as ingratitude, Clare found herself exceedingly uncomfortable, as she searched for words which would not offend him. He reached over and patted her hand.

"There, there, m'dear, didn't mean to put you to the blush, you know. Ah, but, you know your aunt." Here, his face took on a positively worshipful look. "She worries about you, wants to be certain you're cared for. That's why she's so late in coming down tonight," he confided with a wink and a smile. "She thought if we spoke alone, you and I, that I might be able to convince you.

"I told her it wouldn't do one bit of good." He looked at her kindly. "I told Maude that I think you're perfectly capable of caring for yourself, but she wasn't having any of it, so, I agreed to mention it to you this last time. I hope I needn't tell you that I should be only too pleased to have you with us," he added sincerely, "and I must have your promise, my dear, that if you ever change your mind, if you ever need anything, you will come to us without hesitation." He grinned. "Your word, Clare, or I'll not cease plaguing you either."

She raised watery eyes to his smiling face and clasped his hand warmly with both of hers. "You have it, sir."

"Good," he pronounced, leaning over to place an avuncular kiss on her brow. "Now, where is your aunt, for I vow I am famished!"

Ten

The next day, Maude returned to Edwardes Square from one of her frequent shopping trips, calling out gaily, "Only see, Clare, whom I have brought with me!"

From behind a precarious stack of bandboxes and ribbon wrapped parcels came a muffled chuckle. "Afternoon, Clare. I can only assume you're looking as lovely as ever, for I fear that I cannot actually *see* a thing. What say, Miss Beauchamp, where would you like these?"

"Max!"

"Right on target, Clare. I say, was it my boots or my voice that gave me away?"

"Estelle," Maude called, "be good enough to relieve poor Mr. Newmarch of his burden. There, that's better. Well, Clare, you will never imagine. There I was, standing in the milliner's door waiting for the girl to find me a hack, such a dreadful inconvenience, being without one's own carriage, when who should come to my rescue but the gallant Mr. Newmarch. He was kind enough to take me up in his carriage and bring me home, and I have invited him to tea."

Clare was glad to see him again, for his quiet charm and happy disposition always made his company a pleasure, and seeing him again, she found that she had missed him. By the end of that tea, he had convinced her to attend the theatre with him and, so it was that, for the second time that Season, Clare left her seclusion and returned to society.

At the theatre, there was a crush to see the performance

of Edmund Kean, who though still relatively new to the London stage, always drew a great crowd. Newmarch expertly guided his party, which included Maude and Langley, to the box which he had reserved early in the day, and turned to Clare, his gaze warm and admiring. "Clare, you look beautiful tonight. But, then, you always do."

She detected something in his eyes and voice which she had never noticed before and, flushing, she murmured her thanks for the compliment.

"Clare, I am so happy that you honored me by coming out this evening." He paused and wondered why she would not meet his eyes. "I have hoped for the opportunity to speak with you . . ."

"Oh, Max, see, the play is about to begin. They do say that Mr. Kean's Shylock is beyond compare. I am so eager to see him."

Better lighting in the box would have betrayed the hurt that passed over his face. Less noise might not have hidden the sigh of resignation that escaped his lips. Never hesitating, he went on to extol the virtues of the great actor. "Yes, but then it would have to be better than his Romeo," he replied and proceeded to discuss with her the finer points of the actor's talent.

In a box not far away, sat Northrup and Letitia. He had progressed beyond the point of withdrawing from society and had fallen into the habit of escorting her about town. Although he felt no commitment toward her, she was accessible and a woman more of his own station, the latter a quality which had become even more important to him since Clare's betrayal. For her part, Letitia lately had been willing to overlook his habitual coolness and bide her time, but she was becoming restive.

Piqued at his lack of response to her last three questions, she followed his eyes and, to her dismay, found that he was quite engrossed in watching Clare and Newmarch, who were chatting with Maude and Mr. Langley.

"Dearest, is that not Maximillian with the Winchester woman?" she asked sweetly.

"Aye, Letitia, I believe it is." He had not known that Max was back in town. For a minute, he considered seeking him out at the interval to warn him about Clare, but dismissed the thought. Newmarch would catch on to her soon enough.

"How odd. Or—perhaps not. I expect that she is still attempting to work her charms on him." Northrup made no response. "Oh and do but look, Northrup. I am sure that is her aunt and the other gentleman must be the poor fellow whom the old—that is, he must be the man she has somehow managed to attach. They say he's rich as Croesus. Well, it is easy to see whom the niece takes after, is it not? Northrup?"

She turned to look at him. He was staring down at her, silent, his shuttered eyes telling her she had said too much. Letitia could have bitten off her own tongue. *Better be careful,* she warned herself, *or you'll drive him away.* Much to her relief, the din in the theatre had softened to a moderate hum, and the performance began.

"Dear Miss Beauchamp, do allow me to felicitate you on your engagement," Lady Emily said to a beaming Maude. Presiding over the tea tray, Clare sat quietly and listened as the two women discussed the coming nuptials. Maude, sensing an ally, sought to enlist Lady Emily's support in convincing Clare to join her household.

"Really, Lady Emily, I am certain that you can see it is by far the sensible thing for her to do. Well, I am afraid that I must be off, or I shall be late for my fitting. This trousseau will be the death of me, I am convinced. But, I am counting on you," she said conspiratorially, "to intercede when I am gone. Surely you can make Clare see reason."

Lady Emily said nothing for a minute or two after Maude had left. Then, she put down her teacup and turned, fastening a direct gaze on her hostess. "Well?" was all she said.

Clare's eyes sparkled over the rim of her cup and she chuckled. "I beg of you, Lady Emily, not to ring a peal over my head. My aunt is very kind to offer me a home, but I cannot and shall not accept."

"Thank heaven for that!" Lady Emily expostulated. "Good God, girl, do you think me a nodcock? Did you actually think I should support your aunt's position? Oh, I daresay it is the proper, indeed to quote Miss Beauchamp, the sensible thing to do, but I am hardly the person to school you in proper conduct, my dear. Society don't call me eccentric for nothing, you know."

Clare tried to object, but her guest waved a bejeweled hand to silence her.

"No, no, Clare. Did you think I don't know what's said behind my back? As I told you a moment ago, I ain't a nodcock. I may be the daughter of the earl of Buckinghamshire, but I'm not really accepted socially, you know. Why, most people wouldn't even recognize me, but for my dear Robert. But, I'll tell you a secret, Clare; that doesn't really bother me. Most of the people who call themselves quality ain't nothing more than a bunch of hypocritical fools. The truth of it is, I like to shock 'em!" she laughed.

Clare grinned. "And you have been most successful, dear ma'am. Why, the night you wore the viscount's garter on your head overset everyone in the room! People talked for weeks!"

The older woman subsided into unrestrained laughter. "Indeed, they did. Indeed, they did." They enjoyed this reminiscence, Lady Emily relating the horrified reactions of Lady This or Duchess That, one of whom actually fainted at the blasphemous spectacle.

"I offended her sensibilities, don't you know. Ah, but enough of that. I did not come here to talk of my escapades and, to own the truth, I didn't even come here to wish your aunt happy, though I am sure I do. I came here, Clare, to talk of you. Good Lord, child, what has happened? First you go off to Gloucestershire with Northrup—such a promising development, why I was all expectations! And, when you finally return, I hear no announcement, not even a hint of betrothal. I must confess, I am mystified." Ignoring Clare's blushes, she went on in her inimitable, direct fashion.

"Really, dear, it is just too bad, for I am convinced that the two of you would suit so well. After all, the primary reason I suggested you bring out Evelyn was to throw you and him together. But now I find that Evelyn resides in Grosvenor Square with her uncle and, last week, I even saw the girl shopping with that feline, Letitia Marlowe. I must say, neither of them looked remarkably pleased with the other's company.

"As for you, Clare, you seclude yourself here again for months"—Clare contained a smile at this hyperbole—"and when you do come out it is with Max Newmarch. Mind, I do not mean to say that dear Max is not everything he should be, for he is very dear to my heart. Actually," she wondered thoughtfully, "I had rather hoped that he and Leah . . . Well, no matter. The point is that I do not think he is for you, dear. To be blunt, I do not believe for a minute that you cherish any sort of tendre for him." Clare sat miserably, looking at the dregs of tea in her cup.

"I know, you think me an interfering witch, and you may well be right. Still, having the supreme good fortune myself to have the joy of a true love match, unlike most others"— she sniffed disdainfully—"I can recognize the makings of another. And I tell you, I recognized it between you and Evan. And now, he is everywhere with that—that—Letitia Marlowe." She uttered the name with a shudder, as if it nauseated her. "I simply cannot credit it."

"Lady Emily, please, I beg you will stop." All of Clare's resolve, so painfully built up, was rapidly crumbling. "You do not know . . . that is . . . Oh!" Tears sprang willfully to her eyes.

"You are quite right, Clare, I do not know. And I beg you

will enlighten me." She sat beside Clare and took her trembling hands in her own. "Please, dear, I am aware that I appear a blustering, insensitive busybody, but I want only to help. Can you not tell me what has happened? What pains you so?"

Able to speak of the awful scene with Northrup at last, Clare's emotions erupted in a violent burst of sobbing, but she somehow related the whole tale to her friend. Lady Emily cradled her in her arms and patted her head protectively, murmuring the requisite useless platitudes, and raging at what she was hearing.

"The fiend! How dare he? I freely admit I do not understand him. Why, he was ever so gentle and kind, until that minx jilted him. Even so, why would he say such things? Of course! This is all her doing. She is just as calculating as I feared."

She held Clare at arm's length and studied her red face and swollen eyes. Clare lowered her gaze. She had not told Lady Emily of what had occurred in the abandoned cottage. She could not. She had told her merely that they had grown much closer at the Court, close enough for her to expect that he would offer for her. Clare suspected that her listener did not entirely believe this expurgated explanation. For Lady Emily's part, while she believed that there was more to that part of the story, for once, she refrained from pressing the matter. She offered her a handkerchief, for Clare's was sodden, and regarded her as she rose from the settee.

"You, obviously, are very much in love with him—even still." Clare nodded miserably. "Will you do nothing to win him? To convince him of his error?"

"Indeed, ma'am, what would you have me do?" she asked in a soft, numb voice.

Lady Emily silently agreed, for clearly there was nothing Clare could do. If she tried to explain matters to him, she would again leave herself open to his censure for, in his mind, there was no reason why he should believe her.

Clare rose quickly, her hand clutched to her breast. "Lady Emily, I implore you, you will not speak to him of this, will you? I could not bear it. Please, please say nothing to him."

"Clare, how could you think I would ever do such a thing? No, I shall say nothing to him of this, nothing at all, I give you my word."

Clare was just coming downstairs early in the morning, when Estelle opened the door to a stormy-eyed Northrup, who demanded to see her mistress. Clare froze, wishing she could turn and run back to her room, but realized that he had raised his eyes and seen her. Well, she was not about to give him the satisfaction of seeing her run off in her own house like a frightened rabbit, but then, neither did she intend to see him and subject herself to further abuse at his hands. Considering the man's complete lack of manners, she saw no need for politeness on her part. She took a deep breath and, in what she hoped was an authoritative tone, said, "Estelle, tell his lordship that I am not at home." *There,* she thought, *that should put him in his place.*

He strode into the foyer, all at once filling it with his presence, and glared up at her. "Estelle, tell your mistress I would see her. *Now!"*

Estelle looked from one to the other, utterly at a loss. She soon recalled her loyalty, however, and for the first time grasping the duties attached to her position, she overcame her awe of Northrup's rank. Her voice was pathetically brave. "I am sorry, your lordship, Miss Winchester is not receiving callers this morning."

Northrup merely sneered, standing his ground, and Estelle blanched, uncertain what to do next. Clare understood that he would remain where he was until she consented to speak with him and came slowly down the stairs, hoping her posture conveyed some semblance of dignity.

"It is alright, Estelle. I shall see the earl in the drawing room. Do you tell Mrs. Musgrave that I shall be with her directly, for this will take but a moment," she said pointedly.

Removed to the drawing room, they both spoke at once.

"How dare you come to this house?"

"Madam, what have you done with my niece?"

"I?" she asked. "What can I have done with your niece, sir? Have you not deprived me of the pleasure of her company?"

"Let us say that I thought I had done so. Obviously, I was wrong," he bellowed.

"Will you tell me of what I stand accused this time, sir, or do you prefer to continue in these mad ravings?"

"God, there is no end to your deviltry! Do you still think you can get to me through Evelyn?"

"You put too high a price on yourself. I do not want you, and, if I did, I tell you again that I would not use your dear niece to get you," she retorted with a perfect calm which surprised both of them.

He stared at her, for the angry flush that had crept up her cheeks was quite becoming. For a moment, he hesitated. Was it possible that she was not involved?

Clare stared back, intensely aware of his handsomeness, his masculinity. Suddenly, the meaning of his question struck her. "My lord, what is wrong? Has something happened to Evelyn?"

"Indeed, ma'am, that may well be. I can tell you only that when I rose this morning, she was gone," he replied, stricken. "She left a note."

"Oh, no," Clare whispered, sinking into a chair.

He appraised her and, seeing the concern on her face, asked more gently, "Do you, then, truly know nothing of this?"

She turned on him. "I had thought, sir, that you could do nothing more to wound me. I was wrong."

He took a seat next to her and shook his head. "Forgive

me. It is just that I cannot imagine that even that silly child would have the nerve to elope without someone's assistance."

"Elope!"

"Exactly. Oh, I tried to talk sense to the Crowleys, but they wouldn't listen. The note said that she and Peter had decided to take matters into their own hands. I can but assume they have fled to Gretna Green, and I am going after them. I assumed that you must have aided them and, foolishly, I have wasted valuable time by coming here first."

"Take heart, you may not be too late."

"I can but hope," he said, rising. "But I know not exactly when they left, you see."

"Then you must delay here no longer."

"Aye," he said, his eyes lost for a moment in her soft, brown hair. He turned to go.

"My lord, you will let me know what happens?"

He stopped and, without turning, nodded slightly, then hurried away.

It was late the next evening that Molly tapped on Clare's bedroom door and handed her a grey vellum envelope splashed with the wax of the impressive Northrup seal. "Edward, that is, Mr. Reynolds, just arrived with it, miss."

"Thank you. Why don't you take him to the kitchen for some refreshment? I shall let you know how this sorry tale has come out."

"Thank you, miss."

My Dear Miss Winchester,

As you requested, I write to advise you that I was able to overtake my niece and Peter. Their conveyance broke down not far from town and I, unhappily for them, was the first to come to their aid. I hasten to assure you that neither party was injured.

I am taking Evelyn and Peter directly to Gloucestershire, as she has no desire to remain in town. For myself, I have determined to try again to make the boy's parents see reason and permit the union.

Northrup

Clare was greatly relieved by this news and hoped that he would win over the Crowleys. Perhaps, now that they had proof of the depths of Evelyn's and Peter's feelings, they would realize their error and relent. *Why, then,* she asked herself, *do I feel so let down.* She scanned the letter again. There was nothing there to offend, in fact it was ruthlessly correct. Had she expected more? Yes, she admitted, she had hoped that he would soften. She folded the letter again. *Ah, well, at least if he is at the Court, I shall be spared encountering him here in town.*

"Another macaroon, Letitia?"

"Thank you, Lady Emily, but I must decline, although they are delicious. My figure, you know."

"Oh, my dear, surely you have nothing to fear there? Why, you put us all to shame."

"Ma'am, you are too kind." Letitia was most pleased with herself. She had been not a little surprised to receive her first invitation to tea at Lady Emily's, for though she had attended balls there, that had always been because her escort had been invited. To be asked to tea herself was quite a different matter.

She knew that this was not because her hostess harbored any kind feelings for her. Rather, she assumed, smugly, the lady finally saw that she must recognize Letitia's relationship with Northrup. In Letitia's calculating way, she cared not a whit about the motives for the invitation. It mattered only that she be seen in the woman's drawing room. That, at this moment, was worth a good deal more to her than a dozen invitations to the salon at Gore House. Why, had she not told everyone that she was coming here? This acceptance could only serve to promote her in Northrup's regard, and that sweetened the achievement for her.

"And may I say, Letitia," her hostess positively gushed, "that I think your dress lovely. Few women can wear that rich shade of blue—unfortunately, I am not among them—but on you, the effect is very attractive. Do you not agree, Clare?"

Clare started at the question, for she had been lost in thought and, so far, had contributed little to the conversation. She was quite unable to understand why Lady Emily should have asked to tea a woman for whom she professed to have the utmost dislike and even more bewildered by that lady's inviting her, Clare, to join them. Strange, too, that Lady Emily should ask for her opinion on the woman's taste in fashion, just when she was thinking how much nicer Letitia would look with that enormous vase of roses dumped over her head.

"Clare, dear?" Lady Emily prompted.

"Oh! Yes, Lady Emily, forgive me. I quite agree, Mrs. Marlowe's dress is of the first stare."

Letitia's smile broadened. "Why, how kind in you to say so, Miss Winchester. I expect it is the excellent color which has caught your eye, for I have noticed that your wardrobe seems given over to the most—ah, shall I say, quiet shades," she added with a smirk, as she raised a haughty brow to Clare's pale yellow tarlatan. "Perhaps, once your dear aunt is married, you will find yourself in a position to purchase such finery. Doubtless, when that time comes, you will want the assistance of one with experience, and I pray you will have no hesitation in calling on me, for I shall be pleased to give you all the help you need."

Clare glanced at the remainder of this friendly little circle, which consisted of a Mrs. Potter and Sarah Shipley, the latter mother to Helen and Leah, and recently come up to town for a visit. The two ladies were involved in their own conversation and had not heard Letitia's cutting remarks. Next,

she looked to Lady Emily, but her hostess was at that moment
attempting to blot up a few drops of tea which had splashed
onto the table. In that second of time, she thought she could
detect the hint of a smile about the viscountess's lips, but
immediately, she berated herself for being so uncharitable.

She turned a glassy stare on Letitia and hoped that her
indignation could not be seen. "Mrs. Marlowe, I cannot conceive why you should think that I would take advantage of
any change in my aunt's circumstances. As for my clothes,
I assure you that I am entirely satisfied with them."

Letitia gave a breathy laugh. "I daresay you are."

Lady Emily thought it politic to intervene at this point,
and drew her other guests into the conversation. Once again,
Clare swore she espied a smile, but the impression was fleeting. For a while, the talk revolved about the ball which Lady
Emily was planning for her goddaughters, and the latest on-
dits and recent trends in decorating.

Lady Emily allowed that Mrs. Potter had lately redone her
grand drawing room in the classical Greek style, which was
the rage. Almost as if on cue, Mrs. Shipley, remarking that
she was in the throes of redecorating her own home in Kent,
requested the pleasure of seeing the results of Mrs. Potter's
efforts. That lady, flattered by such attention, suggested the
following morning as a suitable time for a call. Casting a
quick eye to her friend, Mrs. Shipley added that she was
eager to see the new furnishings as soon as possible and
begged that they drive to Bedford Square then and there.
Mrs. Potter, a quiet woman, whose opinions were never
sought, was only too willing to submit to this plea, and the
two ladies took their leave. Lady Emily sat back and sipped
her tea complacently, smiling at her two remaining guests.
Really, Sally is such an accommodating friend.

"Well, tell me, you two, you both are coming to my goddaughters' ball, are you not? I intend that it will be the affair
of the Season."

Both assured her that they would attend. Asked who would

escort her, Clare said that she was uncertain. Very likely, she would accompany Maude and Mr. Langley.

Letitia purred. "Surely there must be someone you can count on to escort you, Miss Winchester? I should find it excessively tiresome and, dear me, embarrassing, if I were in the position of having to hunt about for a gentleman to spend an evening with me."

Before Clare could say what she thought of that remark, Lady Emily stepped in. "Really, Letitia? Tell me, then, who will be your partner?"

Letitia's beautiful green eyes registered innocent surprise at such an unnecessary question. "Who? Dear Lady Emily, need you ask? Northrup, of course."

"Really? I confess you have the better of me there, for I have not seen Evan for what seems ages. I had thought him from town."

"Yes, to be sure, he is attending to some tedious business at his estate, I believe."

"You believe? Dear, me, do you not *know?*"

"Well, yes, of course I do, ma'am. He is in Gloucester-shire."

"But, if that is the case, how do you know that he will be here to bring you to the ball?"

Letitia was a little discomfited, but attempted to hide her unease with a laugh and a peremptory wave of her hand. "Be assured that I have no doubts in the matter. If I desire to come to the ball with Northrup, and I do, he will escort me."

"La, but you are confident, Letitia. I have never known him to be so biddable." Letitia smiled, and Lady Emily continued, watching her closely. "I should be careful, if I were you, generally, a lady dares not be this sanguine about a gentleman's attentions unless . . . Why, Letitia, there is something you are not telling!"

Maintaining her secretive smile, Letitia refrained from responding.

"Come," the older woman persisted, "tell me. Clare, do you not think that Letitia is keeping something from us?"

Clare's heart was pounding. Had Northrup offered for Letitia? If so, she was not sure she could bear it. She was spared a reply, however, as her questioner pressed on.

"Oh, Letitia, you are unkind. Confess, I beg you. Northrup has proposed, hasn't he? You are to be married!" Clare held her breath, and it seemed hours before Letitia answered.

"Well, ma'am," she conceded with feigned reluctance, "you and Northrup are *such* old friends, I feel that I can tell you. The truth is out; we are to be wed."

"Say you so? To be married?" Letitia nodded and turned a satisfied smile on Clare. "Why, Clare," Lady Emily cried, "is that not wonderful?"

"Yes, wonderful, ma'am. I wish you happy, Mrs. Marlowe."

Letitia acknowledged the felicitations with a small, triumphant nod. Clare rose, knowing she could no longer remain, or she would disgrace herself. She made her excuses, itching to slap the gloating smile from Letitia's face, and departed.

Much later, Lady Emily sat in her boudoir, sipping another cup of tea and talking with her old friend. "Thank you for your help, Sally," she said, settling back in her chair.

"Not at all, it proved quite simple."

"Oh, yes, well, I knew it would. You see, no one ever asks Samantha Potter's opinion about anything so, naturally, she leapt at the chance to show off her drawing room." Resting her head against a satin cushion, she shut her eyes and sighed. "I can but hope that I did the right thing."

Her companion patted her hand. "Well, Em, I am persuaded you did, and we shall see soon enough, that much is certain. In any event, as you said yourself, 'tis better for a woman to know where she stands, one way or another."

"Did I say that?" she asked drily. "I suppose I did. Never have known when to keep my mouth shut."

Eleven

Lady Emily's ball did turn out to be the acknowledged triumph of the Season. The grand ballroom was opened to its full size on this night and festooned with garlands of flowers and greenery. The room was full despite the lateness of the Season and the heat that generally compelled many folk to remove to their country estates by this time. The windows were thrown wide to receive any hint of a breeze, and the footmen were kept busy refilling the large cut-glass bowls of cool ratafia and lemonade and cracking bottle after bottle of the best champagne. If many of the ladies present tittered behind their fans at Lady Emily's eccentricities or, if not a few of the gentlemen were at odds with the viscount's politics, all of them shrewdly recognized the position which their hosts commanded, for it seemed that not a single invitation had been declined.

Clare had conceded that she would have to face Northrup and his intended eventually, and, in any case, she would never have given Letitia the supreme delight of staying at home. So, when Max offered his escort, she accepted almost happily, even inviting him to dinner before the ball.

She stood up with him for the first waltz, and now, as he handed her to a mutual friend for a quadrille, she saw again a hint of sadness in his eyes. At the last minute, Maude had decided to dine with Mr. Langley, so Clare and Max had taken supper alone. He had been rather quiet during the meal and later, as they sipped coffee, he had sweetly and sincerely proposed marriage. Clare had suspected his intentions ever since their evening at the theatre, but she had hoped desperately that he would change his mind and not declare himself.

It was not that dear Max was not everything a woman could want a husband to be, and the time they passed together was never anything but happy. His was a far cry, she told herself, from the temperament of the earl. They shared many interests, and Clare knew that he loved her. Why then couldn't she marry him? Though she was exceedingly fond of Max, she did not return his love. Whether this was because her heart still tumbled at the thought of a certain pair of dazzling blue eyes, she could not honestly say, but she suspected it was, indeed, the case.

She refused his offer as kindly as possible and thanked him deeply for the honor he had bestowed upon her. Wisely, she refrained from couching her answer in logic, knowing herself that reason and practicality are furthest from the minds of those in love.

He had not been entirely surprised by her reply, he told her gently, as he had suspected that her affections might be engaged elsewhere. He mentioned no names, for he was uncertain himself, and he did not press her when, flustered at his perception, she lowered her eyes and remained silent.

"I quite understand, Clare, being utterly lost in love myself. I shall not be so hard as to press my suit further, for I see it pains you to think that you have hurt me. I will say only that if you change your mind, you have but to tell me." His voice was soft, and, though he never lost his composure, Clare had seen the sadness in his eyes then, as she did now, accompanying her new partner to the dance floor. Dear Max.

He watched her graceful movements for a while, admiring the way the sea-green silk of her dress shimmered in the candlelight, and it occurred to him that his country home must be in urgent need of his attention.

"You're looking pensive, old man."

"Oh, Northrup, didn't see you."

"I know. You seem mighty caught up with Miss Winchester. I don't think you've taken your eyes off her these last five minutes."

Max gave a short, pathetic laugh. "I suppose I have not."

"See here, Max, you and I have been the best of friends since we were in shortcoats, have we not?" His lips were set in a hard line, and he finished off the remainder of his champagne in one gulp. Max smiled and wondered what his friend was about. Could he be in some kind of trouble?

"Evan, what's bothering you? Anything I can do?"

"In a way," Northrup replied cryptically. "Look, I think we may be frank with one another." Max nodded and his friend hurried on. "I wasn't going to speak to you of this, but, I must tell you, for your own good, to keep away from that woman." As he spoke, his eyes darkened, and he glanced about searching for a waiter to refill his glass.

"What woman?"

"What do you mean, 'what woman?' What woman were we talking about? Clare Winchester, of course."

Max's gaze hardened. "What the hell are you saying, Northrup?"

"I'm saying that she'll only hurt you. I'm saying that she's nothing but a little schemer. Got her hooks out for a rich husband."

"Northrup, but for the long-standing friendship of which you were so careful to remind me a few moments ago, I would call you out for that." He kept his voice low, but Clare herself would not have recognized Max's face, which his fury had transformed into that of a stranger.

The same abiding friendship allowed Northrup to overlook the implication about his lack of courage. "I daresay," he drawled, then adopted a more conciliatory tone. "See here, it is precisely because of our friendship that I say this to you. She is unworthy of you, Max, not exactly respectable in her youth, you know. For God's sake, *I* know her. She wants you for your fortune, that is all. I tell you, Max, she's of the basest sort. She's out to make a bloody fool of you."

"So good of you to tell me all this, old friend. Very flattering, too. Spoken out of the true bonds of friendship, I've no doubt," he said evenly.

"Damn it, Max, I didn't mean it like that."

"Who are you to censure her? Don't you remember being foolish when you were young? I can recall, if you cannot, some cloth-headed doings on our part. You weren't always a patterncard of propriety and you weren't always so pompous and so damnably right either! Your pride always has been your greatest vice. Come to that, since when are any of us in this room above reproof? I would venture to say that there are more scandals and closet skeletons here tonight than in the rest of London put together. Why, half the people here are hanging out for a rich husband—or wife," he said with a sneer. "This is really almost laughable, Evan. God, man, what do you suppose that bitch, Letitia, is after?" He had half expected Northrup to deal him a facer for the remark, but the other man remained silent.

"Come to that, who told you these things about Clare?" Northrup did not reply. "Let me guess," he said acidly. "Letitia." The look on Northrup's face confirmed his suspicion.

"Devil take you, Evan, you are the fool. You dare to call Clare a schemer. I'll tell you how devious she is. You say she is after my fortune? Alright, why then did she refuse my offer of marriage earlier this very evening?"

His jaw fell. "She what? But, that's two of you she's turned down, for she refused Tobias Portman, as well."

A flash of humor cut across Max's face. "Oh well, we can't give her any points for that, old boy. That was merely discriminating taste."

Northrup frowned, his mind working feverishly. "If she said no, Max, why are you here together?"

"Because I am not a schoolboy, Evan, who will not join

the game unless it is played by his rules. More importantly, I hope that I may always call her friend, if not wife."

His friend stared at him. "I deserved that. I am sorry, Max. I see that you do love her." They both watched Clare finishing the last steps of the dance. Max looked at his companion from the corner of his eye.

"Oh, I shall come about. I'm going down to the country tomorrow. There's quite enough there to keep me busy, I daresay." He continued to eye Northrup. "Ahem, it would seem that I am not the only chap in love with the lady." Northrup looked shamefaced and could think of nothing to say. "Never mind, I understand."

The dance ended, and Letitia's partner was escorting her back to Northrup. Both men watched her as she tilted her head back in a gay, tinkling laugh. Max grinned and placed a hand on his friend's shoulder. "Good luck!" he said, and walked off to collect Clare.

Letitia saw the telltale glint of anger in Northrup's eyes, but decided it could not be of her doing and chose to ignore it. She was about to suggest that they stroll on the terrace, when Clare and Newmarch approached. Newmarch appeared decidedly confused and Clare, her hand through the crook of his arm, had a determined, polite look about her.

"Northrup," Letitia said hurriedly, "let us get some air, for it is awfully warm in here and, worse, here comes that Winchester woman. I assure you I do not wish to be seen socializing with her."

"Indeed, madam?" his tone was ominous, and he held her arm in an iron grip.

The other couple reached their side and greetings were exchanged, though no one could have said the atmosphere in that particular area of the ballroom was warm, despite the late summer heat.

Clare took a deep breath, wishing to get her self-appointed task done with. "My lord, may I wish you happy on your betrothal," she said softly. Newmarch added his congratulations, not realizing that he was actually gaping at his old friend, and felicitated Letitia.

That lady stammered, and Northrup looked confused. "My betrothal? I am afraid, Miss Winchester, that you must be misinformed. I am not engaged, but I am happy to report that Evelyn and Peter are to be wed in the spring. I'm back to close up the house, since I shall be busy in the country and will not be in town for some time."

"You have prevailed with the Crowleys?"

"I must confess that there was not a great deal of need for my influence. You see, the one person whom we all failed to consider was Kitty. Once we got back to the country and everyone was firmly confronted with the situation, the girl informed both sets of parents that she had no intention of marrying Peter. It seems that her own parents simply had not taken her protests seriously before. When they realized that she was sincere, they said that she need not go through with the marriage. Well, after that, it was easy, for the Crowleys really had no ill feeling toward Evelyn. It was just a silly obsession of Marion. I spoke with Ambrose Crowley, and he convinced her that Peter and Evelyn should be allowed to wed. I expect you'll soon have a letter from her."

Clare beamed. "But, that is wonderful, sir. I am so happy for her. She must be transported!"

"Quite. That is to say the very least of it, as I am sure you can imagine." Clare laughed, and Letitia bristled with jealousy at their familiarity. "But, there you see," the earl went on, "it is Evelyn's whose wedding you must attend, and I hope that you will," he added with a speaking look, "not mine."

Max interjected with obvious relief and satisfaction in his voice. "There, Clare, I told you that you must be mistaken." He attempted to lead her away before she could embarrass herself with another blunder, but her bewildered mind and her heart demanded a solution to this puzzle. She ignored Max's hand on her arm, looked searchingly at the man and woman in front of her, and stood her ground. Letitia visibly paled.

"I do not understand, my lord. Only the other day, Mrs. Marlowe told me of your engagement. To one another," she added by way of explanation, since he seemed so obviously in need of one. Max groaned, and the earl's eyebrows shot up.

"Did she?" Northrup looked at his "intended" as if he would throttle her.

"I said no such thing, you wicked woman! Northrup, there you have the proof of her true character." Letitia managed a pose of righteous indignation. "She lies in order to malign me in your eyes."

"Oh, but you did, my dear. Announce your engagement, that is." All eyes turned to Lady Emily, who had appeared suddenly at Northrup's side. She grinned from ear to ear and nodded vigorously. "Yes, you did, indeed. Allow me to refresh your memory, Letitia. It was just as Clare has said. At tea. At my house. Here in St. James's Square. Correct me if I am wrong, Tuesday, was it not?" she asked sweetly.

It was as if Letitia's gasp were a collective effort, for the entire group seemed to hold its breath. "You—you old crow," she spit. The older woman's grin broadened. The Harpy hovered nearby, scandal-thirsty minions at her side, listening to this melodrama, a look of greedy anticipation on her face, as if she could barely wait to claim the ostracized soul of society's latest Lucifer.

"That is enough, Letitia," Northrup interrupted. She glared back at him stubbornly. "Lady Emily, since Mrs. Marlowe obviously does not have the good grace to apologize, I pray you will excuse us." So saying, he nodded to the others, tightened his grip on her elbow, and led her outside to their carriage.

Neither said a word all the way to Letitia's house. When he led her to the door, she hesitated. It was more than apparent that he was furious, and she was uncertain of the wisdom of asking him in, while he was in such a mood. She was saved the trouble of deciding, however, for upon the butler's opening the door, he stepped in and followed her to the drawing room and slammed the door.

"Letitia, what the hell is the meaning of this?" he thundered.

"Northrup, whatever are you talking about? And please do stop shouting," she replied innocently, dabbing her dry eyes with a handkerchief.

He whirled her about to face him and shook her. "That will not work any longer. Now, answer me. Did you say we are to be married?"

Her chin lifted defiantly. "What if I did?"

"How dare you tell such a blatant lie?"

Immediately, her attitude changed, and she tried to coax him. She put her hands on his shoulders and, drawing his face close to hers, she smiled. "Dearest, what does it matter? I am sorry for anticipating you, my love, for I know that men prefer to take the lead in these matters, but after all, it was only a question of time before you actually would propose so I . . ."

"What are you saying? Madam, you presume too much," he replied, roughly putting her from him. "If I'd had any intention of marrying you, be assured that I have, thankfully, recovered my senses."

Her conciliatory, sweet pose disappeared as quickly as it came and her language became distinctly unladylike. "You dare to speak to me so? I would point out to you, sir, that by morning, our 'betrothal' will be common knowledge. You will have no choice—you will have to marry me."

He leaned casually against the doorjamb, arms folded and one ankle crossed over the other, as he asked softly and with ruthless coolness, "Why?"

"Why? Because—think what people will say! We would be the laughingstock of the ton!"

"We? You, madam. For it was you who made this precipitous and untruthful announcement, not I. I have, at last, come to realize that I do not care tuppence what society says of me. But, in this case, it matters not, for I am but an innocent bystander, while you . . ." He looked down at her lovely face, now contorted with spite, and wondered that he had ever felt anything for this shallow, selfish creature. His voice was nearly a whisper and he spoke slowly.

"Wed you, Letitia? Nothing could persuade me to do anything so unpardonably foolish." She slapped him. "I wish I might say that such behavior is beneath you, madam, but, alas, I cannot."

She came at him then, screaming, her hands raised, but he stepped out of her way and opened the door. She went out after him.

"Where are you going? Don't you dare to leave me. Did you hear what I said? Don't you leave this house!" By the time she reached him, she was shrieking like a banshee. "Answer me, damn you! You're going to that Winchester female, aren't you? I know you are! That little . . ."

"Letitia!" That deep, commanding tone had brought many a man to heel, but she never flinched.

"Northrup, if you go to her, I swear that I'll make both of you regret it for the rest of your lives. I'll . . ."

He shook her until her raven curls fell into disarray about her face, which now was scarlet and unrecognizable.

"You spiteful hellcat! You will do *nothing.* Do you understand? Nothing! If you so much as attempt to sully that woman's name again, I shall ruin you. You have my solemn oath on that, madam."

Something shattered loudly and expensively against the door as it shut behind him, as if she were determined to claim the dubious victory of having had the last word.

After Northrup and Letitia's abrupt departure, Max stood, hands on hips, and gave a raucous laugh. "I'll be damned if she isn't foiled at last. And her own doing, too, that makes it all the sweeter. Oh, pardon my language, ladies, but I confess that I find it impossible to contain my pleasure."

Lady Emily's smile and laughter echoed his. "No need to apologize to me, Max. I promise you that I am just as happy as you are to witness that woman's downfall. Have to admit, for a while, she had me quite worried. Wasn't sure I'd done the right thing."

Max looked puzzled but was too pleased with the present circumstances to bother with questions and went off, whistling, to find the ladies some champagne. Clare now understood what had happened.

"Lady Emily, never say that you planned this?" The viscountess puffed with pride. "Of course, I see it now. You pushed Letitia into saying she and Northrup were to be wed!"

The other woman shook a finger at her. "You will recall that I did not have to push too hard, miss. Letitia is more than capable of hanging herself, dear; I merely hastened the happy occasion by supplying the rope. Actually, I thought I handled the whole thing rather well," she said, highly pleased with herself, "and that was not very easy, you know.

"You see, I wanted you to have the pleasure of seeing her squirm when you congratulated Evan, so I had to make certain that no one but us knew of the 'engagement.' That was where dear Sally came in. She was already my houseguest, and I could hardly not ask her to tea. Besides, if our little party had consisted of just the three of us—you, me and"— she gave a theatrical shudder—"Letitia, one of you might have become suspicious."

Taking a deep breath, she went on with her convoluted tale. *"Then,* I didn't remember until it was too late that I had invited Samantha Potter simply ages ago. Well, she can be such a milk-and-water thing, that I truly hated to cry off so, by prearrangement, I had Sally spirit her away at the appointed time, so that we could be alone. Just the three of us."

Clare was so surprised at the machinations of this complicated, outlandish scheme, that she could not speak. Lady Emily was beckoned to a nearby group of people. "Well, dear, Letitia is out of your way, so I have done all that I can. Now, if you will excuse me," she said with childlike glee, "I am afraid it falls to me to explain her appalling behavior to these fine people." She patted Clare's cheek and swept away, thinking what a delicious coze she and Sally would have once the others had gone.

Clare sat in her bedroom window wrapped in a cool, blue-lawn nightdress, her hair falling about her shoulders, unable to sleep. Her mind was a whirlwind. There was no denying her pleasure at finding the betrothal was a hoax and at seeing Letitia routed, but did Northrup believe she had confronted the woman with the express intention of humiliating her? She could not go to him and try to explain, for she knew she could not endure his rejection again. What would happen now?

The atmosphere at Brooks's was blissfully quiet—quiet enough to permit a man serious thought. It was only a short while after his arrival—short enough for just one glass of port, in fact, that a determined Northrup stepped back into St. James's Street. A bright yellow and clearly inebriated man loomed before him, just outside the door. "Good God," he muttered, "I really must consider changing clubs."

"Hullo, Northrup."

"Portman. You will excuse me, I am otherwise engaged." He smothered a laugh at his own choice of words and attempted to move on, but Portman's bulk blocked the narrow brick walkway. Tobias clapped him soundly on the shoulder.

"Engaged, eh? Heh, heh. I'll wager she's a pretty piece." Northrup gave a slow, appreciative smile. "She is that." "Who is she, eh? Anyone I know?"

"In point of fact, Portman, you do. But, I should be less than a gentleman if I told you her name."

"Won't say a word, I swear it. Perhaps she has a friend?"

"As to that, I am certain that she has many."

"Well then?"

A mischievous gleam shone in Northrup's eye. "See here, Portman, this lady is very special. Her sensibilities are quite delicate. It would be highly improper for me to bring someone with me. You understand."

"Oh ho, by gad I do. 'Pon my soul, I do! But the good lady can hardly blame you if we don't arrive together, eh? Ha, ha!"

Northrup raised his brows in mock outrage. "Really, Portman. If you don't mind, I am late."

Once his carriage had rounded the corner, he instructed the driver to keep a tight rein on the horses until he was certain that Portman's conveyance had spotted them. When he came into view, the earl leaned back lazily against the squabs, a smile on his face and a roguish twinkle in his blue eyes.

The carriage turned into the square, and Northrup snapped shut his father's old hunter watch. Just gone two, he noted. He looked up at her house to see the glow of lamplight emanating from a room on the second floor, and he smiled again. Good. She could not sleep, either.

"Tell your mistress that I am here," he ordered, when his knock was finally answered.

A bleary-eyed Estelle, clutching a dressing gown up to her chin, stared at him. "But, sir, your lordship, it's very late, and I . . ."

"Estelle, believe me when I tell you that I am all too well aware of how late it really is. Call your mistress. Now!"

"Estelle, what is all this racket? I . . . . Oh!"

Northrup looked up to glimpse Clare, clad only in her

nightdress, leaning over the top of the stairs. Seeing the cause of the commotion, she turned and scampered back to her room. Neatly sidestepping the yawning maid, he took the stairs two at a time.

"Your lordship, you can't go up there!"

"Estelle," he hollered over his shoulder, a determined smile on his face, "go to bed!"

He reached her room just as Clare tried, unsuccessfully, to shut the door. She ran behind a chair.

"Sir, I will thank you to leave my room—this house—immediately!"

He smiled slowly. "First, we must talk."

"Out, I tell you!" Her voice was beginning to carry. "We have nothing to say to one another."

Reaching behind him, Northrup swung shut the bedroom door. "I presume you would prefer to preserve the quiet and, er, ignorance of the neighborhood," he explained drily. "Would not you? Perhaps you should close that window as well. For my part," he added rakishly, "I don't give a damn what anyone knows or thinks!"

"Odious man! Open that door at once! I would not have people say I was trying to *trap* you, sir." Her eyes flashed amber now, and her tone was caustic.

Northrup closed the window and advanced toward her slowly. "I deserved that and much more." He paused. "Clare, please listen to me. Please allow me to explain why I acted the way I did."

"There is no need for explanation. I am not a wantwit, sir, and I understood your behavior only too well." She had been unable to dodge him, caught as she was between the chair and the wall, and now he reached for her hands. "Do not touch me," she spit, pulling back, as if burned. "You relinquished that privilege, sir—nay, you tossed it away. It is not yours to pick up again at your pleasure—and never will be!"

"Do you think me a fool that I do not realize that?" He

dropped his hands. "By God, I have been a fool, a bloody fool. I was so wary of being hurt again, of being duped again, that I listened to the one woman who was capable of doing that to me." Speaking of Letitia, his eyes turned stormy and he ran long, slender fingers through his hair. Clare turned from him, her arms crossed and her head high. "Damn, she was the conniver, not you, I see that now."

"Pretty words. One might have expected a gentleman of your discrimination and education to have perceived that from the very first."

He whirled her around to look at him. "Damn it, Clare, listen to me. I'm asking you to forgive me. I know I've no right to ask it and even less to tell you that I love you, but I do. Those awful things I said . . ."

She raised eyes brimming with tears. "Please, do not trifle with me. Have you not hurt me enough?"

He drew her into his arms and looked down into her eyes as she struggled. "My little love," he murmured against her hair, "what have I done? Would that I could cut out my tongue."

She wriggled out of his arms and backed away. "Do not call me that! You told me once, sir, that I do not have the morals of a lightskirt!?" She burst into tears. He crossed the room and put his arms about her once again. This time, she did not protest.

"My little love," he repeated. "Please, I beg you, say that you will forgive me." Her head was resting on his chest and she could hear his heart beating. She sniffed and nestled a little closer.

"Clare," he whispered. She raised her eyes uncertainly to meet his. He kissed her deeply, and she responded with equal ardor. He smiled. "That is much better. You are so lovely. I have been lost without you these past weeks," he said, and kissed her again.

Suddenly, recollecting their surroundings, she jumped away from him and began a frantic search for her dressing gown. "Good heavens, you must leave at once. This is entirely improper!"

Northrup grinned wickedly and his eyes raked her. "Indeed, yes, it is and quite wonderful, don't you agree?" he asked as he recaptured her with one hand and snatched away the intruding wrap with the other.

"Evan, please, you must go."

"I shall not. Not until you say that you forgive me and that you will be my wife. Then—*perhaps*—I shall consider it." His lips wandered about her neck.

"Evan!"

"Clare. My carriage still is standing out front, where I left it," he explained slowly and deliberately, "and it will remain there until you tell me what I wish to hear. It will remain there, Clare, until morning if necessary. Only think what the neighborhood will make of that!"

"Wretch!"

"Oh, yes, my dear, one more thing. I should also tell you that on my way, I met, not intentionally, God knows, that jackass, Portman. And do you know that I have the strangest suspicion that he followed me here. So convenient for my purposes. So, you see, you must marry me, darling, for your reputation is sure to be in tatters by tonight! Well, madam, what is your answer?"

She smiled. "I suppose I must marry you. It would seem you have left me no choice."

"That was my intention."

"Devil!"

"Just so. And, incidentally, I adore you."

"I believe you mentioned that." He looked down at her, a question in his eyes. "Oh, Evan," she sighed, "I do love you so." Raising herself on her toes, she kissed him with surprising passion.

Still holding her close, he grinned again and teased her. "I begin to think you were indeed quite wild in your youth."

Her finger traced his bottom lip, and her eyes twinkled. "Yes, my lord, I am very much afraid that I was."

"Good. I should hate to spend the rest of my days with a dull, predictable wife. And Countess Changeable Rose has a certain—flair to it, don't you agree? Just think what a fascinating life we shall have, my little love," he said, and gathered her into his arms again.

ABOUT THE AUTHOR

Jessie Watson lives in Waltham, Massachusetts. Her second Regency, *The Cat's Bracelet,* will be published in June 1998. She can be contacted in c/o of Zebra Books.

LOOK FOR THESE REGENCY ROMANCES

WATCH FOR THESE ZEBRA REGENCIES

LADY STEPHANIE   (0-8217-5341-X, $4.50)
by Jeanne Savery
Lady Stephanie Morris has only one true love: the family estate she
has managed ever since her mother died. But then Lord Anthony Rider
arrives on her estate, claiming he has plans for both the land and the
woman. Stephanie soon realizes she's fallen in love with a man whose
sensual caresses will plunge her into a world of peril and intrigue . . . a
man as dangerous as he is irresistible.

BRIGHTON BEAUTY   (0-8217-5340-1, $4.50)
by Marilyn Clay
Chelsea Grant, pretty and poor, naively takes school friend Alayna
Marchmont's place and spends a month in the country. The devastating
man had sailed from Honduras to claim his promised bride, Miss
Marchmont. An affair of the heart may lead to disaster . . . unless a
resourceful Brighton beauty finds a way to stop a masquerade and
keep a lord's love.

LORD DIABLO'S DEMISE   (0-8217-5338-X, $4.50)
by Meg-Lynn Roberts
The sinfully handsome Lord Harry Glendower was a gambler and the
black sheep of his family. About to be forced into a marriage of convenience, the devilish fellow engineered his own demise, never having
dreamed that faking his death would lead him to the heavenly refuge
of spirited heiress Gwyn Morgan, the daughter of a physician.

A PERILOUS ATTRACTION   (0-8217-5339-8, $4.50)
by Dawn Aldridge Poore
Alissa Morgan is stunned when a frantic passenger thrusts her baby
into Alissa's arms and flees, having heard rumors that a notorious
highwayman posed a threat to their coach. Handsome stranger Hugh
Sebastian secretly possesses the treasured necklace the highwayman
seeks and volunteers to pose as Alissa's husband to save her reputation.
With a lost baby and missing necklace in their care, the couple embarks
on a journey into peril—and passion.

*Available wherever paperbacks are sold, or order direct from the
Publisher. Send cover price plus 50¢ per copy for mailing and
handling to Penguin USA, P.O. Box 999, c/o Dept. 17109,
Bergenfield, NJ 07621. Residents of New York and Tennessee must
include sales tax. DO NOT SEND CASH.*